SOUTHERN POISON

PREVIOUS WORKS BY T. LYNN OCEAN

Fool Me Once

Sweet Home Carolina

Jersey Barnes Series

Southern Fatality

SOUTHERN POISON

A Jersey Barnes Mystery

T. LYNN OCEAN

THOMAS DUNNE BOOKS
ST. MARTIN'S MINOTAUR ⁂ NEW YORK

This is a work of fiction. All of the characters, organizations, and events portrayed in this novel are either products of the author's imagination or are used fictitiously.

THOMAS DUNNE BOOKS.
An imprint of St. Martin's Press.

www.thomasdunnebooks.com
www.minotaurbooks.com

Library of Congress Cataloging-in-Publication Data

Ocean, T. Lynn.
Southern poison : a Jersey Barnes mystery / T. Lynn Ocean.—1st ed.
p. cm.
ISBN-13: 978-0-312-38346-6 (alk. paper)
ISBN-10: 0-312-38346-0 (alk. paper)
1. Women private investigators—North Carolina—Fiction. 2. Retired military personnel—North Carolina—Fiction. 3. North Carolina—Fiction. 4. Domestic fiction. I. Title.
PS3615.C43S685 2008
813'.6—dc22

2008020639

First Edition: September 2008

10 9 8 7 6 5 4 3 2 1

For Queen Hilda,

who graciously let me camp out in her home—

and take over her study—

when I was between moves and on deadline to finish this book.

Thanks, Mom!

ACKNOWLEDGMENTS

To the dedicated consumer education activists who maintain the informative Web site safecosmetics.org and organize the Campaign for Safe Cosmetics. To all the folks who happily answered hypothetical questions, including Del Cummings, computer guru Charles Cartrell, physican Tracy Nelson, and professional SUTS Steve Lawson. To manuscript readers Dave Barnes and Ted Theocles for their time and input. To Katie, a terrific editor, and all the savvy people at St. Martin's Press.

To all the fiction-loving folks who read *Southern Fatality* and sent e-mails to say they were eagerly awaiting the next Jersey Barnes adventure: Your feedback is my fuel.

And to all the fabulous booksellers who make the publishing world go 'round by putting books in the hands of readers.

Many thanks!

ONE

Men from my past keep reappearing in my life. First it was my best friend from high school, twenty years after we'd been abruptly split apart when we both joined the Marine Corps. Duke Oxendine, a full-blooded Lumbee Indian whom everyone calls Ox, went through a divorce when he took his twenty-year retirement from the military. It took only three or four tequila shots to convince him to manage my bar, which occupies the lower level of a historic building known as the Barter's Block, or more commonly, the Block.

Next it was my father, who'd abandoned my mother and me before I'd even hit puberty. A retired cop who'd lost his driver's license due to deteriorating eyesight, Spud appeared on my doorstep a few years ago and moved into the efficiency apartment that is connected to mine, both of which are on the upper floor of the Block, directly above the pub.

And now it was my handler. Three years into my stint with the marines, I'd been plucked from active duty as an MP to go to work for an antiterrorism tentacle of the government the agents called SWEET—when there weren't any superiors within earshot. The acronym stands for Special Worldwide unit for Entertaining and Exterminating Terrorists. It sounds strange to those who don't know, but often, part of a SWEET agent's job is to entertain the bad guys—even though the bosses prefer to call it infiltration. It was in SWEET that I learned very cool things such as how to identify explosives and carry out surveillance, alter my appearance, meld into an undercover environment, and kill somebody with seemingly innocuous everyday items. In addition to paying for my specialized training, taxpayers also footed the bill for a pair of perfectly round size-D breast implants. They were enhancements, my bosses explained at the time, which along with a brow lift and periodic injections of cosmetic filler into my lips, would help me do my job. I no longer subject myself to the prick of a needle in my mouth—your body reabsorbs the stuff at an amazingly rapid pace anyway—but I do retain the store-bought boobs and have grown rather fond of them. Regardless of my current hair color, I have the dumb blond routine down pat and can turn it on or off with a mental flip of the light switch in my government-conditioned brain.

Moving slowly down the stairwell that leads from my apartment to the Block, I studied Ashton to make sure it was really him. Gazing at the Cape Fear River, he lounged at the bar and blended with the locals and tourists who found temporary haven in the Block. One of my favorite things about the Block, and quite possibly the reason I bought the old building in Wilmington, is the huge industrial-size garage doors that can be opened to take advantage of river-scented breezes and the view of boats gliding by. Unless it is blowing rain or unusually cold, the doors are open every day and today was no exception. It was midday and quite warm outside, but the overhead fans made it comfortable inside the Block.

Ox had called upstairs to tell me I had a visitor, but Ashton was the last person I expected. I hadn't seen him in person for five years—since I lost my sense of invincibility and retired from the government to open my own security agency.

I slid onto the vacant bar stool next to the man and checked out his profile. He'd gained some pudginess and his pale skin made a double chin stand out more than it should have. But Ashton had aged from more than just the passage of time. He turned to study me—face down to my sandaled feet and back up again—before speaking.

"Jersey Barnes." He took a healthy swallow of beer from a frosted mug. "You look just as fabulous as you did five years ago. North Carolina must agree with you."

He stuck his hand out and I shook it, warmly. He'd done a good job of looking out for me during my stint with the government, even through all the dangerous assignments and seemingly absurd plans of action. I am alive, and for that I will always be grateful to him. "Thanks, Ash. I really love it here. The people, the climate, this old building, everything."

Cracker ambled up to sniff my visitor's shoes and wait for a treat.

"This must be your dog. Yellow Lab?"

"White Lab, actually. My father named him Cracker because he is too white to make a good hunting dog."

Ashton didn't give the dog a peanut, and with an audible sigh, Cracker moved on in search of a more promising human, a regular customer who would scratch him behind the ears and shell a few peanuts for him.

Ox placed a beer in front of me and I automatically reached for the glass. It tasted good, better than beer should to a woman who'd vowed to quit guzzling the liquid as though it were sparkling water from the fountain of youth.

Ashton and I drank. There was a reason he'd appeared in my

bar and sooner or later I would find out what it was. It came sooner.

"We need you back, Jersey, for a onetime assignment," he said. "Could take a few months, maybe more."

The beer floating happily in my stomach threatened to inch back up my throat. "What?"

"The agency needs you back."

I kept the brew down by drinking some more, and shook my head. "I don't think so, Ash, but thanks for the offer. I have a standing date with *Incognito,* my boat. I might even learn how to play golf. I'm not working any longer, not even for my own agency. I just brought in another partner to work with Rita."

He nodded knowingly. "Joan Jackson, also known as JJ. Started as an army sharpshooter. She's done some freelance work for us on occasion. Likes to use the lobbyist-slash-activist cover. As I understand it, she actually got some stem-cell research legislation shoved through the system last year. Good choice. She'll do well with the type of clients your agency takes on."

I gave him my patient smile. "You've been checking up on me."

"Far as the agency is concerned, we never stop keeping tabs."

"Should I be flattered or pissed?"

He drank some beer. "Standard operating procedure for all agents of your caliber, active and retired. Doesn't necessarily require an emotional response of any kind."

Ashton always had been dry to the point of seeming callous. I looked more closely at his face and detected something off in his eyes. Worry? Exhaustion? Something else? He laid a sealed manila envelope on the bar. "Take a look at this."

"A file loaded with top secret intel, of course. The theatrics are mildly amusing, but as I said, I'm not interested. Notwithstanding the utmost respect I have for you, I don't *want* an assignment. Seriously, I'm retired." I slid the envelope back toward him.

"During the tenure of the assignment, you'll work on a contractual basis and will be paid one lump-sum check upon completion. Plus, there's an upfront hazard-pay bonus."

I almost wanted to learn more but quickly regained my senses. I had zero desire to do another job for the government. Especially when the words "hazard pay" were involved. "I'm not a wealthy person, but I live comfortably. The Barnes Agency doesn't advertise, yet we still have to turn away business. The Block breaks even, and even surprises us once in awhile by showing a small profit. And I'm happy. You see, I have all the money I need. I got tired of playing chicken with the Grim Reaper. That's why I retired so young."

He smiled, tolerant to the point of condescendence. "I'm not here to ask. I'm here to facilitate."

"What the heck does that mean?"

"You don't have a choice, Jersey." He pushed the envelope back in front of me. "I'm going to order some food and eat while you throw your eyeballs on this. What's good here?"

I passed a menu to Ashton. "The beer-steamed shrimp is excellent, as are the crab cakes. Hush puppies are a house specialty. Burgers are good. And you can't go wrong with whatever the specials of the day are."

"Gumbo, served over brown rice with a side of collards. For the appetizer, spicy fried sweet pickles," Ruby said, hustling by with a plate of hot wings. A fifty-something veteran waitress, she is famous for eavesdropping without being obvious about it.

"Fried what?" Ashton said.

"Southerners will deep fry just about anything. Pickles, jalapeños, tomatoes, squash. You name it."

Without opening it, Ashton returned the menu to Ox. "Think I'll pass on the specials. I don't even know what a collard is. But an order of the crab cakes would be great. Maybe some hush puppies with that."

"You got it," Ox said from behind the bar, his luscious mouth twisting in amusement at me and my rapidly changing retirement plans.

The food issue settled, Ashton returned to business. "Did you read your contract, Jersey? The one you signed when we first recruited you?"

"I'm sure I did." I was young and green back then, three years into my required six with the marines. At that point in my life, I'd have signed anything to get out early.

"You still have it?"

"Probably."

"Good," he said, watching a barge progress slowly beneath the Cape Fear Memorial Bridge. "Read page twelve, paragraphs two through five. You can be called back into service at any time for thirty years after your initial service date, and you can be utilized in a consultant capacity up until your death. As long as you are in good physical health and you're of sound mind, you belong to the agency on a per-assignment basis if the situation warrants."

Until death? Mind racing, I reached for my beer and frantically tried to think of a way out. He'd said something about good health. Surely I could fake an illness if I had to. I have some doctor friends.

"Don't even try," Ashton said. "We have all your current medical records, right up to your last doctor's visit and pap smear results."

"Crap," I mumbled to myself.

"Guess you'd better postpone your upcoming shuffleboard tournament," Ox said, passing by with two frozen drinks. "Might want to cancel your bingo dates, too."

I glared at him. Wicked grin spread across his face, he kept walking.

Like a bad slow-motion scene in a movie, I felt my hands retrieve a file from the manila envelope. I wasn't sure if I'd been reading for a few minutes or half an hour, but when I finished, Ashton was devouring a plate of crab cakes. Ox had served him a small side dish of collards as well.

"What is it that you want me to do?" I heard myself ask after I'd watched him eat for a moment, my ears ringing with a steady buzz, as though the bomb just dropped on me had already exploded.

Ashton sprinkled hot-pepper vinegar on the collards and took a tentative bite before nodding with palatal agreement. "You're familiar with the Sunny Point ammo dump?"

"Vaguely. The Military Ocean Terminal Sunny Point, or MOTSU. Largest ammunition port in the nation. Army-owned. About sixteen thousand acres, just south of Wilmington." I felt myself slipping back in time, to when my knowledge on various subjects was persistently tested. Back then, though, I had a desire to excel by pleasing my bosses and answered their questions with the eagerness of a puppy in training, awaiting praise. Now I was just stuck in a bad dream.

"Right," he said and forked another wad of collards. "It is the Army's primary deep-water port and the only DOD terminal set up to accommodate containerized ammunition."

I waited for the rest.

"We've picked up some high-frequency chatter, which may indicate that one of our nation's ammo dumps is targeted by a terrorist cell. Sunny Point ranks highest on the probability reports and we need you to be a set of eyes and ears. A position in food services has become open, as the current employee will be out on medical leave."

"You want me to work in a cafeteria?" My afternoon had plummeted from pleasant to dreadful and it still hadn't hit bottom.

"You'll actually be working what some folks affectionately term the roach coach. It's a mobile meal truck run by Mama Jean. Makes the rounds by construction sites in the afternoons and has been a fixture at Sunny Point every morning for years. Just about everyone coming or going stops for breakfast, plus you'll get some local drive-by traffic. The truck isn't allowed inside MOTSU but there is a nice scenic spot near the entrance where Mama Jean always parks." His Adam's apple moved rhythmically as he finished the rest of his beer and pushed a napkin across his mouth. "In any event, you will make egg biscuits, hash-brown patties, that sort of thing."

"You have got to be kidding me."

"Negative. The position gives you flexibility and the opportunity to gather information in an informal environment. It's a great cover, since Mama Jean has already told the regulars about her scheduled hysterectomy. She'll be out for at least a month, maybe more. And you don't have to do the afternoon construction-site runs, unless you just want to see some sweaty bodies in hard hats."

"You're funny."

"Seriously. We're turning over all income to Mama Jean, and she'd probably appreciate the lunch income. So, feel free."

Yeah, right. "Am I the only one?"

"Of course not. Other agents are being utilized as eyes and ears in and around Southport."

"What positions? Anybody I know?"

Ashton frowned. His way of telling me I wouldn't have access to that information, unless I needed it. The government never did like for its left hand to know what its right hand was doing. God forbid the two should actually hold the bat at the same time and swing at the ball together.

"I'll need a car," I said. "Anything armored that's being pulled from service and going to auction?" It's how I'd acquired my Mercedes-Benz S-series for a ridiculously low price. Of course, it helped that I am friends with the man in charge of the auctions and had sent him a case of his favorite bourbon.

Ashton grinned. "First of all, we're making a few revisions to the mobile meal truck to give it surveillance capabilities and offer protection, just in case you find yourself in an unpleasant situation. Second of all, you're not in a position to bargain. But just out of curiosity, what happened to the Benz?"

It was my turn to grin. The government obviously hadn't been keeping that close of tabs on me. "It got shot up last month by a crazy woman and her boyfriend." I didn't mention that the fellow had also been my boyfriend. The betrayal still stung, if I let myself think about it too long. "Bullet-resistant glass and armored plates did their job, but the hood and door panels look like Swiss cheese and the windshield is a connect-the-dots puzzle. Car's not worth what the repair bill would cost. Anyway, I'll need something to drive when I'm not slaving away over a hot grill in the back of a truck."

He pushed his empty dishes back and drummed some fingers in thought. "Tell you what. I'll authorize you as a bidder on any current auction vehicles. Get what you want, but you pay out of your own pocket."

"Floyd still running things there?"

"Affirmative. I'm sure he'll take good care of you, just like he did with the Mercedes."

"At least buy me a set of new run-flat tires with Uncle Sam's checkbook." When the set that came with the Benz wore out, I replaced them with much cheaper, regular passenger tires. But I've since decided that there is no use tooling around in an armored car if your tires could easily be shot out.

Frowning, Ashton shook his head.

I twirled a strand of hair around my forefinger, arched out my chest, and produced a sexy bimbette look, complete with fluttering lashes. "Puhlleeeze?"

Ashton held my raised eyebrow stare. He nearly smiled. "I taught you that look and it doesn't work on me. You report for work on Monday. Your name is Jill Burns."

"Can't it be something a little more exotic like Marilyn Tulika or Giana Brenneka?"

He dropped some bills on the counter and stood to leave. "Good to see you again."

"Wish I could say the same."

TWO

Peggy Lee Cooke leisurely opened her eyes and rolled over to face the rays of early morning sun that pressed through the miniblinds. Enjoying the flood of warmth that hit her cheeks, she smiled, and, catlike, stretched her entire body, starting with her toes. She couldn't remember when she'd last awakened happy and now that she thought about it, maybe she'd never before had anything worth being happy about. But now that a meaningful project sizzled on the burner and she had the love of an amazing man, she couldn't imagine *not* feeling cheerful.

No longer did she feel like a childless outcast. She wasn't even bothered by her three-year-long failed attempt to find a cure for her type of infertility, working with the wild leafy shiff bush found in South America. She used to think that a man would never marry her if she couldn't give him a family. Men wanted heirs to immortalize their name and she planned to mother hordes of children. Two or three, anyway. But like a promising slot machine that pays off just enough to keep the gambler from moving on to the next flashing machine, her research project ultimately ended up a loser. It sucked up all her energy and left her barren and dry. Until *he* came along, that is. Her lover and life mate. Chuck was a surprise jackpot.

A good chemist, he told her, didn't accept failure. He'd held her face between his strong hands and explained how a fruitless research project could be redirected—and resurrected—as a winner. Which is exactly what he did with her wild leafy shiff bush research. She'd chosen the right slot machine, after all, and it promised to pay handsomely.

Pushing herself upright on the edge of the bed, Peggy felt beautiful, despite her plainness. The genetic outcome of her mother and father's union hadn't bestowed her with alluring physical features, but it hadn't been totally unkind. Her skin was blemish-free, her eyes were set apart by seven-point-four centimeters, pupil to pupil, and her thick hair grew fast. Using how-to tips from a magazine, she'd tried applying makeup before her dates with Chuck, but the result was always clownish so she no longer bothered. Even so, he had called her brainy and gorgeous, and she'd been pleasantly giddy since. She was the best of both worlds, he proclaimed, as they'd made love in his hotel room and watched a movie and made love again. He was a visionary with big dreams and now she was a part of something that might change the world. She was *someone.*

Stripping off a T-shirt and shorts, Peggy stepped into the shower and thought back to her geeky high school years, when nobody—not even the other girls—wanted anything to do with her. Fueled by a craving to learn more about chemistry, the only subject that made perfect sense of the world that surrounded her, Peggy plodded steadily through years of higher education until she could put the word *doctor* in front of her name.

She gloated in the proof that her stepmother had been wrong all those years ago to scold her for growing crystals in a brand-new

Easy-Bake Oven. She didn't even cry when she got spanked over the incident, because seven-year-old Peggy knew that Santa Claus would have put a chemistry set beneath their scraggly tree, had he only known. A career in chemistry was her destiny, as sure as beautiful crystals will grow from simple charcoal, ammonia, and salt.

Now, twenty-five years later, Peggy Lee gleefully acknowledged that it was also her destiny to become a wife. There was a reason she remained lonely for so many years, because just as the best crystals use more advanced ingredients and take the longest to develop, the best relationships happen in due time. Chuck was elated to learn of her virginity and wasted no time in teaching her precisely how to please him. Since her first gynecological exam at age thirteen, she'd known of her sterility—one category in which the DNA crapshoot had been unreasonably cruel to her—but now she felt feminine for the first time in her life. Her defective eggs didn't matter anymore, and in hindsight, they hadn't mattered all along. Chuck didn't want children. The world was already overpopulated, he'd said. It was fate that put the two of them in the same hotel for a weekend conference. Fate that seated them side by side at a keynote speaker luncheon. Fate that merged discussions of two entirely separate projects, hers and his, both of which flopped during field trials. One pharmaceutical dud and one commercial-glue fiasco that, merged together, had changed futility and frustration into promise and progress. Peggy wasn't sure whether she believed in God or not, but a higher power of some distinction had to be at work. Everything happened for a reason, she learned, and her life was meant to be exactly the way it was turning out.

Chuck had been so impressed with Peggy that he built a satellite laboratory in Wilmington and hired her to head up the first stage of Project Antisis. She'd been willing to move to Roanoke, Virginia, where ECH Chemical Engineering & Consulting resided. For privacy reasons, though, Chuck chose to run Project Antisis from a satellite location and found the perfect spot right in Wilmington. Peggy Lee manufactured the synthetic plant-based chemical, which she added to a nontoxic adhesive, and shipped the raw material to a production and packaging facility in Virginia.

The pieces were rapidly and efficiently falling into place. Chuck traveled to Wilmington almost weekly, and she anticipated his visits like a military wife waiting for her soldier to come home. Even though they couldn't truly be together until phase one of Project Antisis was fully implemented, she was happy. Blissfully happy, she realized, toweling dry, deciding what she would wear to the lab that day. As she pulled a pair of jeans and cotton top out of a drawer, Peggy Lee's mind wandered to other clothing. A wedding dress, for starters. He was simply waiting for the right time to propose. She just knew it.

THREE

"*When are they* gonna haul away that damn hunk of junk, for crying out loud?" Spud complained, asking nobody in particular. People think he looks like a much older, shrunken version of Wolfgang Puck. Except my father's demeanor is much different from the famous chef's, and right now, agitation was the flavor of the moment. "That stupid car is still causing me headaches."

Spud and Bobby, one of my father's poker buddies, had joined Ox and me for a midday snack at the Block. It was well past lunchtime and too early for the happy-hour crowd, and a smattering of low-maintenance customers sat around eating peanuts and drinking beers. Ruby tended to everyone and still had plenty of time to catch up on local gossip with the regulars.

"The insurance adjuster was a young kid, and once he took a look at your Chrysler, he wasn't sure how to write up the report. Said he had to send a senior adjuster out," I explained to my father for the third or fourth time. "Should be sometime this week."

After deteriorating eyesight claimed Spud's driver's license, he'd embarked on a mission to get rid of his Chrysler LHS. Unfortunately, his valuation of the vehicle was much higher than anyone else's and he couldn't sell it. Mad at the state of North Carolina and obsessed with getting rid of the car, he'd schemed ways to lose it so he could collect the insurance money, right up until a local cop offered to buy it. When Spud finally snagged a buyer with cash in hand—a buyer willing to pay the full asking price—my father had an epiphany: he would keep the car so his friends could tote him around in it. Minutes later, somebody drove a garbage truck into the Block, ripping right through one of the giant metal garage doors. Spud's car was parked outside said garage door and the huge truck's front-end forks had pierced it like toothpicks going through a fat olive. After being forked and crushed, the Chrysler was peppered with incoming rounds from no fewer than twenty handguns. When the firestorm ended, the tow-truck driver couldn't figure out how to safely haul away the garbage truck with Spud's car attached—and suspended a foot off the ground. A forward-thinking kind of guy, he called a welder to cut through the metal prongs, effectively amputating them from the truck. Victorious, he towed the garbage truck away, leaving the impaled, smashed, shot-up Chrysler sitting in a patch of grass outside my bar, two long forked rods protruding through its belly.

Spud retrieved his walking cane so he could poke it into the concrete floor a few times. "Well, I'm tired of waiting! It's been almost a month now. That car was fully insured and I want my money. Any idiot can see that it's totaled, for crying out loud." That was an understatement. Demolished would be more like it.

I bit a hush puppy in half and let it melt on my tongue. "Calm down, Spud. They're probably just reviewing the police report. Maybe they found out that the car had been sunk, burned, and almost stolen during your failed foray into insurance fraud."

"Yeah." Bobby spurred it on. "Maybe they've launched an official investigation."

"Well the insurance company can launch this." Spud shoved his cane in the air, in lieu of an arthritic middle finger.

Before he could get into a full-blown tirade about the insurance industry, Hal and Trip showed up. My father and his three poker friends—after much old-age shuffling and grunting—headed upstairs to Spud's kitchen table for a round of Texas hold 'em.

I tried to focus on the information in front of me but couldn't help but to look at Ox instead and wonder—if my budding retirement hadn't been so rudely interrupted—whether we might have finished what we started. The night of the shootout at the Block, he had stayed with me and I distinctly remember the glorious sensation of being enveloped in his arms as I drifted into the deepest sleep I'd had in a long time. Physically and emotionally drained from the week's events and relaxed by too much alcohol, my body wouldn't cooperate with my mind's desire to ravage Ox's body. Awakening beside him the next morning, I quickly came to my senses. He was certainly willing, but sex with my best friend could change everything. There might be no turning back. Ox is tall and has traditional Native American features with some surprises tossed into his DNA, such as the dimple set into a square chin and a unique cinnamon eye color that changes with his mood. Just hearing him speak sometimes drives me crazy. A Lumbee can be anywhere in the country and immediately recognize another Lumbee, simply by hearing the other speak. Their unique dialect is sort of Southern, but influenced by several ancestral sources and Ox retained the distinctive manner of speaking even though he'd led a mobile military life. When he first appeared in Wilmington, I didn't fall into bed with Ox because he needed time to heal after a nasty divorce. In the years to follow, he always had a gorgeous woman on his arm and I always had a somewhat steady male companion. The timing had never been right. Either that, or the spirits had different plans for us.

"What's on your mind?" he said.

"Oh, uh, nothing really." *Just thinking how good it would feel to press our naked bodies together.* "I'm still blown away by this assignment. I feel like a commodity, like they own me or something."

"You're mad because you are accustomed to doing things your own way, on your own terms." He had a knack for seeing through bullshit. Hopefully, though, he didn't know what was *really* on my mind. Him. Naked.

"I suppose."

"Let's get you in place and get this thing figured out so we can be finished with it. Then you can go play on your boat and ponder life after retirement."

I smiled. "We?"

"I've got a feeling you may need me on this one." He looked outside, at the placid river. "Oddly, I've got a feeling that we may need each other more than usual in the coming weeks."

Ox's predictions were always right on target. "I don't understand," I said.

"I don't, either." He opened the file and together, we scoured my notes and the computer printouts.

In typical covert fashion, an envelope had been delivered earlier by a woman I thought was a tourist. She handed it to me personally, saying only, "Don't leave this shit lying around." Inside I found a dossier containing detailed information on all Sunny Point personnel, or in government lingo, "the population served." There are soldiers and Army reserve units, as expected, but few in comparison to the more than two hundred civilians who work at the facility.

The packet also contained general operating info on Sunny Point and a fairly detailed blueprint. Built along Highway 133, it is surrounded by a huge buffer zone of undeveloped land and large sand dunes, and at sixteen thousand acres and more than two hundred thousand square feet of buildings, it is the largest ammunition port in the nation. The facility receives ammunition, explosives, and various other hazardous cargo by both train and truck, and loads the stuff on outgoing ships.

We went over the report detailing possible terrorist scenarios and potential weak spots in MOTSU security. Nothing jumped out and said, "Look at me! I'm an open invitation for a terrorist!" Other than familiarizing myself with the information, there wasn't anything to do except park the roach coach as scheduled and cook some eggs.

"I don't even cook breakfast for myself and now I'm supposed to go cook for a bunch of strangers every morning?"

"Least they didn't make you a janitor," Ox said.

The Block had slowly filled up while we concentrated on the task at hand, and another server and bartender arrived for the evening shift. The noise level climbed accordingly and soon leveled off to steady hum of good-natured chatter. All heads suddenly swung in Ruby's direction when her entire body erupted into a loud, jiggling belly laugh. Two confused tourists stood by her side, and like the rest of us, didn't understand what was so funny.

Ruby stopped laughing and pointed at me. "That there is the Block's owner, Jersey, and the manager, Ox. I'm sure one of them can help you out."

I stood to greet the couple, reminding myself to let Ruby know that Ox was an owner, too. I'd finally gotten him to agree to accept 50 percent ownership in the Block, which I took as a good sign. It meant that he didn't have plans to leave Wilmington anytime soon.

"What can we do for you?"

"We'd like to find out who the artist is," the man said.

"Artist?"

He pointed outside, at the pathetic remains of Spud's car. "It's a really incredible piece. Makes a statement, you know?"

Stupefied at their interpretation of art, I forced myself to nod.

"I just love the way he patterned all the bullet holes," the woman chimed in. "And the giant fork prongs must symbolize that humans are really insignificant in the overall scheme of things. Like maybe we're really *not* at the top of the food chain."

"Right," the man agreed. "Anyway, we couldn't find a signature plate on the sculpture and my wife wants to know who created it. Does the artist have a gallery around here?"

I looked at the twisted, impaled monstrosity that used to be Spud's car. "It was a coordinated effort by a group of local artists."

"They're actually law-enforcement officers who dabble in art," Ox confided to the couple with a straight face.

"Really? Wow. That would make a great story." The woman pulled a camera phone out of her handbag. "I've got to tell my editor about this. I write for *Eclectic Arts & Leisure* magazine. We have a national subscriber base."

The man led his wife outside, where the couple started taking digital photographs of the Chrysler from various angles. Ox let loose with a deep throaty laugh.

"Think they'll notice that Cracker uses the sculpture as his personal fire hydrant?" I said.

He laughed harder.

FOUR

John Mason prided himself on his appreciation for discipline. A complete lack of discipline had made Americans weak and dishonorable, in his opinion. That, and all the greedy politicians who pretended to work for the public good, when all they really cared about was padding their pockets and jetting around the country, gorging themselves at Ruth's Chris Steak Houses and shopping at Saks Fifth Avenue stores for their mistresses. In an obscene display of indulgence, the U.S. Congress had just voted themselves a pay raise and continued to up their already fat pensions while sending other people's family members into combat zones without the proper equipment.

He knew the exact moment his twin was killed, even though he lay in bed asleep, on the other side of the globe. He'd been awakened by an alarming blanket of dismay that slammed into him as though it were woven of lead and dropped from fifty feet. He died right then and there along with his brother, and only a pounding heart and sweaty body made him realize that he remained physically alive.

There were plenty more like him—people who lost family members for no good reason. God-fearing, hard-working Americans who'd been screwed by their own government.

Veins bulged in his temples as he grunted out a final military press and let the chrome weight bar drop to the carpeted floor in his den. He loved the old, utilitarian house because it was surrounded by trees and set on a large lot that offered plenty of privacy. He was especially pleased with the old hidden root cellar that was left from the original house built on the property. Inside, he'd converted the living room into a gym and stocked it with free weights, a pull-up bar, and a treadmill. Just like a real health club, mirrors covered one wall so he could study his contracting muscle groups and monitor his form. A stack of neatly folded and bleached towels were within easy reach on a table, along with a bottled-water dispenser. A by-product of discipline, self-sufficiency made one stronger and that was the basis of his spiritualism. Stay disciplined and self-sufficient. A reflection in the mirror grabbed his attention and the image staring back almost seemed a stranger. Weekly injections of steroids had produced thirty added pounds of sheer muscle, and shaving off the wavy hair gave him a commanding appearance.

John removed the forty-five-pound plates and returned them to their proper rack, toweled off, and dropped to the floor to complete his workout with one hundred sit-ups. Knees bent, he wedged his feet beneath a worn sofa, and, holding a twenty-five-pound weight over his chest, proceeded to count out rapid sit-ups. He reveled in his daily workouts and never missed one, even when away from home. At this point, it was crucial to stay in top physical condition and keep his eye on the prize. The success of his mission depended on it.

Breathing deep, John willed his heartbeat back to normal and stretched for exactly five minutes. His Luminox watch, the same model many Navy SEALs wore, indicated it was time to drink a liter of water and prepare for the night's assemblage that should have been a total of five men but would be just as effective with four.

He couldn't be happier with the location and event they would disrupt in less than a month. The guest list was even better than he'd originally hoped. His maneuver, the plan he'd been working on for nearly a year, would get the attention of those who mattered. Most—if not all—of them would be dead, but he'd get the attention of their cohorts and associates and maybe *those* people would realize what their job was supposed to be. Serve the public, not themselves, the greedy bastards. Maybe in the future, they'd be a little more disciplined in the choices they made.

Before he showered, John decided to dispose of the body sprawled on his sofa. To keep things tidy, he'd asphyxiated the man with a simple choke hold. A slight but steady drizzling rain would keep the pleasure boaters indoors, and the marina should be relatively quiet. Before he carried the body to his boat, he'd be sure to get a photo of the would-be tattler, eyes still open and bulging. A good reminder to the remaining three men that discipline must be served above all else, and that rats would be squashed dead. They had a mission to accomplish, and variances from the original plan would not be tolerated.

FIVE

Not being privy to labor-force specifics, I didn't have a clue how many people were working to intercept a potential terrorist action in Wilmington. But somebody was churning out a lot of theories. SWEET liked to keep things neat and organized by putting a number on anything that could conceivably have a figure attached to it. In relation to all the military ammunition storage facilities in the country, somebody decided, a 70 percent probability of a potential terrorist action was awarded to MOTSU. Conjecture is imperfect, however. The same number crunchers couldn't suggest who, how, and when. Or exactly what, for that matter.

In addition to the personnel info for all Sunny Point employees, I had a list of everyone who'd had access during the past year—right down to the folks who'd serviced the air-conditioning units—and was instructed to be on the lookout for both employees and MOTSU visitors while working the roach coach. Extra security measures had quietly been implemented at the ammo dump, and while some Washington brains were thoroughly vetting all relevant military personnel, other Washington drones were executing background investigations on every civilian employee. So far, though, nobody stood out as a strong person of interest.

I had thought about going to the Barnes Agency for a quiet place to work, but opted instead for my kitchen table. Heading to the office in stretch lace panties and a Victoria's Secret satin, white fur-trimmed robe might draw unwanted attention to the nondescript building that houses my agency. I have a penchant for quality lingerie and collect camisoles, chemises, and bras with abandon. One of my prized pieces is a custom-sewn bodice that includes a leather holster for my standard backup weapon, a Sig Sauer P232. Seriously. An Arizona friend makes the quick-release holsters with ultrathin cowhide that is first softened and then vacuum molded around the gun. He'd originally made two for me: a thigh holster and an ankle holster. My partner Rita commissioned the third holster—the bodice—as an official retirement gift for me, attaching a card that read, "Just in case you start jonesin' for the feel of steel." Her attempt at humor. It is a perfect fit, though.

Happy to be working in my sexy jammies—even if only for one day before reporting to work in the food truck—I peeled a banana, gave Cracker his customary bite, and called my friend Soup, knowing he'd pulled off seemingly impossible feats before. Strong coffee loaded with cream and sugar poked at the motivation sensors in my brain and I tried to think like a terrorist.

It stood to reason that a bad guy eyeballing MOTSU would desire one of two things: disable the facility to interrupt operations, or blow something up to kill lots of people. The planning and resources required to disable the facility would overwhelm even the most dedicated of terrorist cells, so I figured the goal had to be a body count. Question was, who were the targeted bodies?

"Hey, Jersey," Soup answered. "Since you only call when you need something, I assume you're back in the workforce. I knew the retirement thing wouldn't stick. Did you get tired of eating early bird specials at four o'clock? Or was it the nasty taste of all those fiber supplements?"

I ignored the retirement barbs. "It's a long story. By the way, how are you enjoying the cushy job for Chesterfield Financial?" Soup is a technology junkie and one of the best hackers in the country. After helping me on my last case, he was hired by Samuel Chesterfield, head of a national brokerage firm, to overhaul their online security system.

Keyboard clacks were rapid and nonstop. "Pays a helluva lot better than working for you."

"If you hadn't been working a job for me, you never would have met Samuel Chesterfield."

"True." He slurped something—probably soup, which is how he got his nickname—and a loud swallow traveled through the fiber-optic cable.

"And," I said, "you wouldn't have just enjoyed a fabulous week on *Incognito* with your friends." My one extravagance, the forty-eight-foot sport fishing yacht was a gift from a grateful client. As a thank-you to Soup, I had the boat fully stocked with food and booze, and hired Captain Pete to haul Soup and company anywhere they wanted to go.

He blew out a long sigh and stopped keyboarding. "Okay, lay it on me. What do you need?"

I needed a complete schedule of events that were happening within a two-hundred-mile radius of Wilmington, I told him. Anything, public or private, that involved more than one hundred people or anything that would be attended by high-profile power figures. For the upcoming four months.

"That'll cost you more than a return favor, Jersey. You're talking some major time consumption."

"Let's shave the parameters, then. How about a hundred-and-fifty-mile radius for the next three months?"

"How about fifty miles and one month?" Soup said, admitting that he could in fact produce the information. He is brilliant that way. He just doesn't like to work harder than necessary. And he would uncover some nifty details that Ashton's people would overlook.

"One-hundred-mile radius and two months out," I countered.

"Done. What do I get out of it?"

"The opportunity to save lives."

"Anything else?" Keyboard sounds started up again and I knew his mind was already figuring out which databases he'd have to hack to fulfill my request.

"The who-owes-whom-a-favor pendulum swings back in your direction," I said.

He snorted out a laugh. "By the way, we gave your boat a few tweaks. *Incognito*'s GPS navigation system and depth finders are now coupled with a voice feature. Your radar screen is hooked up to a DVD player for those long trips. Oh, and the plasma flat screen in the salon? It gets satellite reception pretty much anywhere you go in the world. Same for the onboard emergency mobile phone."

"I don't have an onboard emergency mobile phone."

"You do now."

"Are you crazy? I don't want to pay every month for those satellite services."

"You're not. I wouldn't burden you with a satellite phone bill, you being on a fixed income and all," he chided and hung up.

I ran a foot back and forth over Cracker's fur. "Remind me to never turn Soup loose on my boat again," I said to the dog. He flopped onto his back and would have started snoring if not for timid knocking on my kitchen door at the top of stairs that went down to the Block. Thinking it was probably a stray customer in search of restrooms, I flipped on the security monitor and was surprised to see Ox's daughter.

I rushed to hug the girl and her chin was nearly even with mine. I am taller than average at five eight, and she is a still-growing teen. Cracker nosed his way between us and wiggled his hello. "Lindsey, how are you? Your dad didn't mention you were visiting this week."

Ox's only child, Lindsey is high-energy and beautiful. Even though her mother, Louise, was awarded full-time custody after the divorce, Lindsey spends her summers with Ox and she and I are pretty tight. When she'd gotten out of school for the summer a few months back and informed us that she was staying in California with her mom, Ox was understandably upset. But he didn't pressure her and although Lindsey never did tell us exactly why she'd decided to remain on the West Coast for her summer break, I suspected it had something to do with a boyfriend.

"I didn't tell him I was coming," she said in a small voice, sniffled, and came through the door, dragging a wheeled piece of luggage behind her. She'd been crying, but even with red-rimmed eyes and slumped shoulders, she was a stunner. Anyone who didn't know would assume her to be twenty instead of sixteen years old. Every time I see her, she looks more and more like Ox. Olive skin, the same cinnamon-speckled eyes, dimpled chin, and knockout smile—when she chooses to display it.

Her gaze narrowed when she looked at my attire. "You realize an animal had to die to make that robe, right?"

"It's faux fur."

Her eyes moved to my boobs. "Well it suits you, then."

"Thanks," I said, unsure if her comment was a compliment or a cut on my store-boughts. "You want a cold drink?"

"You have anything diet?" Like she needed something diet.

"No. How about a regular Coke?"

She shrugged.

I retrieved two cans of Coke from the fridge and we sat down. Lindsey knew that she could tell me anything. We'd been hiking, camping, kayaking, and seen tons of movies together. I'd gone on weeklong summer vacations with her and Ox, taught her how to shoot, and comforted her when she broke her arm and couldn't play in the softball state finals. I have been her friend, guardian, and sometimes disciplinarian. But she was a well-adjusted kid and had never before just shown up unexpected.

"What's going on, Lindsey?"

"I can't live with my mom anymore and I came here to live with Dad. I thought he'd be happy, but when I told him, he was, like, shocked. He sort of went pale and that's pretty tough for an Oxendine to do, you know? I guess he just doesn't want to deal with me. Even though Mom probably wouldn't fight him this time." She shrugged. "So I left and came here."

"Wait a minute, let's back up. First of all, does your mother know where you are?"

Lindsey shook her head. "I told her I was staying over at a friend's."

"How did you get here from the airport?"

She popped the tab on her soda. "I'm not a *baby,* Jersey. I took a cab to Dad's place. Then I walked here. It's only a mile or so."

"Honey, your father loves you more than you'll ever know. What you saw on his face was probably surprise. You did sort of blindside him."

Her wide-set eyes darkened, much like Ox's do on occasion. "I won't go back to California."

Cracker's tail started wagging a second before Ox beeped in the security code and came through my door without knocking. Ox is not one to lose his cool, ever, but he was flustered to say the least. The two Oxendines stared at each other until he broke the silence.

"Lindsey, what is going on?"

She slumped lower in her seat. "You don't want me, that's what's going on."

"What are you talking about?"

"I want to live with you, but it's clear you don't want me."

Ox pulled his daughter out of the chair and hugged her tight. "Never think I don't want you," he said in a low voice I almost didn't recognize. "You just surprised me, is all."

Eyes downcast, Lindsey drank some soda. Ox looked at me, silently asking what was going on. I did a palms up. I was as clueless as he was.

"Why don't you guys go into the living room, where it's more comfortable," I said.

At my urging, Lindsey moped her way out of the kitchen.

"Go talk to her," I whispered to Ox. "I'll leave you two alone."

He caught my arm. "Please, stay. I don't know what to say to an upset sixteen-year-old."

"I think she had a fight with Louise," I said, retying the sash on my robe that had worked its way loose.

Ox's eyes moved over my satiny, fur-lined outfit. "Nice."

"Thanks. Your daughter wasn't as impressed by it."

He smiled. "Will you help me out here?"

"Let me put on some clothes first." So much for enjoying a leisurely morning in my jam jams. I found Lindsey sitting on the floor with Cracker, letting him exuberantly lick her face. Ox watched them from the sofa. Even when he and Louise were still married, Ox had always let his wife deal with the emotional, sometimes irrational side of their daughter. He still didn't quite know how to deal with this side of Lindsey.

I settled into a chair. "Since you are two of my favorite people in the world and I love you both, I will moderate the discussion," I said, hoping to lighten the tension a notch. "Lindsey, you can start by telling us what happened. Did you have a fight with your mother?"

She shook her head. "Not really. But her boyfriend is a total jerk.

Dealing with him coming over to the house was bad enough, but now he's moved in."

Ox's jaw clenched. "Roger moved into your and your mother's house?" It was the house he'd paid for, the one Louise got as part of the divorce settlement. Ox could have made her sell, but he chose to give her what she wanted and walk away, once his ex said she no longer loved him.

"Not him. Her new boyfriend. *Albert.* She calls him Allie. It's disgusting."

"So, your mom has a new boyfriend who is at the house a lot?" I said to clarify.

Lindsey pushed Cracker away from her face and the dog settled his wide head across her lap. She absentmindedly rubbed his neck. "I told you, he *moved in.* He lives there and he's a pig. The game room is now his office—he made Mom get rid of the pool table—and now I'm not even allowed in there. It's like his private Zen space, or something. He totally rearranged our furniture to enhance the energy flow. And there are like, new phone rules and stuff. She's cooking tofu and seaweed for God's sake, because he's a health nut."

My eyes flicked to Ox, wondering if this was all news to him. It was.

"When did Albert move in?" he asked.

She shrugged. "Maybe two weeks ago?"

I slid into the role of counselor. "So it's understandably a big adjustment. You must feel left out of the whole equation."

"Duh!"

Ox's jaw muscles were working overtime, but his words came out calm. "Clearly, you don't like this man, but what exactly makes him so unbearable?" After all, his ex wife was free to do what she wished, as long as his daughter wasn't neglected or in danger.

Lindsey threw her hands up. "You don't get it! This weirdo has moved into my house and brought all his things and he's changed everything around and now we have to live by his rules and eat that nasty stuff he calls food and Mom just runs around fussing over him like he's royalty or something!" She wiped her eyes with a sleeve before tears had a chance to roll down her face. "I don't want to live there anymore. I want to live here, in Wilmington, with you."

I hated to ask but we had to know. "Did Albert do anything to hurt you, Lindsey?"

"Hello? He's destroyed my life! Does that count?"

"Has he done anything to physically harm you?"

"You mean like come on to me or something? No way. I'd kill him if he ever tried to touch me."

"If I didn't get to him first," Ox said under his breath. He flipped open his cell phone and dialed.

"Louise, it's Duke," Ox said when his ex answered. "Lindsey is here with me and everything is fine." He paused to listen before walking back into the kitchen, to get out of earshot. Lindsey looked at me with raised eyebrows. Sound carries relatively unobstructed between my kitchen and living area, and Ox's voice was faint but clearly decipherable.

I tried to start a conversation with Lindsey but she shushed me, preferring to eavesdrop instead. I couldn't blame her. I wanted to hear his side of the conversation, too.

"No, she's not at her friend's house," we heard Ox say. "She's here in Wilmington." Pause. "Yes, she told me all about Albert." Pause. "Really, Louise. Your personal life is your business. But this . . . sudden new live-in is a bit much to force on our daughter, don't you think?"

Lindsey unfolded her long limbs from the floor and plopped down on the sofa to get a better vantage point from which to hear.

"Are you planning to marry him?" Ox continued. Long pause. "I think I do have a right to know since it involves Lindsey. Not to mention that I send you an alimony check every month and continue to pay the tax bill for the house that he now lives in." Another pause. "Seriously, Louise. I'd be happy for you and your new husband, if marriage is in the cards for you."

Louise's voice must have risen to a shout because Lindsey and I could actually hear faint sounds coming out of the handset when Ox paused to listen. The girl's mouth twisted with amusement.

"Now is not the time to discuss it," Ox finally said. "Lindsey is fine and we'll take good care of her, as always. Let's talk later." He hung up without listening to her reply.

Ox came back into the living room to find me petting Cracker and Lindsey immersed in a magazine. We looked up.

"I'm not saying one way or the other, but if your mother agrees to let you move here, we'll have to enroll you in school right away. Summer is almost over, and classes at New Hanover High School start the last week in August. That's only a few weeks away. Are you prepared to leave all your friends behind?"

"Absolutely. I mean, they can come and visit, right? And it's not like I haven't changed schools before. I am, after all, a military brat." Lindsey jumped off the sofa to give her father a kiss. "Can we go get a pizza?"

"Sure," Ox and I both said at the same time Spud ambled in.

"Lindsey! Get over here, doodlebug, and give me a hug!"

She ran to my father, swiped the beret from his head to put in on her own, and threw her long arms around him. He was a good head shorter than Lindsey and she had to bend her knees. My father and Ox's daughter had hit it off the very first time they met. I imagine that, if I had a son or daughter, Spud would be a fabulous grandfather. Odd, since he'd been a complete loser as a father when I was a kid.

"Did I hear the word *pizza*?" Spud snatched his cap back from Lindsey. "Let's go. Anybody 'round here got a car that ain't wrecked?"

"Dad will drive," Lindsey announced, prior crisis forgotten.

Ox mouthed a thank-you to me and we headed for A Slice of Life Pizzeria in Ox's four-door Ford truck.

SIX

"*I hear you've* got a few good armored cars to peddle," I said to Floyd, the man who handles vehicle and boat auctions for SWEET and several other low-profile agencies. Feeling domestic, I'd put a meat loaf in the oven and phoned him while I waited. "Ashton says he authorized me as a bidder."

"Jersey? Is that you? Where have you been hiding?"

"I'm not in hiding, Floyd. It's called retiring young." I peered through the oven door at the meat loaf. It didn't appear to be doing anything. "Well, at least I *was* retired."

He chuckled. "Yeah, you're on the authorized bidder list. I've got a nice Volvo XC70, color is lunar gold. Papers say the steel was done by Alpine Armoring, an outfit in Virginia. Level A9."

"Excellent. That'll stop a high-powered rifle, right?" Not that I planned on getting caught between a sniper's crosshairs, but A9 was a pretty good armor job. And lunar gold sounded pretty, in a New Age sort of way. I punched the speakerphone button to be hands-free, so I could go online to find a photograph of the Volvo.

"Stop pretty much anything, except armor-piercing ammo from a high-powered weapon. And maybe a shotgun slug fired at close range."

I found the Volvo Web site and waited for the photo I wanted. A tan station wagon appeared on the computer screen. "You did say XC70, right?"

"Yup. It's an all-wheel drive. Take you anywhere, on most any terrain."

"Sorry, I can't bring myself to drive a station wagon, even if the marketing folks at Volvo call it something else. And AARP beige just isn't my color, even if I am trying to retire."

He shuffled through some papers and told me the Volvo was the only armored vehicle up for auction.

"Well, crap."

"I thought you retired. Why do you need an armored set of wheels?"

"I am retired. But SWEET coerced me back to drive a mobile food truck and whip up bacon and egg biscuits on the side of the road."

He let out a laugh that climaxed with a cough. "Never mind. I don't want to know."

Exiting the Volvo site, I decided he was right. I did retire, from both the government, and more recently, from my own agency. I didn't need armor. And tooling around in a regular car would cut my fuel bill by half. "Forget about the Volvo. What else have you got?"

He rambled off several vehicles, paused, let out a low whistle, and mentioned an unavailable BMW X5. It was a beauty of a crossover vehicle—sedan bred with SUV—but it wouldn't be for sale until next month, he said.

"That's perfect, Floyd. I'll take it."

He blew out an emphatic sigh that ended in another cough. "What do you think I am? An eBay Buy It Now icon?"

"Of course not. And you really should quit smoking."

"I'm going on the patch next week," he said.

I waited to hear more about the X5.

"This thing is practically new, less than fifteen thousand miles. Seized from a stock broker who was selling confidential tidbits to a group of revolutionaries. It will land in the driveway of a higher-up before it ever hits the auction block."

"What color is it?"

"Black."

A shiver of excitement made my shoulders do the wave. I love black vehicles. Especially luxury ones.

I smiled. "I'd look way better driving that X5 than some old blowhard in a pinstripe."

He didn't respond. Maybe I was wearing him down.

I looked at the meat loaf again, willing it to cook. "I really do need a new car, Floyd. The Benz is toast and I can't afford the repair bill. I've been driving borrowed cars for a month. Can you hook me up?"

I heard the click of a lighter and his toke on a cigarette, which meant he'd made a decision. "Ten grand and I'll have it delivered to that bar of yours in a week or so."

"Can you do seven—"

"On paper, I'm going have to say the vehicle needs an engine and a transmission just to make ten fly. Seriously."

I waited.

"Jersey, this thing is in pristine condition."

"You still drinking Maker's Mark?"

"Mmm huh."

"Well, I'm sure the car has a few door dings. Seven thousand seems reasonable to me."

"Christ." He disconnected. I'd have to remember to send him a case of bourbon.

Victorious, I replaced the handset and checked the meat loaf again. It still wasn't doing anything. Consulting the recipe, I set the oven timer for one hour and headed downstairs to see if the Block's kitchen had any vegetables to go with my meat loaf.

Hanging behind the bar, Ox chummed with Pete, a local boat captain and one of the Block's regulars. Ox threw his head back to laugh at something Pete said and a rush of arousal fired through me at the glimpse of his squarish jaw and near-perfect teeth. I mentally scolded myself. I had to quit thinking of him that way. Or maybe not. It wasn't hurting anything. Fantasies of getting frisky with Ox were a harmless distraction.

"Got any mashed potatoes?" I said, walking up.

"Nope. Baked potatoes. Steamed broccoli."

"Can I have some of both? In fact, why don't you and Lindsey join me and Spud for dinner? I'm cooking meat loaf."

His dimple deepened when he smiled. "You do remember what happened last time you attempted to cook meat loaf?"

"Yeah, but this time I used a recipe."

Pete's hands gestured outward. "Hello? What am I, invisible?"

"I'm still mad at you for letting Soup have his way with *Incognito.* She was violated."

"To the contrary. Your boat has been pampered." He rolled his head to stretch the neck muscles. "Anyway, the voice feature on the depth finder is very hip."

"Okay, I'm over it." I gave him a greeting hug. "Want to join us for dinner?"

"Be much obliged," he agreed. "The wife has taken the girls back-to-school-clothes shopping, so I'm on my own tonight."

Lindsey scooted up to us, clutching a handful of dollar bills. "Can I get some more quarters, Dad?"

"You still losing?" Ox asked his daughter and opened the register to make change. A curious question, since there aren't arcade games in the Block. She took the coins with an outstretched hand. A colorful bracelet was tattooed around her wrist. I'd never noticed any tattoos during all her previous visits, and couldn't believe that Louise would have let her get one.

"Nope, I'm winning now that I've learned how to bluff. Fierce!" She skipped off to join Spud and Bobby at a corner booth, where playing cards and coins were spread among the used napkins and half-full glasses.

"She is her own person, isn't she?" Ox mused. "Growing up so fast it's almost scary."

"Growing up is a good thing," I said. "But aren't you upset that my father is teaching her to play poker? Or that she has a tattoo?"

"Some good life lessons to be learned in the strategy of gambling, Barnes. And the bracelet isn't a real tattoo. It's called Derma-Zing, which comes off. All the rage among the teen crowd. What rock have you been hiding under?"

I raised an eyebrow. "Lindsey just explain the Derma-Zing thing to you?"

Ox grinned.

"Hey, I'm out of touch with what's hip, too, and I've got three teenagers," Pete said. "I'd still be listening to the Doobie Brothers and wearing knee-high tube socks if it weren't for them."

"Being out of touch with what's cool is one thing. But I think I'm missing way too much of my daughter's life," Ox said. "She's like a different person in such a short amount of time."

Nobody had any feel-good words to say about that, so we set a time for dinner, Pete joined Spud's poker game, Ox left to make a bank deposit, and I walked upstairs to check on the meat loaf.

Ox and Lindsey arrived with a basket of bread, baked potatoes, and a container of steamed broccoli. Spud followed, carrying a deck of cards. Pete brought up the tail, grumbling about all the money that Lindsey swindled from him.

"How much did you win?" I asked her.

"Eight dollars and fifty cents. It would have been closer to twelve, but Spud cheated on the last hand."

"Girl can play some poker, I'm telling you," Spud said. "She's a natural."

I smeared some tomato paste across the top of the meat loaf and set the platter in the center of the table with a flourish. "Your gourmet meal is served."

Spud said grace, throwing in a gratitude for not only the food we were about to eat, but also the daughter who'd prepared it. I felt a sense of pride, something that almost bordered on maternal. Had my career and family path taken a different course, I'd be a whiz in the kitchen by now. Everyone passed the food and quickly dug in.

Spud abruptly stopped chewing and clutched his throat in the universal symbol for choking. He coughed up a half-swallowed mess of meat loaf and spit it into his napkin.

"You okay, Spud?"

He sucked down gulps of tea and gargled with the last swallow. "No I'm not okay! This meat loaf would gag a hog, for crying out loud."

I surveyed the faces around my table. They collectively wore a tortured expression.

"Thought you used a recipe this time," Ox said.

"I did, but I had to substitute for a few things I'm out of. Soy sauce for worcestershire. Regular sugar instead of brown sugar. Pepperoncinis instead of green peppers. Nothing major."

Everybody stared at me as though I'd just served them rabbit droppings.

"Oh, come on. It can't be that bad. Lindsey?"

"Maybe you have some tuna or something we can make sandwiches with?" she offered.

I cut an oversized piece of meat loaf, shoved it into my mouth, and chewed. "It tastes fine to me. Just a little salty, maybe, and a little spicy." I ate some more. "Bit of a vinegar aftertaste. But it's not *that* bad. And for your information, Spud, a hog can eat anything without gagging."

Ox excused himself from the table and returned minutes later with a plate-load of barbecued chicken breasts. Everyone dug in for the second time and the world was righted on its axis.

"So, have you decided whether or not I can live with you?" Lindsey asked her father without preamble. Accustomed to teenage crises, Pete smiled and helped himself to a second piece of chicken.

"I will talk to your mother and see if we can work something out."

"Is that a yes or a no?" Lindsey persisted.

"If she's agreeable, then yes, of course."

I changed the subject before the mood turned heavy. "You've got another tattoo thing, like the bracelet on your other arm."

"It's a Derma-Zing design. Tattoos are so, like, *out*," she said around a bite of bread, in a tone that silently added "you moron."

I examined the girl's forearm and ran my fingers over a bright purple rose with a green, thorny stem. The lines were slightly raised, almost like the text on an embossed business card, but thicker. "Nice detail on the rose. Did you do it?"

"I guess you could do your own designs but it's a lot more fun if you do each other's. Like, my best friend Marla did this one. Last month, all the girls on my tennis team had a pizza party and everybody got the same design on their left shoulder so it would show through our T-back uniform tops. And, like, if you're tight with a guy, then he would do a design on you. But you wouldn't do one on him, unless it was hidden, cuz guys don't get Derma-Zing designs. It would be like wearing mascara or something, you know?"

"Sure," I said, not really knowing, but intrigued nonetheless. "And these tattoos—"

"They're *designs,* Jerz," Lindsey cut in with an eye roll.

"The designs. How long do they last?"

She shrugged. "Maybe two weeks. After that, they peel off like a sunburn." She scooted her chair back and produced a bare foot. "See my ankle? That one just came off and you can't tell anything was there."

To prove a point to my ungrateful guests, I made a show of eating a second helping of meat loaf and tried to ignore the gag reflex. "Cool. So maybe I could do another design there for you."

"Uh, hello? Totally *not* cool." She shook her head and returned her attention to the grilled chicken breast on her plate.

Ox caught my eyes and we instantly knew what the other thought. He would have his hands full, for sure. Not only was Lindsey a hormonal teenager, but she'd virtually grown up on the West Coast. Now that the girl had sprouted breasts and curves, it was like she'd dropped in to visit from another planet.

Pete offered to take Lindsey out on my boat, Spud agreed to give her poker lessons, everyone thanked Ox for dinner, and Ox delivered a standing toast to me and my new job on the roach coach.

Before my dinner party disbanded, Lindsey reminded her father to settle things with her mother. He agreed to call Louise the next day.

"I love you, Dad."

He smiled. "Love you, too."

Ox stayed to help me with the dishes and we harmoniously worked side by side, enjoying the blues music I'd put on the CD player, mentally recapping the evening's events. When we finished, he slipped a leash on Cracker and we headed outside. Strolling along the sidewalks without a destination, we found ourselves in downtown's old residential area in front of the Camellia Cottage bed and breakfast. Its bloom-laden veranda caught our attention, as did the laughing couple stretched on their backs in a giant rope hammock. Arms extended, the young man held a giggling toddler up in the air above them.

"It's a little scary," Ox said, "the prospect of being solely responsible for a vibrant, opinionated, self-sufficient girl. You always hear people say how fast they grow up, but the sentiment never hits home until you're suddenly looking into the face of your own sixteen-year-old daughter, wondering when she stopped playing with matchbox cars and started wearing eyeliner."

I found his hand. "I'm here to help."

His fingers tightened around mine. "Thanks. That means a lot."

SEVEN

A thermos of spicy Bloody Marys would have been excellent liquid courage for my foray into the mobile food cart business but I resolved to drink bottled water instead. Sobriety might come in handy. I'd familiarized myself with the compact grill, lunchbox-sized steamer, cash register, and more important, the electronic toys Ashton had installed, including hidden video cams and a nifty miniature fluoroscope imaging system mounted inconspicuously beneath the fold-down serving counter on the passenger side of the truck. With the push of a button, it would give me a flash outline of a customer's body on a small notebook computer, which of course would reveal any metal objects—translation: weaponry. It is the same technology that has some airline passengers complaining about a lack of privacy, since fluoroscope images can reveal surprising detail of private body parts. I could learn, for example, whether a walk-up male customer tucked it to the left or the right as I served his coffee with extra sugar. Not that I would use an expensive antiterrorism contraption for such petty purposes. Unless I got really bored. Or the man was particularly hunky.

The drive to Sunny Point carried me through Southport and the passing scenery could have been any small beach town with a hodgepodge of shops and lots of signage: directional road signs for the ferry that cruised between Southport and Fort Fisher, colorful advertisements hawking sunset cruises, kayak rentals, and deep-sea fishing excursions, and an array of real estate billboards. I cruised past a few groceries, the all-important high-pressure car wash to remove sand and salt, and a liquor store, which most certainly had all the fixings for a good Bloody Mary. I ignored the impulse to turn in. A mix of older, modest homes with crushed oyster shell drives and newer, much bigger homes with elaborate entrances occupied the land bordering the Cape Fear River. A touch of early post-dawn chill blew from an awakening sky and, other than the fact that it was six thirty in the morning, it was a pretty decent day to sell food on the side of the road.

I reached my destination and swung in, just off the intersection of Highway 133 and Sunny Point Road. A large brown sign on elevated posts declared: UNITED STATES ARMY MILITARY OCEAN TERMINAL SUNNY POINT MAIN GATE. Just for kicks, I continued east toward the bowels of the ammo dump. It was another mile to the two real main gates: one for general admission and the other for truck deliveries. The general gate was closed up tight so I forked right to the other gate, which was guarded by several square badges from AJAT Security. They weren't soldiers, but they weren't your average contract security workers, either. There were five of them and these well-paid men were armed with everything from holstered semiautomatic pistols to a Mossberg shotgun, and that's just what was visible. During the Clinton administration when military bases across the country closed, a large number of military positions were eliminated. In many cases, they were simply replaced by civilians.

"Hi, guys." I gave them my friendly and eager-to-please smile from the window of my oversized, boxy truck. "I'm taking over for Mama Jean and I know she serves a lot of people who work here, but I'm not sure where she parked," I lied, knowing she parked a mile back, just off the intersection.

A man with the last name of Henson—according to his name badge—leaned back on his heels and grinned. "Looks like Jean is leaving her business in very good hands, Miss . . ."

"I'm Jill. Jill Burns."

"Well, Jill, you'll need to park this baby off-property." The man leaning against a guard shack paid close attention but his face remained impassive, almost hostile. Three others openly followed the conversation, but were content to let their buddy deal with me. Henson lowered his voice. "That's the official answer. But really, you can probably get away with setting up just inside the first gate you came through, by the intersection. Mama Jean's been parking there for years, so I doubt anybody will hassle you."

"Great, thanks."

All five men watched as I pulled forward and made a slow U-turn. I waved as I passed. Nobody waved back, but Henson nodded once.

I drove back toward the main intersection and angled the truck into a well-used horseshoe on the side of the road. As Mama Jean instructed during our telephone training session, I prepped everything before I flipped up my side flaps and lowered out the serving counter. When I opened for business, a few cars stopped almost immediately, and not surprisingly, they inquired about Mama Jean and her condition. She was fine, I reported, and resting comfortably. By nine o'clock, I'd small-talked myself into a slightly dazed, smiling stupor. And I'd only checked out somebody's private parts once. My first three hours back into undercover work and all I'd learned was that some men don't tuck it either way. Apparently, straight down works, too.

I also learned from one particularly gossipy group of three carpooling women that Mama Jean consistently overcooked eggs and had a reputation for serving stale biscuits, which explained why most people purchased only coffee or bottled juice and prepackaged muffins. The preparation instruction manual supplied by a helpful food distributor offered several nifty hints, such as, place the thawed-out biscuits in the steamer for twelve seconds before serving and use the round egg mold for perfectly cooked eggs every time. Apparently, Mama Jean hadn't bothered to read the manual, which meant that nobody would expect too much out of me. I had nowhere to go but up with my breakfast cooking skills.

By the time I dropped the truck at the designated warehouse, swapped it for my economy-sized rental car, and drove home, exhaustion had set in and it wasn't yet eleven in the morning. I grabbed the newspaper and a beverage and had just gotten comfortable in a chaise lounge on my outside balcony when Soup phoned.

"How was your first day on the vomit van?"

"I learned that sometimes they just hang straight down. And I made nineteen dollars in tips."

"I'm not going to ask about your newfound knowledge on perpendicularity, and you should probably turn over all of your tips."

I planned to turn the bills over, all right. As I stuffed them in my wallet. "What's up?"

"Hacked into Lady Lizzy's computer."

"The gossip columnist?" Lady Lizzy is who locals turn to for the latest Wilmington-area scoop. She has a column, a radio talk show, and a blog.

"Yep. Her home computer is set to allow remote access, probably so she can get in from her work computer. Or maybe to get technical help. Anyway, I tiptoed in and found her calendar of upcoming events to be most interesting."

I popped the tab on a Coors Light, promising myself that it would be my only one for the day. Even though it wasn't yet lunchtime, it sure felt like it. "Soup, you're amazing."

"Tell me something I don't know."

"And you're cocky."

"Like I said, tell me—"

"Yeah, yeah. I know that I'm going to owe you. Watcha got?"

"Using the *Star-News* and the *State Port Pilot* event blurbs, the chamber of commerce calendar, and Lizzy's juicy stuff, I've compiled a list of potentially suspect activities. Those with celebs, high-profile politicians, and a large planned attendance. Hundred-mile radius and two months out, as requested."

"With exact dates and locations?"

"Of course. Even have the contact person or event planner for most."

The beer cooled my insides as it slid down and pooled satisfyingly in my stomach while my brain wrapped itself around the good news I'd just received. I'd have to get a Sunny Point delivery schedule along with the rail and road routes used. "So then, I can map out the location of the events and see if any correspond with travel routes of incoming shipments to the ammo dump."

"You betcha. If you can work that in between your bridge clubs and bingo nights."

"For your information, even when I do manage to retire for real, I won't be hanging out in a bingo hall. And I don't know how to play bridge," I said.

"You could always form a shuffleboard league."

"I owe you, guy."

"No shit," he said before hanging up.

EIGHT

Daydreaming, Peggy Lee Cooke let her outstretched palms caress the rows of hanging gowns as she roamed the aisles of Llewellyn's Bridal Shoppe. She loved the satiny feel of the fabrics and the delicate lace and beads that could make a person appear sexy and virginal all at the same time. She stopped to watch a young woman and her mother, undeniably jealous of the fact that this girl already had a wedding date. Not to mention a mother who was obviously involved in her daughter's life.

Peggy couldn't stand the stepmother who'd raised her and she wouldn't have the benefit of a doting mother-in-law, either. Chuck's parents were both killed in Bangladesh, along with more than two hundred other employees and residents, during an industrial explosion. The only reason Chuck didn't die with them, he'd told her, is because he lived in the States at the time, earning a chemical engineering degree. Bond Chemical had transferred his father from Connecticut to head up the new overseas operation. It was a lucky career advancement, people said back then. But now, everyone knew better. Chuck had spit on the employer-paid life insurance benefit check with plans to send it back when he realized that he could put the money to good use. Combined with the settlement funds from a class-action lawsuit, it was enough capital to start a business. Today, Chuck's company was hugely successful and, thanks to his old Ivy League fraternity friends, boasted a heavy-hitting client list that included several government contracts. But Chuck still thought of his dead parents every day, he'd confided to Peggy. He imagined the terror they must have felt during the last minutes of their lives. And every flashback of the parents he lost made Chuck even more angry at all the manufacturers who continued to churn out loads of nonessentials for product-hungry Americans—everything from expensive cosmetics to cheap trinkets. It was all so senseless, he'd said, and Peggy agreed. People were materialistic and wasteful, he'd explained, and Peggy agreed. She agreed with everything he voiced. She loved him. And even though Chuck continued to mourn, Peggy knew she could help him heal.

Watching the mother-daughter pair shop, Peggy experienced a flash of resentment at having been cheated out of the mother-in-law she'd never know. She missed Chuck's parents, too, and she'd never even met them.

"We can have any gown delivered right to the wedding location," a clerk was telling the pair. "It's a residence, yes?" The woman rattled off a street address and the clerk replied that she could deliver to any location within thirty miles. They discussed details of the wedding after which the mother dismissed the sales clerk with a few curt words.

"Mom, there is plenty of time, really," Peggy heard the college coed-looking girl say. "My gown is the main thing that matters."

"Your wedding is next month. That's only three weeks away, and right now, everything matters! We need to finalize the menu by tomorrow. The wedding planner is threatening to quit if we don't sit down with him and finish choosing the flowers and decorations. And whichever gown you get, it will probably have to be altered. Seriously, Janie, there is a lot to do."

The girl held a bright white strapless gown against her body and studied the effect in a full-length mirror. "You're just freaking out because Daddy's entourage will be there. Everything has to be perfect since it's a great photo op for the press. And of course you want to impress all his supporters, with your big dreams of being the first lady if he actually runs in the next election. And the mayor of New York City? Whoop-di-do. Daryl and I could care less if he's there, even if he is best friends with Daddy." The girl spun sideways to get a better view of the gown's detachable train. "You don't care about what I want."

The mother turned her daughter around by the shoulders and spoke in a low controlled voice, but it was loud enough so that Peggy could keep eavesdropping. "First of all, you will *not* speak to me like that. And second of all, your father and I are spending a fortune on this wedding. The only reason we're doing it here is because it's what you wanted, even though I've had the Starlight Roof at the Waldorf-Astoria reserved for a year. If this was all about what I wanted, you'd be getting married in Manhattan instead of here. So quit being bratty about everything and for God's sake, pick out a gown already!"

The girl sighed, dropped the dress. "I'm sorry, Mom. I like the other dress, the one they're holding at that little bridal boutique on Oleander Drive."

Mother and daughter hustled out the front door without bothering to thank anyone. Peggy picked up the discarded strapless number and held it up with one hand while scrunching her hair in a makeshift twist with the other.

"Would you like to try it on?" a saleswoman asked.

Peggy checked the price tag. Twenty-seven hundred and sixty-five dollars. "No thanks, not today."

She left the store with a smile, thinking that soon, a three-thousand-dollar dress wouldn't be a problem. Heck, when her time came, Chuck would spend *thirty-three* thousand dollars for a dress if that's what she wanted. Once Project Antisis took off, there would be no limit to what she could have. They would be rich.

NINE

It was a great day and then it wasn't, and then it was again. My used—but new to me—BMW X5 arrived and she was a beauty. Shiny black on the outside and creamy soft tan leather on the inside. To my delight, Floyd had even put a brand-new set of tires on it for me. I found a note in the glove box that read: "Try not to get this one shot up, will you? Floyd." With Ox riding shotgun and Lindsey in the back, I immediately went for a test drive through Wilmington's historic residential district and fell in love. The delivery made my day.

But then Ashton ruined a perfectly good natural high by refusing to give me the information I wanted. I didn't need the details on incoming or outgoing container loads of ammo, he told me. Furthermore, he said, I had no need to know the routes they'd travel, much less the time of day they'd be traversing rail or road. Before disconnecting, Ashton reminded me that I was in place as a trained observer, not an investigator. *Whatever,* as Lindsey would say. Simply asking for information is the easy way to acquire it, but there are plenty of other methods.

"Fine, that's just fine," I grumbled to Ox. After our test drive, Lindsey had disappeared to explore the riverwalk on foot and Ox and I had plopped down at a round table outside the Block. The Block's patio is constructed of wide bricks over a bed of sand, and small greenish brown chameleons darted among the tables and chairs, hunting insects only they could see. Word is, they eat mosquitoes, too, so I like the reptiles. "If SWEET wants to pay me nineteen hundred dollars a week to serve freakin' egg biscuits out of a truck, then that's what I'll do."

"Uh-huh," Ox said. "You'll keep digging."

I wiped at a miniscule stream of perspiration that intermittently dropped between my breasts, tickling the crevice over my breastbone. July is supposedly the hottest month in Wilmington, but August always seems hotter to me. Something about the month of August feels sensual, or maybe the long days are just plain sweaty and sticky. Perhaps it depends upon one's mood. Despite the day's heat index, though, outdoor breezes and stimulating smells had drawn a gathering of patio customers.

Relaxing beneath the shade of an umbrella and passively observing the activity around us was indulgent, and aside from being disgruntled, I physically felt perfectly content. "Ashton said they are closely monitoring all movement of munitions and have added extra security. Like that's a good reason I can't have the requested route and delivery schedule."

With a wave, Ox acknowledged a couple of regulars entering the pub. "Guess Ashton is big on the need-to-know-basis concept."

I handed over the calendar of social events that Soup compiled. "You make anything of this?"

Ox scanned the data. The list was comprehensive and included political fund-raisers, charitable fund-raisers, grand-opening events, various festivals, a number of private functions, and an invitation-only showing of a soon-to-be-released film that had been shot in

Wilmington. We discussed the movie—a harmless romantic comedy—and went over each event in some detail.

"What are the three double-starred entries?" Ox said.

"They came from Lady Lizzy's computer. Scheduled events marked with stars, but no additional details. Based on her columns, I'd guess they are happenings where somebody big is expected to attend. A celebrity, maybe."

"Think the three events are connected?"

"It's a possibility."

"Maybe we should go talk to her."

"Sure," I agreed. "But we'll need something to trade. Lizzy won't give anything away unless she gets something in return. And we certainly can't mention the phrase 'terrorist attack' or she'd write a panic column that would evacuate the entire peninsula."

Ox poured some ice water over a thick napkin and wiped the back of his neck. Either I was sun-drunk, or the move was sexy. Undeniably sexy. Crazy, abandon-all-reason, undeniably sexy. It made me want to finish what he started by wiping down his face and chest, slowly, with an icy cold cloth. Like I said, August is a sensual month.

"So, back to my original question." I held up the stapled papers and shook them. "You make anything of this list?"

"Other than the logical assumptions we've already discussed? No."

I cut my eyes up to the sky. "What about them?"

"The spirits?"

"Yeah, your protective spirits, your instincts, your uniquely accurate gut feelings? All of them. What do they say about my list?"

Ox leaned back to reposition his legs, crossing them at the ankles after kicking off a pair of leather boat shoes. He wore Bermuda shorts and a nearly hairless, well-muscled leg brushed mine when he settled into his new position. I almost wanted to forget about work in lieu of determining how my relatively light skin would look next to his golden-olive pigmentation. The vivid thought pricked at my nerve endings. All of them.

Ox caressed my bare leg with a naked foot. "Your own instincts are just fine, Jersey Barnes, and you should trust them. What are they telling you right now?"

I slid my feet out of their sandals and returned the toe caress. "That playing footsies with my best friend and business partner is much more fun than thinking about terrorists?"

The arch of his right foot traveled up the inside of my left leg, stopping just below my knee. A vibration of energy continued upward. My eyes closed in response and when I opened them, Ox was staring at my mouth. His eyes radiated pure appetite.

"Want to play more than footsies?" he said.

In high school, we'd simply been too young to concern ourselves with sex and were quite content to hit each other with gloved fists in the boxing ring as he taught me how to fight. My recollections fast-forwarded to five years ago, when he'd divorced and moved to Wilmington. The desire had revved up on several occasions, but there had always been some germane reason to avoid sex with each other. Mainly, I suppose, we didn't want to mess up a good thing. But now, the August heat had disabled all reasoning capabilities and I couldn't think. To heck with worrying about ruining a friendship.

"That's a most enticing suggestion, Duke Oxendine."

We headed upstairs to my bedroom, stripped off every thread of clothing, and didn't emerge until the late afternoon heat gave way to a pastel-colored duskish sky. We knew each other better than anyone else in the entire world and the physical closeness, mouth against mouth, skin against skin, culminated a twenty-seven-year friendship. My earlier prediction had been accurate: sex with Ox is indescribable.

TEN

Ox's scent clung to the sensors in my nose and my aura hovered somewhere near giddy. I was in such a good mood that I didn't even mind my unplanned return to undercover work. It had taken several shifts on the roach coach for me to fall into a comfortable rhythm, and more important, for the regulars to become chummy with me. They stopped in clumps and hung around for several minutes to laugh, bitch, and talk about their upcoming workdays. I'd identified three civilians who were on Ashton's persons of interest list, but all seemed like ordinary hard-working tax-paying citizens to me and none, according to the fluoroscope, were packing heat. Why they'd been identified as POIs made no sense to me, but as instructed, I completed my daily reports and e-mailed them from the onboard laptop computer. In addition to keeping a vehicle traffic count and gleaning intelligence information during five-minute chunks of conversation, I became a master with the grill—using the egg molds—and customers started ordering breakfast biscuits. Just for kicks, I ran a two-for-one special and discovered a direct correlation between free food and the number of bills in my tip jar.

Into my ninth or tenth morning on duty, I sat on a stool inside Mama Jean's truck, skimming the newspaper, when John's sedan pulled in. He is the AJAT contractor who heads up day-to-day security at MOTSU, but unlike the gate guards, he doesn't wear a uniform and looks pretty darn good in a white button-down and tie.

"Hey, Jill," he called through the serving window. "You still doing two-for-one biscuits? If so, I'll take a couple of sausage."

I guessed him to be in his late forties, even though a muscular body and entirely flat stomach made him appear younger. He'd passed Ashton's background check and hadn't been identified as anything other than what he appeared to be. Still, since he was in a position to oversee the movement of shipments through Sunny Point, I'd been paying him special attention in hopes of learning something that resembled a clue.

"For you? Sure." I pulled out two precooked frozen sausage patties and tossed them on the grill. "What are you up to today?"

"The usual. Shipments come and shipments go. I keep everything secure during the process."

"Drinking coffee this morning?" I asked and shifted into wide-eyed, admiring bimbette mode.

"Please."

I served his coffee and added three creamers, just like he drank it. "You make your job sound so easy. But it must be high pressure. I mean, it's a lot of responsibility, right?"

He grinned. "Somebody's got to do it."

The sausage patties started to sizzle so I flipped them and dropped a few biscuits into the steamer. Twelve seconds later a sounder buzzed. I removed the biscuits, added the sausage, and stuck each in a foil wrapper.

I punched some numbers into the cash register. "That's three dollars and eighty-five cents."

He produced a five and told me to keep the change.

I gave him my earnest smile. "Thanks."

"Why don't you come out here and sit with me for a minute while I eat?"

I'd added four folding plastic chairs to the roach coach supplies, and set them up outside Mama Jean's truck every morning, along with a small plastic table that was perfect for setting drinks on.

"Sure," I agreed. It was nearing time for me to close, so there probably wouldn't be any additional sales for the day.

We discussed the hot temperatures, last weekend's king mackerel fishing tournament, and a newspaper article about the expanded walking paths at Orton Plantation and Gardens. He finished his second biscuit before broaching the subject of me.

"So tell me, Jill, I'm curious." He blew on his coffee before sipping it and I noticed that he was missing part of his ring finger, enough to make it shorter than his pinky. "How did you end up working for Mama Jean?"

I'd already been asked the same question several times. "I heard about the job through a temp agency and the hours are perfect for me. I serve a few biscuits, muffins, and coffee and then I've got the rest of the day off to do whatever I want. I paint, for example. Nothing I'd show anybody, but I enjoy throwing some oil colors on a canvas."

"You're an artist, then. But working for Mama Jean can't pay all that well."

"Pays enough for me. Besides, I don't want a real job. If I had one of those, I'd have to actually work." I made an icky face. "Yuk."

He laughed, sipped more coffee. "You're a lot of fun, Jill. What say we meet for a drink this evening, after I finish my shift? Nothing fancy. Just a cocktail and a snack somewhere."

"Sure." There could be worse things than having a drink with an athletic and charming fellow. Plus, if I could get a few drinks in him, I might learn something useful. I gave him the mobile number that Ashton had issued me. It rang into a nifty slim camera phone, which also served as a GPS tracking device so that SWEET could keep up with me. Of course, it only worked if the phone was powered on.

Nobody else stopped for food or coffee so I closed up shop and headed to the warehouse where I kept the truck parked. The day hadn't yet warmed up to hot status, so I drove home from the warehouse in my X5 with all the windows down and sunroof open, thoroughly enjoying the fresh air and sunshine. My light mood dissipated when I arrived at the Block to find Ashton. It was probably not good news.

"Mama Jean is dead," he said. "Her neighbor found her on the sofa, unresponsive. Cause of death not yet known, but it doesn't appear to be a homicide."

I retrieved a couple bottled waters and joined him at a table. "You believe that?"

"I just saw her yesterday to give her your week's deposit. She was perfectly fine then. Almost bubbly. Told me that she felt great and had even stopped taking the prescribed painkillers."

"What's your take?"

He grimaced. "Something isn't right. Far as Mama Jean knew, I own a temp agency and provided you to work the truck. She was thrilled with everything, especially the fact that I would personally drop by once a week to bring her money. Oh, she also said that you've increased breakfast sales thirty percent and that I should give you a raise."

My shoulders went up. "Can't argue with that."

"Mentioned that she earned thirty-five to forty dollars a day in her tip jar, between breakfast and lunch. Said you were probably making twenty a day, just doing breakfast." His head cocked slightly and he squinted at me through raised eyebrows.

"There's a tip jar?" I said.

The brows went down and he shook his head. "Is there a chance that your cover has been compromised?"

"I don't see how." I'd been careful and always made sure I wasn't followed when going to and from the warehouse, where the food truck was garaged. And while the Block is a popular Wilmington hangout, people working and living around Southport had plenty of their own hangouts and rarely traveled to Wilmington just for a meal. Plus, even if a Sunny Point employee did spot me at the Block, they'd have no reason to suspect I owned the place.

My handler frowned. "There will be an obituary in *The State Port Pilot.*"

I nodded.

"She lived in a mobile home on Long Beach. Local PD is handling the investigation, but I've got one of our people on it and another overseeing the autopsy. You'll be updated shortly. Meanwhile, let me know if you make any connections with anyone who might have motive."

I nodded again and Ashton—never one to waste time or words—disappeared without bidding me good-bye. I felt sad for a woman I'd never met in person and wondered what she might have known that could have gotten her killed. Mama Jean had been serving food along roadsides and at construction sites around Southport for more than fifteen years. She'd experienced firsthand the new construction growth and she knew a lot of locals. And since working the truck, I'd learned that people treated me like a hairdresser or cab driver, when it came to talking. They disclosed things they'd probably never say to a coworker or a neighbor. Perhaps Mama Jean had learned something that could have been dangerous to someone. My head buzzed with ifs and unknowns. I changed clothes—stuffing my boobs into my favorite hot-pink sports bra—and headed to the gym for a weight workout. I threw a pair of flip-flops into my bag so I could go for a manicure and pedicure afterward.

I met John at Fishy Fishy Cafe in Southport and was pleased to see that he looked even better in jeans and a Tommy Bahama silk shirt than he did in business attire. All other things being equal, it never hurt to have nice scenery while doing undercover work. Or eat great food.

"Wow," John said when he saw me in a tan linen skirt and wedge sandals. My everyday piece, a .45 caliber Glock, was concealed inside a matching short-sleeve cropped jacket that buttoned at the waist. The getup was complimented by an ultra-low-cut stretchy white top with beaded trim. Since I have the big implants, I figure that I may as well show them off and the majority of my dress-up clothes do just that. "Don't you look beautiful."

"Thanks," I said. "I clean up well."

We ordered fish tacos for an appetizer and an entrée of paella—chicken, clams, and spicy sausage cooked in rice—plus a couple of icy Land Shark Lagers to cut the burn. A group of construction contractors all similarly clad in work jeans, tees, and baseball caps were just finishing their end-of-day happy hour and spotting them was a sure sign of good food and cheap beer. Fishy Fishy butts up to the water and its small bar serves double duty by opening to the outside docks and to the indoor clientele. We chose to sit on the outdoor covered pier to take advantage of the water view, as pelicans swooped in to claim a post.

When our beers were served, we clinked to Jimmy Buffett's marketing prowess, as he partnered with Anheuser-Busch to produce the Land Shark Lager under the Margaritaville Brewing Company label. The beers were light and smooth and quite good. Then again,

I've never tried a new beer I didn't like. John took another swig, drawing my attention to his missing piece of ring finger. "What happened to your hand?"

His expression froze in distaste, as though I'd asked something very personal. After a few beats, he held up his hand, fingers outstretched and palm toward me. His hands were huge and the fingers thick with muscle, like a football jock. "Lost it in an accident. No big deal."

"Okay. I don't mean to pry, John. I was just curious."

He studied something invisible to me, something hanging in the air, a vivid flashback maybe. "We grew up on a small farm. When we were teenagers, my brother was feeding stalks of corn through the chopper and his shirt got caught. Almost pulled him in."

"So you saved him?"

John drank, nodded. "Back then, not all machines had emergency shutoffs, and there wasn't time to do anything other than cut his shirt away to free him. I didn't even realize I'd hurt myself until we saw the blood. He said I was his hero. And he was real upset that a piece of my finger was cut off." John drank a third of the bottle with one tilt. "What he didn't realize is that I would have gladly lost my entire hand, or even my arm, to save him."

I nodded. "Where does he live?"

John's eyes cut sharply to mine. "He doesn't. He's dead."

"Oh. I'm sorry to hear that." John didn't want to talk about it so I didn't push.

Our appetizer arrived and we ordered a second round of lagers. He spooned one of the grouper-and-avocado-stuffed flour tortillas onto a small plate for me before serving himself. "Since we're learning a bit about each other, tell me, Jill. Who do you really work for?"

"Excuse me?" My hearing is fine, but he'd caught me completely off guard.

"My guess is Homeland Security, even though you don't look the type."

I showed him my puzzled smile. "You think I work for Homeland Security? That's the craziest thing I've ever heard. Why would you say that?"

"Just a guess. But what I do know is that the temp agency you supposedly work for doesn't exist. Mama Jean gave me the number when I stopped by to bring her flowers. I need to hire some laborers to do a renovation project at my condo, but when I called, the person on the other end of that number said she was short staffed and didn't have anyone available, even though I told her I was flexible on the days. What's more strange is the fact that there is no business listing anywhere in this area for the temp agency."

"You've got quite an imagination. Besides, the temp agency is brand new."

John smiled and the skin around his eyes crinkled, giving his eyes a friendly, almost mischievous appeal. I noticed that the hair at his temples was slightly gray, but on him, it looked distinguished. "I don't believe you," he said.

"Why not?"

"The miniature cameras mounted beneath your truck's overhang, for starters. Most people would never bother to look, much less recognize them as digital recording devices. But I'm trained to notice things."

I brushed my hair back and styled it with my fingers, unconcerned. "That's weird, because I've never noticed anything even resembling a camera anywhere on Mama Jean's truck."

"I oversee day-to-day security for MOTSU. I know pretty much everything that goes on. And I've seen several new additions in personnel that happened all at once." I started to interrupt but he stopped me with an upheld hand. "Plus I was instructed to have my men on alert for anything unusual and report any deviances—regardless of how slight—from normal operating procedures. Security measures are tighter than before. It's obvious that a potential threat has been detected."

My eyes went wide. "What kind of threat?"

"Don't know, wasn't told."

I gave him my brightest smile. "Well anyway, I just sell food from a truck to earn a little lipstick money. For something to do, really. I lead a simple life."

He reached across the small table to take my hand. "You are anything but simple, Jill. If that's your real name."

Our paella arrived and he let go of my hand. "Regardless of who you work for, it's clear that we are both in the business of keeping people safe. Maybe we can help each other out by sharing information."

I'd have to notify Ashton of John's suspicions and there would be hell to pay for somebody. Probably the genius who first made contact with Mama Jean and created my undercover role. "Jill is my real name. And, sure, I'm all for sharing information. That could be fun. Whatcha got for me?"

"Nothing right now. What do you have for me?"

"Nothing right now."

He nodded to himself. "Well then, I guess there's nothing to do but eat and enjoy each other's company."

We did just that and my thoughts only strayed to Ox two or three times. John was entertaining, but I would have rather been sitting across from my best-friend-turned-lover. Ox loves spicy food as much as I do. And we might have started playing footsies under the table again.

ELEVEN

Napping isn't my thing, but that's exactly what I was doing when Lindsey awakened me by pounding on the door.

"Lindsey, hey, what's up," I said, letting her in, not believing I'd been asleep on the sofa for more than an hour.

"Can I stay here for a few days?"

I stretched my sleepy muscles as her request sunk in. "Sure, I guess, if it's okay with your dad. But why don't you want to stay where you are, at his place?"

She opened the refrigerator and peered at the contents for a full minute before selecting a bottle of water. "Mom showed up this morning. Flew in on the red-eye."

My stomach balled up. "Louise is here, in Wilmington?"

Lindsey gulped half the water with one tilt of her head. "Yep. She was all stressed out because one of the gifts she brought in her carry-on had broken, and then they confiscated her hair trimming scissors at the airport, and then the flight was delayed. But that's just Mom. She's easily excited, you know? Anyway, she had Dad put her luggage in my room and made a big deal about how she'll sleep in there, with me. Like I care which bed she crawls in. But I think she wants to try and work things out with Dad. She probably got sick of cooking all that tofu and seaweed shit for Albert."

"You shouldn't use that kind of language, doodlebug," Spud said, coming into the kitchen with a yawn. He'd just awakened from his own nap. "Although I ate tofu chili one time, and it did taste like shit."

"Anyway," Lindsey continued, "Mom is all, like, emotional or something and I don't want to be in the middle of that little dog-and-pony show, you know?"

Before I had a chance to answer Lindsey's request, Ox knocked once and punched in the security code to enter. "Thought I might find you here, Lin."

"Hi Dad. Jersey said it's cool if I stay here."

I had?

Lindsey plowed on. "It's actually closer to the high school and besides, I'd see you every day, right?" She and Ox both knew that I loved the girl like my own family. Of course she could stay with me, just as she had a few times before. This time, though, the reason for her request was already gnawing a tiny hole in the lining of my stomach.

I felt Ox's eyes on me, but I couldn't look at him. The passionate hours we'd spent together just a few days ago were fresh and vivid, and I didn't want to contemplate the possibility of Ox reuniting with his ex. "Sure, Lindsey can stay here as long as she'd like if that's good with you, Ox."

"Thanks, Jerz, that's perfect! Maybe I can even work at the Block a few hours a day, after school."

"Lindsey, honey, why don't you and Spud play some cards while Jersey and I go downstairs to talk?"

"No problem." She practically skipped to Spud and gave him a hug. "Hey, teach! Will you show me how poker side cards—I mean kickers—work?"

Chatting it up like old buddies, they plopped down at the kitchen table and Lindsey expertly shuffled a deck of cards, just like my father taught her. I watched, thinking about what it would have been like for me to spend time with Spud, back when I was Lindsey's age. And why, I wondered as self-pity turned my bones to rubber, why did Ox's ex-wife decide to come after him now, when she'd never wanted anything from him before except money? Life suddenly sucked and my soul felt flat, deflated. Wordless, I walked through the door while Ox held it open. We headed down the stairs, to the Block's outdoor patio.

"Louise said she had to divorce me to find herself," Ox said, once we'd settled ourselves into swiveling chairs. "Now that she's learned she can survive on her own, and now that she's sharing the house with this Albert fellow, she realizes that she can open herself up to someone again. Become half of a couple, she said."

My abdominal muscles relaxed and I realized I'd been holding my breath. "That's good, right? If she marries her live-in, you won't have to pay alimony any longer."

His eyes held mine for so long that I could see the pupils dilate and constrict as they focused. "She flew here because she had to see me. To be sure."

My stomach contracted again. "To be sure that she is completely over you?"

"Yes."

I wrapped my mind around his single-word answer and thought about the laws of reciprocity. "And, you? Do you need to find out if you're completely over her?"

Ruby sashayed by our table to see if we wanted anything. Neither of us did. Sensing the conversation to be private, she kept moving.

"Jersey, the other day with you was incredible and I haven't been able to stop thinking about it—and you—since. What we might be, if we decide we want to be together. But I can't just turn Louise away."

Yes you can, I thought. *She dumped you and broke your heart.*

"We had a lot of good years together and she's the mother of my daughter."

A daughter who will be college-bound in a few more years.

"We don't talk about it, you and I," he continued, "but we both know that we love each other. We've been tight since high school and our relationship is something special, something magical. I'd do anything in the world for you."

Apparently not anything, since you're letting Louise barrel her way back into your life, I mused.

"Say *something,* Jersey. Say anything. Talk to me."

I breathed deep and corralled my emotions into a small place where I hoped they'd stay dormant. "There's nothing to say, Ox. You have to do what's right for you. Lindsey is welcome to stay here. And as for me, I'm off to have a chat with Lady Lizzy."

"Want me to ride along with—"

"No, thanks," I interrupted. "I'm all set."

I left before he could protest, thinking that the dynamics of our relationship were irreversibly damaged. Ox and I were no longer tuned to the same frequency. Being around him suddenly felt clumsy and awkward. I didn't even bother to ask what information he had planned to trade with Lady Lizzy, to get her to tell all about her calendar. I had something of my own to use and didn't need his help. Or maybe I did need it, but I damn sure wasn't going to ask for it.

The gossip columnist agreed to meet with me at the Thalian Hall/City Hall complex in Wilmington, a venue built in the mid-1800s that includes a three-level theater—one of the oldest in the country. Visitors find it odd that the historic structure serves as both a cultural and political center, but locals love the building enough to have fought for its preservation. Simply approaching the stately, ornate entrance made me feel dignified and I reflexively checked my posture. Head up, shoulders back, boobs out, weapon snugly holstered.

Standing tall, I found Lady Lizzy in the ballroom, which is not only the regular meeting space for the Wilmington City Council but also an elegant, two-story room for rent that is well known to wedding planners. The famous columnist reminded me of Joan Rivers on speed: more flamboyant than the original, louder, and flaunting perhaps twice as many plastic surgeries. Her eyes held a perpetually surprised expression. She was covering tonight's celebration of matrimonial bliss for some reason and I hoped to find out why, especially since it just so happened to be one of the starred dates that Soup rooted out of her computerized calendar database.

"Dahling." She hustled my way with petite steps. "You must be Jersey!" She leaned in to do the double air-kiss thing on my cheeks. I hate the double air-kiss, but I can pretend otherwise.

"Lady Lizzy," I gushed right back, "it's so *fabulous* to meet you in person. Just love your column."

Not, I thought. I'd never even read her column, but I could suck up when necessary.

"I don't have much time because the guests will start arriving soon and I'll have to make the rounds. It's rumored that Dale Earnhardt, Jr. will be here, since he's friends with the groom because they grew up together around Kannapolis!" Her eyebrows bobbed up and down as she spoke. "Plus I've got a definite that Sharon Lawrence is coming! She played Sylvia Sipowicz on *NYPD Blue,* you know. Family friend of the bride! But you've got me all to yourself for ten or fifteen minutes!"

The woman was a walking exclamation point. Ten or fifteen

minutes would be all I could handle. We sat at a linen-covered round table that was topped with an arrangement of bright flowers and miniature candles. There were about twenty other identical tables, but ours had a direct view of downtown through huge Palladian windows. Caterers scurried about, attending to last-minute details. A server wearing black and white stopped to ask if we'd like a glass of champagne.

"That would be just lovely, doll," Lizzy crooned.

I told the waiter I'd have some champagne, too, thinking that Lady Lizzy might fall out of her chair if I asked for a beer.

As soon as the server left, Lady Lizzy leaned in and lowered her voice even though I didn't see anybody within earshot. "So what do you have for me, Jersey?"

I lowered my voice, too. "Something that is juicy enough to cause a huge wave of chatter from your readers, and soak them with delicious speculation. But I'd like to ask you a question or two first."

She frowned and fluttered long, spiky, glued-on eyelashes my way. "I do hope you're not wasting my time."

Sliding into my sorority sister role—the type of sister who honored the woman-to-woman alliance—I showed her my sincere smile. "Of course I didn't come here to waste your time. I've got some great scoop and it's exclusively yours, if you want it. All you have to do is answer a few teeny questions about some upcoming social events, since you're the expert on these things. Consider it a trade—my scoop for your social calendar."

"You own the Barnes Agency, right? It's some sort of security agency!" She gulped half the flute of champagne and scanned the room for a server. "What on earth do you want with my social calendar?"

"It figures you'd have checked up on me, and yes, you're right. I own the Barnes Agency." I gave her my respectful smile. "See, I'm trying to obtain some high-profile business clients. My agency has started to offer specialized, private bodyguards to VIPs—politicians, movie stars, the ultra-elites. You know the type. They're the same ones you cover in your columns."

She leaned back, appraising. "You're a sharp one, Jersey. Of course I can help you out with that, but it's not good for business to reveal details prior to publication."

She flagged down a server, held up her empty flute. "What are you after?"

I needed a guest list of some specific events, I told her, including the two other starred dates on Soup's list. Of course, I only mentioned the dates themselves—not the fact that my buddy had hacked into her personal computer.

"Why are you interested only in weddings? And how did you get those particular dates?"

Another glass of champagne appeared and Lady Lizzy quickly applied a layer of lip gloss before drinking some. I sipped on mine with bare lips and let the bubbles dance on the back of my tongue while I formulated a feasible explanation.

"Lady Lizzy, I've got sources, too. And wedding receptions aren't the only gatherings I'm interested in. I'd like the names of any high-profile folks who will be attending any sort of event in the upcoming few months. Parties, fund-raisers, the works. I'm a woman trying to earn a living, just like you. You peddle gossip while I'm trying to peddle bodyguard services."

She drank her champagne, more slowly than the first glass, and thought about the trade. "Okay, I'll play your game, dahling. But you go first. I hate to get ripped off."

Her eyes lit up at the name Jared Chesterfield, much-sought-after bachelor son of celebrity financier Samuel Chesterfield, and she not-so-subtly reached into a beaded handbag.

I shook my head. "No recording this conversation, or you don't get the rest."

Her jeweled hand quickly retreated. "Sorry, it's habit."

"No problem," I said and served up my scoop.

She audibly gasped when I revealed that Jared is gay and her mouth actually made a round O when I told her that he would be attending a public event with his equally handsome boyfriend of two years. Jared planned to come out, and he would do it in grand style, at a black-tie fund-raiser for the arts. The information was especially valuable to Lizzy, since Jared had recently been front-page news across the nation. Shortly after moving to Wilmington to open a new branch office of Chesterfield Financial, he'd been kidnapped and nearly murdered. Although Ox and I had saved his life, we were content to let law enforcement accept the accolades and face the press.

"Amazing! Does his father know? How did you get this?" Lizzy asked, hand dramatically resting over her heart.

"As I said, I have my sources, too." My informant had actually been Jared himself. I'd been staying in touch with both Jared and his father, and after learning of Jared's newfound zest for life in the open, I asked his permission to "leak" his story. He thought it was a fantastic idea, and was looking forward to the media coverage of him being out with his boyfriend. But Lady Lizzy didn't know that. And thanks to her, Wilmington and the rest of the country would be abuzz the day after the fund-raiser.

Freshly bathed, oiled, and perfumed people began roaming about, laughing and drinking, expectantly waiting for the bride and groom to arrive. A screech of feedback sounded through an amplifier when the band fired up their equipment. As I didn't think terrorists would have reason to blow up a NASCAR driver or a television actress, it was time for me to go.

"Your turn, Lady Lizzy, and make it quick. The party's about to start."

She threw some names at me off the top of her head and promised to e-mail a complete list of everybody who was anyone at all, and rumored to attend an upcoming event in either Brunswick or New Hanover County, which covered Southport to Wilmington. I made it clear that I'd leak my tidbit of news to someone else if she didn't come through, and she agreed to send the e-mail the following day.

We did the double air-kiss again and I headed to the parking lot. For some weird reason, the rich smell of leather in my X5 made me think of Ox. Irony not lost on me, I silently thanked God for work, even though I was supposed to be retired. It had kept my mind off my business partner for an entire hour and a half. Navigating the short drive home, I debated whether or not I should start doing some lunch runs with Mama Jean's truck, just to keep myself occupied and away from the Block. Which made me think about the additional income—slight though it would be—and who would get it. Did Mama Jean have children? Or a will? Was somebody going to show up to sell off her small mobile vending business? I knew nothing about the woman, but decided I would have very much liked her, had we known each other.

TWELVE

Ox enrolled Lindsey in the local high school, where classes would start in a few days. Growing up, I never started school until mid-September, and helping her purchase back-to-school supplies in August seemed odd. Ox agreed to let her work at the Block and she'd already started her job as a hostess, even though our customers always seat themselves. I had to admit, though, that Lindsey's bubbly enthusiasm brightened up the place. And although too young to serve drinks, she could help Ruby and the other servers run food as needed.

I'd finished my roach coach shift and was at the Block, teaching Lindsey how to greet customers, promote the menu, and be on alert for anyone who'd had too much to drink. It was a basic employee training session that Ox would have normally handled, but he'd taken the day off, presumably to spend it with his ex. Which set my stomach off like a blender filled with razor blades, if I thought about it too long. I resisted the urge to quiz Lindsey on the status of her father and mother's reunion. Find out what the two of them were doing today. And ask if she knew which bed Louise was sleeping in.

"Get yourself over to the corner table, for crying out loud," Spud said to Lindsey, shuffling up with the aid of a cane shaped like a long female arm and hand. The fingers were the floor tips and the shoulder was carved into a hand grip. His collection of walking canes is legendary around the Block. "The boys are coming to play some cards and you're the fifth. No coins this time; we're playing with chips only. Big lunch day for the cops and they don't like to see money changing hands."

"Spud, I'm working. I can't play until I finish my shift"—she consulted her watch—"which will be in twenty minutes. Oh, and by the way, I scheduled a photo shoot with some magazine lady who called this morning. She wants shots of you and the other artists posing with the Chrysler. Actually, she called the car a 'magnificent sculptural juxtaposition of real crime and heartfelt humanity,' whatever that means."

"You did what?" I asked, even though I'd heard her just fine. Cracker sauntered over, and he looked at the girl with a cocked head, too.

"I went ahead and set up Spud's photo shoot for next week. The lady—Sally Stillwell—said that her editor at *Eclectic Arts & Leisure* might even use Spud's picture as the magazine cover. How cool is that?"

Spud hemmed and hawed. "For crying out loud, doodlebug. I ain't no artist."

"Everybody has some artist in them. Mom always says that. Of course, she's big on reincarnation, so I guess if you're enough people, at some point you probably would have been a real artist. Anyway, the magazine lady called you an innovative sculptor—not a plain ol' artist."

"She did?"

"Yep. Said she's like, never seen anything quite like your work. Oh, and she can't wait to see the rest of it."

Bobby appeared. "We can shoot something else to smithereens, if that's all it takes to make a sculpture."

"Well, when you put it that way, I can be an artist." Spud used his cane like an orchestra director's wand. "We can use somebody's garage as a workshop and Bobby's van will be good to haul stuff. Might have to find us an old abandoned appliance or lawn mower or some such. We can shoot it up at the firing range." He paused to rub a hand over his wrinkled face. "I'll probably need to grow a ponytail and a goatee, if I'm gonna be an artist."

By the time we finished not-quite-arguing about my father's venture into professional metal sculpting, twenty minutes had passed and Lindsey's shift was over.

"You're the best, Jerz!" She gave me a hug and then squatted to do the same to Cracker. "Thanks for letting me work at the Block, and crash at your place for a while. Wilmington really rocks!"

It is hard to stay out of sorts with someone who has so much genuine charisma, even if she is an ignition button for trouble. I told her she was welcome, once again struck by the observation that her features were her father's. The girl was gorgeous.

"Excuse me," a man said, handing over a business card. "I couldn't help but to notice your daughter's Derma-Zing design." Average height, he was well-groomed, well-spoken and dressed in well-fitting business attire. I read the card, which declared him to be Dr. Edward C. Holloman, president of Derma-Zing. The address was out of state and there was a copyright symbol next to the word Derma-Zing. I didn't correct his assumption that I was Lindsey's mom.

"My name is Jersey and this is Lindsey," I said, taking his proffered hand.

"Can we sit for a moment? I'd like to talk to you."

Lindsey told Spud that she'd join the poker game later and

returned with three ice waters on a tray. "Would you like something to drink besides water?"

The man didn't. I thought about a beer, but refrained. The three of us slid into an empty booth.

"This is going to sound strange, I know, but I promise I'm legit." He opened his briefcase, pulled out a large envelope, and dropped it on the table. "As you see from my business card, my company owns Derma-Zing, which is a new product that is popular among teenagers."

Lindsey nodded. "Yeah, it's totally excellent. I'd never heard about it, until one of my friends told me, like, maybe a couple of months ago. Now, everybody at my school in California wears designs."

"Exactly my problem," Holloman said. "Derma-Zing is all the rage among teenage girls who've been exposed to the product, but in some parts of the country, kids have never heard of it. It's time to take Derma-Zing to the next level. I've decided to go with some print ads in *Teen* and *Cosmo Girl* magazines, plus air a month-long campaign of thirty-second television spots on MTV, VH1, and the Disney Channel."

Lindsey crossed her arms and leaned back to listen. A move I'd seen her father make a hundred times when hearing a pitch from a stranger. I drank my water, thinking that such an advertising campaign would require a sizable budget.

"I've been searching for a spokesmodel for a month now, and haven't found her." He removed a stack of eight-by-ten glossies from the envelope and spread them across the tabletop. "This is what the talent agency keeps sending me. Totally generic. These girls are pretty, sure. But I need a face that makes a *statement.* I need someone with *personality.* Someone who is unique, but someone who other girls will identify with." He waved a hand at the model cards. "These aren't what Derma-Zing is all about."

Lindsey pulled a sheet out of the stack. "This one looks a lot like

Lindsay Lohan. What's wrong with her? And, what kind of a doctor are you?"

The man laughed. "I'm not a medical doctor. I have a Ph.D. in chemistry, and I guess my secretary thought the 'Dr.' looked impressive when she had my cards printed."

"Seems kind of silly to me, since your cards are for Derma-Zing—not an orthopedic medical group or something," Lindsey said.

"Well, maybe I'll have that changed next time I need business cards. As for the Lindsay Lohan look-alike, I don't want to use her because she's not the real deal. I'd love to hire an actual celebrity like Lohan, or Hilary Duff, but I don't have that kind of money."

"This has all been quite interesting, Dr. Holloman, but why did you want to speak with us?" I asked, even though I had a good guess as to where the conversation was headed.

"I just stopped in for a sandwich. But as I was eating and saw Lindsey, I said to myself, that's her. That's the face of my spokesmodel. And when I noticed a Derma-Zing design on her shoulder, I took it as a sign."

Lindsey sat up. "Really? You want me to be your model for, like, Derma-Zing?"

"Well, yes, as long as the test footage looks good. Though I can't see why it wouldn't. I imagine you're still in high school, but we can work around your schedule and do both the magazine photo shoots and the TV commercials right here in Wilmington. And the money the job pays would be enough for a year's worth of college tuition."

"Sweet! What do I have to do?"

"Whoa, hold on," I said. "Before you agree to anything, Lindsey, you'll need to ask your father."

"Sure I do, but he'll say yes as long as I keep my grades up!"

"Of course we have to get parental-consent forms signed. But let me assure you that this is a legitimate product and a legitimate company. And as the mother, you'd get to approve everything before we print or air it. We can put that in the contract."

"Oh, she's not my mom," Lindsey corrected. "She's my dad's business partner."

"Is your father or mother here?"

"Not right now."

I held up a hand to slow things down. "Why don't you leave all the information with us, and Lindsey and I will talk it over with her parents. Somebody will get back to you in a day or so."

He agreed, produced a pile of information from the guts of his briefcase, and answered Lindsey's questions for another half-hour before standing to leave. We learned that Derma-Zing is one division under a large umbrella of products that his company manufactured.

"By the way," he said. "What is your nationality, Lindsey? Well, you're obviously an American so I should say, what is your heritage? You have a most unique look, but I can't quite place my finger on it."

Lindsey displayed a brilliant smile. "I'm a card-carrying Indian, Doc. My mom is purebred Californian but my dad is a full-blooded Lumbee." I didn't bother to explain her reference to the fact that Lumbees carry identification cards, issued by the tribal council. It was Lindsey's way of expressing that she is the real deal—a genuine Lumbee—and proud of it.

"Super, that's super. You're the opposite of all these generic girls the agency keeps trying to push on me. You're the face I've been searching for."

"Thanks, Doc." Lindsey shook his proffered hand. "Hey, by the way. I do get all the free Derma-Zing I can use for me and my friends, right? I mean, the stuff isn't cheap."

He chuckled. "Absolutely."

"Sweet. Well, I've to get in on the poker game before Spud blows a gasket. He keeps waving me over. Later," she said and hurried to the corner booth where the card game was in progress, leaving me to deal with the stack of print collateral and the Derma-Zing president.

"She plays poker, too?"

I nodded.

"She's priceless! She's going to be just perfect. I hope her parents will agree, and please do let them know that I'm available to meet with them anytime."

"Sure thing," I said and walked him out of my bar.

Living with my capricious father over the past few years had proven to be interesting, but living with Spud *and* a spirited teenager might be downright challenging.

THIRTEEN

I received Lady Lizzy's confidential e-mail, and as promised, it contained enough details to fully round out Soup's list of events. Now I just needed a MOTSU shipment schedule, and John was one person who had access to it. I might have been on the wrong track altogether, but I had to do something to stay sane. Even after I'd reported that John suspected I worked for Homeland Security, Ashton instructed me to continue what I'd been doing: observe and report. Unfortunately, doing that had become repetitive and boring. Plus, Ox had said I had good instincts, and something told me that the detected terrorist chatter was indeed tied to a Sunny Point shipment.

Soup's background check on John Mason revealed some interesting details, but nothing out of the ordinary other than his twin brother had died in combat, fourteen years into a military career. It was his only brother—the one he'd saved when they were kids by cutting the boy loose from a corn chopper. After earning a two-year college degree, John went through police academy training and had gone to work in law enforcement. He became a detective and later moved to SBI, North Carolina's State Bureau of Investigation. It was shortly after his twin brother died that he went to work for AJAT Security. I'd spoken with John's former boss at SBI and learned that John left because he needed a change of pace, but that his work ethic had been exemplary. Very disciplined. I decided to throw caution to the wind and ask for John's help. The worst thing that could happen was that Ashton would find out and fire me from an assignment I hadn't wanted to take anyway.

"So, what say you give me a peek at your incoming and outgoing shipment schedule?" I said to John, going for broke as I refilled his coffee. It was time to shut down the roach coach for the day, send my report to Ashton, return the truck to the warehouse, and head home.

"What say you tell me who you work for?" he countered, eyes bright.

I finished cleaning up, secured all containers and bins, and stepped outside the truck. Stacking the plastic chairs, I sighed as loudly as I could. "John, you know I can't do that. So don't even ask."

He blew on his coffee, sipped. "Why do you want to see the schedules? And why don't you just get the information from whomever you work for? Surely they have top-level security access to the terminal."

I loaded the chairs into the rear cargo bay and leaned against the truck to rest, on the shaded side. The morning was rapidly growing hot as the sun centered itself above North Carolina's lower coast. "To answer your first question, I just want to see if anything appears unusual or abnormal. As for your second question, no, the folks I work for don't have access to the internal workings of MOTSU, believe it or not." I hoped he believed me. SWEET was privy to anything and everything happening at MOTSU, including details on toilet paper usage, if they wanted it.

Arms crossed over his chest, John gave me a blatant once-over, but the look was more playful than crude. "Okay, no problem on the incoming shipments schedule. I'll give you everything, rail and road. But what do I get in return?"

I morphed into bimbette mode and threw a sexy smile his way. "Free sausage biscuits?"

His eyes moved to my chest. "Doesn't seem like a fair trade to me."

I breathed deep, to give him a better look. "And free coffee?"

"How about a real dinner date? Maybe somewhere in downtown Wilmington so we can walk around, catch some live music. You're not married, are you?"

"Nope. But I have this rule about mixing my personal life with my work life."

He smirked, slid on a pair of mirrored shades so I couldn't see his eyes. "Yeah, well, I have this rule about sharing confidential information."

I imagined that John was too much of a professional to hand over schedules to a near stranger. On the other hand, he probably expected sex as a return favor. He wasn't going to get it, but I could certainly play along for now. Besides, Ox had tossed me to the proverbial curb ever since Louise came calling. If nothing else, John might give me something else to think about. "Elijah's, tonight, seven thirty? I can meet you there."

He finished his coffee, handed me the empty paper cup. "That's more like it."

"And you'll bring my schedules?"

"Yes."

"Outgoing, as well?"

He shook his head no. "Incoming schedules are reliable and usually on time. Outgoing shipments are much more unpredictable. Besides, outgoing cargo is containerized and sent by ship. If you're worried about an ambush or something, it would happen while a shipment was being transported to the facility, don't you think?"

I wasn't so sure, but agreed with him anyway.

"Don't be late." Only slightly swaggering, he headed to his car with a backhanded wave.

Elijah's is a waterfront restaurant and oyster bar in downtown Wilmington that is a short distance south of the Block. John waited for me in the parking area and acted as though he'd just arrived. He probably got there early to get a look at my vehicle and tag number. In case he had ideas of perusing my true identity, I'd put a fake license plate on the X5, and covered the VIN by stashing a spiral notebook on the dash.

Greeting me with a kiss on the check, as though we were a couple, John handed me a folder containing the inventory printout of product coming to MOTSU. I secured it in the glove compartment and locked my doors.

"Sweet ride," he said, checking out my auction car. "Selling biscuits must pay more than I imagined."

"Oh, it's just a lease," I fibbed. "Life's too unpredictable to not enjoy a few material pleasures."

"I agree. Though carnal pleasures are always good, too."

"Right," I said, ignoring his reference to sex. "I can't wait to eat. The food here is terrific."

We ended up sitting on the outside covered deck to take advantage of the fresh breeze, even though the humidity level hovered at the top of the register. A server found us almost instantly and we ordered a crab dip starter and stuffed shrimp entrees. Without looking at a wine menu, John ordered a bottle of white Bordeaux.

"You copycatting me again?" I teased. "You chose the same thing I did at Fishy Fishy, too."

"I guess we have similar tastes. Besides, that's the only way I can guarantee that I won't have to share my food. Order the same thing your date does and she won't be asking to taste yours."

We worked our way through the crab dip that was served with giant croutons in lieu of crackers and half a bottle of the wine when John's phone buzzed. He consulted the caller ID display and his watch. "Sorry, I've got to take this one. You mind?"

"Not at all."

He headed toward the walkway by the water—either for privacy or politeness—and when he returned ten minutes later, our shrimp had arrived. He apologized for taking so long.

"But the good news," he added, spreading a napkin over his lap," is that the problem is resolved, so I don't need to head in to work."

"And I thought I might get to eat two plates of shrimp."

"No such luck." He held his wineglass up and we clinked to good food and good health.

I didn't learn much about MOTSU, AJAT Security, or John—other than the fact that he didn't like to talk about himself and immediately redirected the conversation whenever I steered it toward him. Even though the dinner was a waste of time from an intel standpoint, John turned out to be a witty conversationalist as long as we discussed movies or books or restaurants. He refused to let me chip in on the tab and, gentlemanlike, walked me to my car.

Before we reached the X5, somebody let out a sloppy cat whistle. "That is one major piece of fine-looking ass."

A group of men—six to be exact—stood around a beat-up work van, smoking cigarettes. I guessed them to be either dock workers or perhaps fishermen just in from several days at sea. With slurred words, another man joined in, ignoring John and leering at me. "Man, would I like to get me a piece of that. Maybe she'd do us both."

"Maybe she'd do us all, being as though the rest of you assholes wouldn't be but ten seconds apiece," another said, and drank straight from a brown-bagged pint liquor bottle. "I'll take up the rear."

"You so horny, you'd take one up the rear," somebody said and they all laughed, much louder than necessary.

"You ought to be a little more respectful around a lady," John said calmly, "before you get yourselves in trouble."

"Guess he wants to keep his piece of ass all to himself," the first one said to the others.

"Oooh, I'm scared," another said. "I'm so scared I might just piss my pants."

The six men banded into a tight group and walked our way, slightly off-kilter. They were drunk enough to lose all sense of reasoning, but sober enough to connect fists with a target. And all were laden with the wiry type of hard muscle conditioned by a labor-intensive job.

"Get in your car, Jill, and lock the doors," John said. He carried an autoloader in a shoulder holster the times I'd fluoroscoped him from the roach coach, so I figured him to be carrying now. Still, there were six of them. And I wasn't in a mood to dodge bullets. If John pulled his gun, one of the bullies might respond in kind.

"No, thanks," I replied. "Think I'll just hang right here."

John moved in front of me, in a sweet, protective sort of way. "You boys have had too much to drink. Why don't you head on home?"

"Seems to me," one said, "you ought to head home and leave her with us." He shoved John, hard, in the chest.

"Shouldn't have done that," John said and threw a punch to the fisherman's jaw that put him on the ground. Thinking they were supposed to back up their buddy, the other five came at us.

"Get in the car, Jill!" John repeated and ducked beneath a swinging fist.

I threw a high roundhouse kick over John's back and clipped a man in the face, spun around and placed a low kick into the knee of another drunk who'd picked up a tree limb and was preparing to swing it. Stunned, both men dropped out of the fight and one went down with a groan. John did a quick double-take before launching himself into the remaining drunks while I stood back to watch. No need to ruin a good manicure if I didn't have to. There was a flurry of fists, grunts, and moans as he took the remaining three men down, one at a time, with practiced precision. The brawl was over in less than thirty seconds.

"Nice moves, Jill," he said, brushing himself off and smoothing his shirt. "Now I'm really curious who you work for."

"I told you, I lead a simple life selling biscuits. And, thanks for the compliment. You've got some great moves, yourself."

He rubbed his knuckles. "I could have handled them all, you know."

"I'm sure. But why should you have all the fun?"

Either too stupid or too stubborn to stay down, one man lumbered upright. "Try an' take me now, you son of a bitch." He held a long-bladed fishing knife with a curved tip. Confident of John's hand-to-hand abilities, I moved out of the way.

John waited for the attack and when it came, he used the man's momentum to disarm him by sidestepping the weapon and pressure-twisting the wrist. In the next instant, John held his attacker by the throat, one-handed, his thumb and fingers squeezing from opposite sides. The fact that it was his left hand, the one with the damaged finger, didn't affect his strength and I became alarmed when John didn't let go, even after the man's knees buckled from a lack of oxygen. He was going to choke him to death. I started to intervene when John snapped out of it and released his grip. The man melted into the asphalt, coughed once, and started wheezing. At least he still breathed. Being around a dead person completely creeps me out.

"Let's get out of here," John said.

"No argument from me."

We walked the rest of the way to my car and once there, he gave me a strange look that I couldn't quite read. "Feel like a drink or a cup of coffee somewhere? Might catch some live music."

Anything to keep me from envisioning Ox and Louise together, and feeling sorry for myself. I'd never been jealous of a woman with Ox before. Not ever. But that was before I'd given in to my cravings and slept with the man. And, Louise was different. He had a history with her. The thought of Ox planning a future with the woman was something I wouldn't allow myself to consider. The more I thought about it, the better an after-dinner drink sounded.

"That works for me."

I rode with him to the Rusty Nail, where we sipped coffees laden with Godiva chocolate liqueur and took in some live jazz music. When the clock approached midnight, he drove me back to my car and kissed me on the lips. It was a quick kiss, one that stopped before I had a chance to think about it. Or protest.

"We should go out again," he said. "I had a great time."

"It was a lot of fun," I said, realizing I'd only thought of Ox and Louise once. Or maybe twice. "Thanks for dinner."

"You're welcome."

I stepped into the X5. "See you around." I drove to the Block, taking several unnecessary turns to ensure that he wasn't following. Just because I was starting to like the AJAT Security worker didn't mean that I could let my guard down. I had a job to do, and gleaning information from knowledgeable sources was simply part of the deal.

FOURTEEN

High school classes started in two days, on Monday, and Lindsey's life was jam-packed. Ox and Louise agreed to let her contract with Derma-Zing and, with help from Spud—self-appointed agent—had negotiated the fee up to an even eighteen thousand dollars. The advertising brains decided on a "down-to-earth real look with jazzed-up graphics" for both the print ads and the television spots. They'd also decided not to use a studio, opting instead for several Wilmington locations, including the riverwalk, the Cape Fear Run bicycle route, and the Block.

Holloman, or Doc, as Lindsey called him, had joined us at my bar to watch a video shoot, and we'd taken a break for lunch. Between his efficient-looking associate, Ox, the media project director, the creative people with lighting and camera equipment, and the extras—teenagers from a local modeling agency with parents in tow—we had a big crowd. Louise—who'd just breezed in fashionably late—added to our number. Only Spud and his poker group were absent because they'd gone shopping, or so they said.

As she professionally schmoozed her way through the crowd, I studied Lindsey's mother. She was a beautiful woman, in a very well-kept sort of way. I recognized the sexy poof of an injected upper lip because I used to have one just like it, back when Uncle Sam was paying for it. I also recognized the store-boughts. They accented her full, curvy hips very nicely. But Louise had much more: flawless tanning-bed tan, styled short blond hair without an iota of dark roots showing, laser-whitened teeth, California-casual bead-trimmed outfit, and a surgically lifted face that caused the corners of her mouth to upturn just a fraction. She caught me looking and headed my way.

"Jersey, it's great to see finally see you," she said.

It was? I hadn't seen her in person for years, and then, she'd all but glared at me.

"You look terrific," she added.

I was wearing torn jeans and a T-shirt baggy enough to conceal the weapon in my paddle holster. "Thanks, Louise. You look great yourself."

She tucked some hair behind her pierced ears, probably so I could get a better look at the huge emerald-cut diamonds clinging to each lobe. "Lindsey tells me that she really loves Wilmington and that you guys have been having a lot of fun together."

That was true. "She's a great kid."

We were sizing each other up when Louise looked down and screamed. She moved in place for a moment, tiny little feet doing their own version of an Irish step dance. "Eeeow!"

A tiny green lizard had found its way into the Block and appeared to be darting toward an exit.

Ox was there in an instant. "What's wrong?"

Louise pointed at the retreating offender, but was too panicked to speak.

"Just a lizard taking a shortcut through our bar," I explained.

Ox rubbed his ex's back, between her shoulder blades. "It's okay, Louise. It's gone now."

I shut my eyes for a long second to keep from rolling them.

"She's petrified of bugs and such," Ox explained.

Puhlleeeze. "Lizards *eat* bugs, Louise."

She cocked her head like a poodle recognizing its name. "They do? Really?"

"Really." I pointed at an insect that existed solely in my imagination. "Just like that spider over there. Spiders are like filet mignon to a lizard."

She spun around and did the dance again. "Eeeow!"

Trying to hold in a smile, I excused myself and left Ox to comfort her.

Once everyone settled in, our group occupied five square tables, pushed together, and I'd asked Ruby to keep the finger foods and fresh fruit coming. Drinks being consumed ranged from black coffee to straight vodka. It was an eclectic gathering but all the fuss centered around Lindsey and she beamed like a true headliner. Louise recovered from the lizard incident and returned to flutter around like an annoying helicopter mom, but Ox hung back and watched the activity with an amused twist to his mouth. Earlier, he and I had spoken about the Block, a problem with one of the employees, and his daughter's newfound fame, but something tangible had slithered between us. Not to mention that I couldn't get the vision of him rubbing his ex's back out of my mind. Before my thoughts could worm their way to the corner of my cerebrum, where I'd corralled all emotions concerning Ox, I tuned in to the conversation flowing around me.

"Have you considered expanding your target market for Derma-Zing?" the project director was saying to Holloman. "I ask because the possibilities for marketing to a wider consumer base are out there."

"Such as?"

"Well, take for example the Harley-Davidson bikers. Several *hundred thousand* riders attend weeklong rallies every year in cities across the country, such as Sturgis, South Dakota, and Myrtle Beach, South Carolina. You could work out a licensing deal with Harley-Davidson to sell a stencil kit of their logos, with tubes of Derma-Zing in black and Harley orange."

Lindsey spat out a sigh of revulsion. "Oh, gross!"

"Why gross?" the agency gal said.

"You don't have teenagers, do you?" I asked the woman. "See, the quickest way to turn a teenager against anything they consider way cool is to have them see the same thing on an 'old' person."

"Hello?" Lindsey added. "Derma-Zing on some scraggly, tattooed biker dude who's like, fifty or something, with a beer gut hanging over his belt? I don't think so."

Two golf ball–sized circles of pink appeared on the woman's cheeks and Holloman laughed. "Not only is our spokesperson a beauty with a unique personality, but she's got marketing savvy, too."

"The stencil idea may have some merit, though." I finished a peeled shrimp and washed it down with a gulp of Carolina Blonde, a tasty light ale brewed in Mooresville, North Carolina. "What if you offered stencil kits to all the major universities that have strong athletic programs? The students could logo each other before a big game."

"Hmm. I want to keep my target market relatively tight, from teenage girls to those in their young twenties," Holloman said. "So the college thing could work."

The entire table looked at Lindsey, awaiting her reaction.

"Yeah, sure. I mean, education is in, you know? I'm going to college. For that matter, most high school girls want to look like college girls, and can't wait to date an older, college-aged guy."

Ox drew his daughter's attention with narrowed eyes.

"Not me, Dad. I said *most* girls. I'm sick of boys, period. Trust me, I'd rather spend Friday nights with Cracker than go out on a date with a guy. At least I don't have to listen to the dog talk about himself all night."

That drew a collective laugh and the project director regained her composure. She clapped her hands. "Well, let's finish this shoot and we can talk about the college market later. You ready, Lindsey? Let Mary have a swipe at you with the makeup brushes, and we're ready to go. Guys? Crew? Extras?" she called.

There was a bustle of activity as a variety of bright portable lights were switched on, two studio cameras were locked into tripods attached to rolling dollies, and all traces of alcoholic beverages, clutter, and beer signage were cleared from the background. A smattering of laid-back locals and a few wide-eyed tourists were content to enjoy their food and beverages in the half of the Block that wasn't cordoned off. Wilmington is home to EUE Screen Gems Studio and is the country's third largest film and television production site, so it's not uncommon to spot film crews or celebrities. But you can always tell a tourist from a local, because a tourist will request autographs from anyone placed in front of a studio camera. Locals don't get too excited until they see the likes of a genuine big-screen star.

Ox found me sitting at a corner bistro table, where I'd attempted to move out of the way.

"We should get some photographs of this shoot for our wall of fame and shame," he said. "Maybe I'll give the camera to one of the regulars and ask them to do it."

"Sure, good idea."

"Lindsey said you got in late last night," he said. "She and Spud played cards until after eleven and you still weren't back. Is everything okay?"

"Just out on a date," I said. "Figure I may as well have a little fun while I'm gathering information."

Ox's face hardened. "Anyone I know?"

Did I detect jealousy? As if he had a right to be jealous.

"Doubtful," I said. "Just somebody who works at Sunny Point."

"You learn anything new?"

"Not really."

He took my shoulder, forcing me to look at him. "Please don't shut me out, Jersey."

"I'm not shutting you out. I'm just staying out of the way while you figure things out with your ex. Besides, between SWEET and Spud and Lindsey, I'm staying pretty busy."

"Any developments at MOTSU?"

"No."

"How'd it go with Lady Lizzy?"

"Fine."

"Ashton keeping you on the roach coach?"

"Far as I know."

With a heavy sigh, he strolled off. Of course I'd shut him out, but I couldn't help it. We never should have had sex. Especially not extraordinary, minds-on, addictive sex. Two indulgent hours had changed everything and so far, it wasn't for the better.

FIFTEEN

In honor of Lindsey's first day back to school, Ox cooked everyone an early breakfast of eggs and waffles at the Block, after which he and Louise planned to drive Lindsey to New Hanover High. Louise, blond hair gelled and blown-dry into a sassy poof around her face, spent most of the meal poring through real estate magazines rather than celebrating Lindsey's new status as a high school senior. Spud asked if she planned to buy property in Wilmington and Louise said something about Ox needing a bigger place. If Ox wanted to get back with his ex and move into a new house, then I was all for it. But I sure as heck didn't have to listen to the details. I thanked Ox for breakfast and made my escape.

Other than getting a late start on the roach coach, it turned out to be a relaxing day and I found myself enjoying the camaraderie as I fed drive-ups, even though there was a lot of conversation about Mama Jean's death. Some regulars had seen the obituary and word of mouth spread the news to most everyone who knew her. As it turned out, she didn't have children or a husband, and had willed her estate to local charities. When it was time to close shop, I called Ashton.

After determining I'd called from the truck, he immediately called me back on a secure line that fed through my onboard laptop computer. I plugged in a headset and we did the secret code pleasantries to ensure him that I was indeed alone.

"Can you take another look at John Mason?" I said.

"Talk to me."

"We had dinner the other night, and while he is both pleasant and quite handsome, I've picked up on a few inconsistencies. Nothing major, but the more I think about it, the more I realize you might want to check it out."

"Go on."

John said he asked for the temp agency's phone number from Mama Jean because he needed work done at his condo, I told Ashton. But John's address on file belonged to a four-bedroom home on seven acres, according to the tax records. He didn't have a condo, unless he'd rented one somewhere. And why would someone pay to have work done on a rental? They wouldn't. Furthermore, I said, John totally clammed up when I asked about his family. Unlike most men, he refused to talk about himself. Plus, there was the whole business of John asking who I really worked for. When I finished telling my handler of my suspicions, I asked about Mama Jean's autopsy results.

"She was asphyxiated. Some bruises appeared that weren't there when we first viewed the scene—consistent with a struggle—and there were petechia hemorrhages in the eyes, face, and lungs. Time of death is estimated to be about four o'clock in the afternoon, day before the neighbor found her. I saw her around one thirty the day she died, when I brought her the week's deposit. In any event, forensics is going back over her condo, inch by inch. I suppose you want to see the report and autopsy photos?"

"Might trigger something," I said. "I've had a lot of conversations with a lot of customers about Mama Jean."

"I'll send a courier to the Block."

"Thanks. You find any flowers in her place?" I asked.

"Of course. Eight arrangements of cut flowers and three green plants, all with the note cards still attached. Made a list of the names and we're following up with each of the well-wishers."

"John's name on that list?"

"Negative," Ashton said.

"He told me that he'd gone to see Mama Jean to bring her flowers. That's supposedly when he asked how she came to hire me."

"Anything else?" Ashton said.

"Nope, other than I'd like to learn more about the death of John's twin. He actually saved his brother's life when they were teenagers, you know."

"Need I reiterate that you are in place to observe and report—not investigate?"

"No, sir."

"Was I unclear in explaining your assignment?"

I busied myself securing the truck's refrigerator and freezer compartments. "No, sir."

Ashton cleared his throat, a sure sign of agitation. "I'm pulling you off mobile meal truck duty. Go straight to the warehouse and secure Mama Jean's truck as usual. Stay away from the ammo dump. And if Mason calls you, make an excuse as to why you can't see him."

"But he's actually a lot of fun," I protested. "Maybe another date or two? I might learn something useful."

"Negative."

Why had the mention of John Mason spooked my handler?

"At least let me stay on the roach coach another week? I think I'm getting close to learning something."

"Again, no."

"But I'm just getting good at cooking breakfast biscuits. I was going to expand the menu to croissants!" Not to mention that my tips had already added up to nearly three hundred dollars and I was saving for a new La Perla camisole with matching boy shorts and silk striped robe. Another week of tips would put me there.

Ashton hung up.

I made the drive and, after stashing Mama Jean's truck inside the warehouse, headed to the Barnes Agency in my Beemer. Both Rita and our new partner, JJ, were in the office, as was the masseur that came in three days a week to answer phones and revive tired muscles. His portable massage table stood in the middle of the room and JJ was prone on top of it. Instead of hiring a temp to replace our secretary, who was out on maternity leave, Rita had chosen to spend the money on stress reduction.

"Hey, Jersey," JJ said, facedown. "Those are your feet, aren't they? How ya doing?"

"I should ask you the same thing."

"I'm doing great." She lifted her head. "Gotta love a job where I can get a deep-tissue massage in the office, even if I did get thrown off a moving bus last week in Savannah."

"She's fine," Rita told me. "The bus wasn't going that fast. Besides, she wasn't pushed off. She fell off."

JJ settled her head back into the massage table and the masseur went to work on her neck. "Thrown, fell, whatever. I caught the woman when she got off at the next stop. And she had the DVD in her beach bag, which made for another satisfied Barnes Agency client."

Rita handed me some mail. "We're still getting a few clients that refuse to deal with anyone except you, but they mostly come around. You enjoying retirement?"

"Not exactly," I said. "I've been cooking and selling breakfast out of a truck on the side of the road for the past two weeks."

"Did I forget to direct deposit your profit-share check last month?"

"You're funny, Rita. I got called back into service for Uncle Sammy and that's my cover."

"Do they know you can't cook?"

I stayed long enough to get a neck and back massage, and left feeling good about the status quo at the Barnes Agency. Rita and JJ were doing a great job without me. But I didn't feel good at all about the status of munitions shipments being processed through the ammo dump. I ended up at my kitchen table, nursing a beer, rubbing Cracker with my feet, and mapping out the locations of upcoming social events. Once done, I compared the dates with incoming munitions shipments. For my trouble, I ended up with nothing. I studied Mama Jean's autopsy report and photos, that—as Ashton had promised—had just been delivered to the Block. I came up with more of the same: nothing. And I wasn't sure if my nauseous stomach was due to stress over Ox's love life or due to the fact that I was missing something obvious. I felt sure I'd gotten close to uncovering one of Ashton's so-called pointers, or clues. I could almost taste it. Like a hungry junkyard dog, I'd caught a scent of something rotten. When that happens, it's against my nature to just let go. Stubborn might equate to stupid, but time would tell. I went over the shipment schedule and social calendar for a second time with the same result.

"Well, crap," I said to the dog. "You think John gave me a bogus schedule? Or, do you think the schedule is legit, but I'm not looking in the right place?"

Cracker yawned and flipped over so my feet could reach his other side.

SIXTEEN

"*I won't see* you around Sunny Point anymore," I told John over orange juice and sweet rolls. As I expected, he called to ask why Mama Jean's truck was absent and I agreed to meet him at a café. I wasn't ignoring Ashton's orders—not really—since breakfast doesn't qualify as a date unless it's a continuation of the prior night.

"That's too bad. I'm going to miss seeing you every morning. Not to mention your sausage biscuits," John said. "You working the food truck somewhere else?"

I shook my head and tried to think of something plausible. "Nope. Since Mama Jean died and she has no heirs, there's no reason to keep the truck operating. I guess it will be sold or given away with the rest of her estate."

John thought about that. "Are you still on Sunny Point duty, then?"

I put on my indulgent smile. "As I've already told you, I'm just a simple person leading a simple life. I don't know what you mean by Sunny Point duty."

"You're still not going to tell me who you work for, are you?"

I shook my head.

"Well, it doesn't matter anyway." He finished his juice. "I'm thinking about taking today off. Why don't you follow me to the mall, park your car, and then we'll go take a drive? Do something fun. Maybe hit a museum or go bowling."

Before I could agree, my personal cell rang. "Your daddy needs a ride," Dirk said when I answered, "and I'm not putting his belligerent ass in the back of my unmarked unless he pipes down." Lieutenant Dirk Thompson is a Wilmington cop who has a soft spot when it comes to Spud. Or a tolerant spot, at least.

"Good grief. What's he done now?"

"It's actually all four of 'em." Dirk paused to tell Spud to be quiet. "In Bobby's van. They didn't feel like taking the seats out of the back to create a cargo area, so they strapped a"—he paused to quiz Bobby—"a giant alligator to the van's roof. Came from a minigolf that shut down. Oh, there were also planks of scrap metal and four life-sized mannequins up there, too. Bought those at a thrift shop."

"Oh, hell," I said. When his friends had collected Spud earlier in the morning, they said they were going shopping. I assumed they meant for staples like Bengay sports cream and prescription drug refills at the CVS and pork loin specials at the Piggly Wiggly. Not alligators and mannequins.

"The whole lot of it fell off. Had traffic backed up in both eastbound lanes. Not all that horrible in itself, but then Spud went and got himself in a fight with a woman on a Vespa scooter."

Spud's voice came over the line. "She mowed down one of my mannequins! Tore both its arms right off, she did. And I still can't find the head, for crying—"

Dirk took the phone back from my father. "The woman is eighty, she swerved trying to miss what she thought was a dead body lying in the road, and Spud ought to be glad that she didn't hurt herself. There's still a hand stuck in the front wheel spokes of her gas-powered scooter."

I told Dirk I'd get there as soon as I could.

"Listen, thanks for the invite John, but I've got to run."

"Anything I can help with?"

"No, thanks." I dropped some bills on the table and rushed out, thinking that—while I was smart enough not to involve John with my personal business—it would be great to have Ox along. He was accustomed to dealing with Spud crises and would have gotten a good laugh out of this one. I thought about calling him to meet me. But I'd been purposely keeping my distance, and martyr-like, I couldn't stop now.

By the time I got to the scene, Bobby, Hal, and Trip were sitting on the rear edge of the van, back hatch open, laughing and drinking Pepsi. Spud stood on a grassy median, staring at the pile of debris that Dirk had cleared from the road: an animatronic alligator with the tip of its tail slowly moving back and forth, scrap metal, and various body parts. A silver-haired woman in a bright orange, long sundress sat on her Vespa, arms crossed, watching my father. Her eyes were covered by oversized black sunglasses. A slim plaster hand, detached at the wrist, was wedged in her front wheel.

"Well, at least he's quieted down," I said to Dirk and gave him a hug. "Thanks for calling me."

"Nobody was injured, so if Spud settles things with Miss"—Dirk consulted a notepad—"Fran Cutter, he's free to go. Of course, somebody's going to need to haul this trash to the dump."

"It ain't trash," Spud said, thumping his way over with a mermaid walking cane. When angry, he always pokes his walking stick into the ground much harder than necessary. "It's supplies to make another sculpture. That is the makings of *art.*"

"Oh, you're a metal sculptor?" Fran asked, fluffing her short hair.

"For crying out loud, woman! Of course I'm a sculptor. Why else would we have been hauling this stuff to my workshop?"

"What workshop?" I said.

Ignoring me, Spud thumped his way back to the pile of debris and stood there, talking to himself. We managed to fold down all the van seats and shove everything in. Dirk separated the alligator's long tail from its body and the two pieces of the damaged animal fit perfectly. We stuffed the mannequin parts anywhere they'd go. Before he left, Dirk got the hand out of Fran's wheel by breaking off the fingers. After Spud settled down, he promised to repay Fran for any repairs the scooter would need. They exchanged phone numbers, Fran fluffing and my father grumbling. Bobby drove Spud in the van and I followed, toting Hal and Trip.

I quizzed them about our destination—the workshop.

"Your daddy leased an old welder's place," Trip explained. "We were on our way there when Bobby swerved to miss a squirrel and everything went kaplooey."

It was another ten minutes to Spud's rented workshop, which turned out to be a dilapidated building about the size of a large two-car garage. When we'd all piled in, Spud pointed out that he was allowed to use the welding equipment and tools, as long as everything was accounted for at the end of his lease.

"Isn't it great?" my father said, arms outstretched until he lost his balance and almost fell over. "We can use the power tools, weld, and do whatever we want in here. It's a perfect art studio."

It was a dingy, cobweb-coated structure with a roof that appeared to have several leaks. And the words "power tools" and "weld" do not belong in any sentence referencing Spud and his poker buddies.

I envisioned more than just mannequin parts lying around. "Just be careful in here, will you?"

"I know everything there is to know about welding and such,"

Trip assured me. "I was a shop teacher before I retired, so I'll keep an eye on your daddy."

Trip's announcement made me feel an infinitesimal bit better about Spud's newfound hobby. We unloaded the road-rash-coated alligator and its tail—which had ceased moving—and the anatomically correct human body parts. I left the four artists sitting around a folding table, collaborating about their sculpture.

Ignoring Ashton's orders, I pointed the X5 toward John's house. I wasn't going to stop and search anything, but I wanted to see where the AJAT contractor lived, partly due to curiosity but mainly because I felt there was more to him than met the eye. Maybe something would jump out and announce itself as a clue. Since I'd turned down his offer to spend the day playing hooky, John probably went to work. If I happened to run into him, I'd just say I changed my mind about spending the day together.

According to the address in his personnel file, John's place sat in an unincorporated area of the county, just outside the town of Boiling Spring Lakes, which put his house a five-minute drive to Sunny Point. I took the same route I'd driven when going to work in the boxy truck. The roads proved much more pleasurable in my road-hugging BMW with the sunroof open and speakers blasting Santana. When my mobile rang and the caller ID told me it was Ox, I punched the ignore button to send the call to voicemail. The phone immediately sounded again, caller ID the same.

"What's up," I answered, leaving the music volume up. Any news in his world would involve Louise and I didn't really want to hear it, unless the woman was on a plane headed back to California.

"Where are you?" he asked.

"Heading south. Just out for a drive, enjoying the day."

"Are you alone?"

As if he had a right to ask, or care. "Yup."

"Is everything okay?"

I muted the music. "Sure, why?"

"I don't know," he said. "I've got a bad feeling."

I made the left turn onto Highway 87. "Oh, please, Ox. What, did you have a vision or something? If so, maybe it's Louise you need to check on. *I'm* perfectly fine." I snapped the phone shut and had barely gotten the volume back up when he called again.

"Yes, I did have a vision, sort of. Somebody wants to hurt you."

"So what else it new?" I said, knowing that I was being a total bitch but unable to stop myself.

"I think you should stop whatever you're doing and come home."

"I told you, I'm not doing anything except driving."

"Then you should stop doing that. I'm serious, Jersey. Let me come pick you up."

I spotted a high-pressure car wash and, just to humor him, pulled into one of the concrete bays. The Beemer needed a bath, anyway. I hopped out and fished through my handbag for some quarters. One spilled out of my wallet and rolled into the parking lot. I jogged after it. "Okay, I've stopped driving. Are you happy now?"

"Where are you?" he demanded and the urgency in his voice spooked me. Before I could answer, a rumbling explosion sounded and I felt a hot pain sear into my back as a wave of force slammed me several feet through the air and into a patch of grass and weeds. I still gripped the cell phone when I landed, and heard Ox's voice, faint and tinny, calling my name as my world got smaller and smaller and then went dark.

SEVENTEEN

The electronic hum of machinery and unpleasant tinny odor of antiseptic penetrated the fog in my brain before I fully came to and realized I was in a hospital room. Ox smiled down at me. "Welcome back."

I tried to speak, but my throat was too dry to make any sounds. He lifted my head with a large hand and held a cup of lukewarm water to my mouth. I gulped it down and my vocal cords worked again. "Tell Ashton I want my hazard pay bonus."

Ox laughed. "You just missed him."

I tried to sit up. A blast of nausea instantly rolled through my midsection, sweat popped out on my entire body, and the walls moved. Breathing hard, I dropped back to the pillow and felt a padded bandage on my back.

"You've got a few scrapes and bruises. A piece of sheet metal was lodged in your back, beneath your shoulder blade, but it didn't puncture anything vital. Nineteen staples to close you up." He refilled my water cup and helped me drink some more. "The reason you feel so crummy is the concussion. Took a pretty rough hit to the back of your head."

"What time is it?"

"Your car exploded at eleven o'clock this morning and it's now almost midnight. Good job, by the way, pulling into that car wash. Owner's not too happy. But it contained the explosion and nobody was hurt. Except you."

"I only pulled in because my car was dirty. That, and to humor you."

"Well then, that dirty car saved your life."

I reached for his hand and when our palms met, my body relaxed as though I'd had a shot of morphine. It was his phone call that had kept me alive. Not a dirty vehicle. It wasn't the first time Ox had saved my life, either. "Thanks," I said, thinking the single word to be most inadequate but unable to come up with something better.

He squeezed my hand. "No problem."

I started to apologize for acting like a bitch since his ex had shown up, but he stopped me. "I was being stupid, too, Barnes. Trying to accommodate Louise without considering your feelings. It's a tough situation for everyone."

At once, the wall of awkwardness between us crumbled. I wanted to talk more, but there'd be time for that later. "Help me get dressed and drive me home? I hate hospitals. There's always a dead person hanging around somewhere." I can handle blood and gore, but completely freak out around a dead person. Totally irrational, I know, but I can't even stand to be near a crime scene until the bodies are hauled away. My government-appointed shrink labeled the condition necrophobia, back when I was active with SWEET. That aside, she'd given me a clean bill of mental health.

Ox shook his head. "No can do. You're spending the night so they can scan your brain again tomorrow, to make sure there's no swelling."

"Well, crap."

A nurse entered the room, followed by Spud and Lindsey.

"You're awake! How ya feeling, Jerz?" Lindsey leaned in to give me a hug and I tried not to grimace when a stab of pain ran through my back.

On my other side, Spud leaned over the bed rails to look at me. He held up some knobby fingers and wiggled them in front of my face. "How many fingers do you see, kid? Who's the president? What year is it? Do you know your name?"

"My brain is fine, Spud. Thanks for coming to see me."

His walking cane shrugged. "Doodlebug here wouldn't go to bed until we came to get a look at ya, make sure you're still in one piece."

"They've both been at the hospital since Lindsey got out of school at three o'clock," Ox confided. "Lindsey's driving Bobby's van. She just got her California license, so she's up for driving anyone anywhere, anytime."

"In this traffic?" I said.

Lindsey whipped out the laminated card to show me. "I've been driving in California on a provisional permit for, like, a year before I got this. Trust me, the traffic at home makes Wilmington seem like the kiddie car rides at an amusement park."

Everyone stood back while the nurse checked my vitals and injected something into my IV line. She asked how I felt—an absurd question considering my condition—and made a quick exit. Ox reminded Lindsey that it was a school night and time for her to go. Spud said he was ready, too, since he had a big day planned at his art studio. After another ten minutes of high-energy chatter and well-wishing, they left and the room was quiet once again.

"His dilapidated workshop is now a studio?" I asked Ox.

"Like I always say, your father is one hell of a thinker."

A uniformed man poked his head through the door to ask if

there'd be any more visitors for the night. Ox said no. The door shut.

"Ashton put a guard on me?" I asked.

"Round the clock."

"Well if you're not going to help me break out of this joint, at least give me an update before you go."

Ashton's people were going through the remains of my X5 looking for evidence, Ox told me, but it appeared that a car bomb had been strapped to the underside and remotely detonated.

"I knew it! I mean, I obviously didn't know about the bomb. But I knew I was getting close to uncovering something. I could feel it, and this proves it."

A frown flashed on his face. "It does appear that you've made someone nervous."

"How did you know about the bomb?"

"Difficult to explain," he said. "But I saw—or rather I felt—it happening. I sensed an emptiness, like you were gone, and I knew something bad was about to happen."

Tokens, or toat'ns as the Lumbees call them, are signs that a spirit is present. Such experiences are a regular part of Ox's life and can be as simple as an unusual smell or as intense as a full-out vision. My best friend also has an uncanny sense of future events that borders on psychic. I don't understand it, but I certainly can't argue with it.

"Was the explosive military-issue stuff?" I asked.

"Made from common industrial stuff. It just so happens that a road construction crew reported a theft of several sticks of explosive to ATF last week."

That didn't necessarily rule out someone who had access to MOTSU inventory. It just meant they chose not to use it. "Who would want to blow me up? Who have I met recently that might think I'm anything other than a woman filling in for Mama Jean?" I asked aloud, but kept the answer to myself: John.

"They swept Mama Jean's truck and found a bug, just inside the little push-out triangle window on the driver's side. Ashton said it had to have been placed while you were parked and on the job."

My whole body throbbed and it hurt to think. "He left the table for about ten minutes when we were eating at Elijah's the other night."

"Who?"

"John. The security guy that I've been out with a few times."

"You really need to be more careful about who you date," Ox teased, but the comment hit close to home. My last boyfriend was involved with the woman who shot up the Block and nearly killed me.

"John said he had to take a phone call, but he could have easily gone to the parking lot. Working beneath my car to strap on the bomb, he'd have gone unnoticed, since it was nearly dark. As for the bug, he could have popped that in place anytime I was parked and cooking. From the serving area, the driver's seat is blocked from view." My breaths were coming short and fast and I felt helplessly weak. But I'd take weak over dead any day. "I always locked the front doors, but left those little windows cracked for some air circulation. They're just big enough for a man to get his forearm through."

"You served a lot of coffee and biscuits to a lot of different people in two weeks' time," Ox said.

"Right, but I only voiced suspicions about one person—John. I called Ashton from Mama Jean's truck. Whoever planted the bug could have been listening in."

"When was that?"

"Yesterday, after I finished the morning shift. Once I spoke with Ash, he pulled me off mobile meal truck duty. Told me to stay away from John and the ammo dump until I received further instruction."

"Where were you driving this morning, when your car blew up?"

"To check out John's place."

While I ate some applesauce, Ox told me that John—along with several other supervisors—had been interrogated by the local police chief and one of the head honchos at MOTSU, with an AJAT Security representative and Ashton looking on. Again, John had come up clean. He had an answer for everything, including why there wasn't a paper trail for the flowers he took Mama Jean. He'd cut them from his yard.

The bosses at AJAT and supervisors at the ammo dump claimed that John's work ethic had been exemplary and they stood behind the man 100 percent. John continued to work his scheduled shifts and politely offered himself to be questioned further if he could help in any way.

But Ashton was not one to buy into seemingly friendly cooperation and, based on the teeny little detail that I'd almost been car-bombed, was in the process of obtaining a warrant to search John's home. When it comes to terrorism and public safety, traditional rights don't always apply to suspects. Even though there was no real evidence, Ashton would have his warrant within hours.

"Where's the best place for a guilty person to hide?" I said, my eyelids suddenly leaden.

"Out in the open," Ox said. He dropped a soft kiss on my mouth and disappeared.

My head pounding as though clamped in a vise, I flipped on the wall-mounted television and barely caught a glimpse of Jay Leno before heavenly sleep overtook me.

EIGHTEEN

John leaned against a wall to watch while a swarm of important-acting people searched his house. Just as he thought, Ashton was too much of a coward to join them.

After the police first questioned him, John figured it was only a matter of time before they would show up with a warrant. They'd already searched some of his coworkers' houses. They showed up at his place sooner than he would have guessed, but he didn't really care. If these assholes wanted to dig through his underwear and search the packaged goods in his freezer, then so be it. He didn't even mind when they took the tank lids off the toilets, removed air vents from the ceiling, and pawed through his tools in the garage. They would leave a mess for him to clean up, but that was a minor inconvenience.

Watching a stern-looking woman with a clipboard who was apparently taking inventory, he grinned, thinking that they'd never find his underground supply room. An old root cellar a few hundred yards from the house, John only found it by accident, when he was clearing brush and heard a hollow sound beneath the tractor. The cellar was dug by the original farming family who owned the land. But as the house was handed down, the younger generations no longer worked the land, and the cellar was forgotten. John lined his secret place with bricks, replaced the rotted shelves, and made a new camouflaged entry door—which he covered with pine straw and leaves. The reinforced door was thicker than the original and actually held a layer of dirt, complete with weeds growing out of it. His small team of men kept supplies in a separate storage facility, but the root cellar was known only to John.

Yes, they could spend the entire morning rummaging through his belongings for all John cared. There wasn't a thing to link him to Mama Jean's murder. Or the Jill Burns bitch. He'd planted the car bomb as an insurance policy and, after he heard her voicing accusations about him, he was glad he'd had the foresight to do so. He couldn't believe his eyes when he saw the BMW suddenly pull into a car wash and saw her jog into the parking lot to chase something during the ten-second remote detonation delay. The blast hadn't killed her as planned, but right now, John had more urgent matters to deal with. Just two days away, the big wedding would be here before he knew it. He'd deal with Jill later.

NINETEEN

My father could play a role and Sally Stillwell of *Eclectic Arts & Leisure* magazine hovered around him as though Spud were a modern-day Leonardo da Vinci. Once he learned that he was going to be on the cover, he threw himself into character: charming, eccentric ex-cop turned brilliant creator. Enamored by the concept of emblematic human frailty, the magazine writer bought into the explanation that, for confidentiality reasons, Spud couldn't reveal the details of where and how the Chrysler had been *transitioned* from reliable transportation into a bold, artistic statement. Which was good, since publicizing the deadly shootout at my pub would not have conformed to Wilmington's Southern, genteel image.

Dirk, Ox, Ruby, and I looked on while Sally interviewed Spud at the Block. Only Ruby had trouble keeping a straight face. The rest of us were stupefied and listened in amazement at the words coming out of my father's mouth.

"Excellent, excellent," Sally said to herself and scribbled on a pad. "This is really good stuff. So then, Spud, how did your group get together? And are any of the other law-enforcement artists coming today? We'd love to get their photos, too."

Spud's walking cane waved back and forth. "No, the other officers are active duty and they like to keep a low profile. But, see, we're like a rock band and I'm the lead singer. The helpers might change, but I envision the sculptures. *Road Rage* was actually my personal vehicle."

"Really? How interesting." She scribbled. "What do you drive now?"

Before Spud could launch into a rampage about the state of North Carolina taking away his driver's license, Dirk intervened. "He's decided not to drive at all, to reduce his carbon imprint."

Spud is about as environmentally conscious as a Texas oilman toting himself around in a Hummer. The original Hummer.

"Er, right," Spud agreed, trying to figure out what a carbon imprint was. "My friends carry me to appointments and such. And to my studio. We carpool."

When asked why his work hadn't been on display in any galleries, Spud told her that nobody wanted his work because he is too old. Gallery owners just didn't have any respect for aging artists, he said, even though eighty was the new fifty and he had plenty of good years left in him.

"The shit's getting thick around here and these are new shoes," Ruby whispered and sashayed off, shaking her head.

Asking me a question about what it was like to live with such a talented man, Sally mistakenly thought I was Spud's granddaughter. She didn't realize that he'd impregnated my mother when he was twice her age, and I didn't mention that he'd walked out on both of us several years later. I gently declined to be interviewed and tossed her questions back to Spud. Ox and Dirk did the same. If Sally thought it odd that nobody wanted to talk with her except the artist himself, she didn't show it. The interview went on for another hour, with Sally quizzing Spud about his views on everything from global warming to crime prevention.

"You are quite the visionary and a fabulous example for senior citizens everywhere," she said and finally closed her notepad.

My father managed to look modest. "Thank you."

"We're flying out tomorrow but we've contracted with a local photographer to get some shots of the current sculpture you're working on. Of course, *Road Rage* will be on the cover with an inset body shot of you, but the editor wants additional shots of your other work. You said it will be finished next week, right?"

Spud's cane shrugged. "Sure, next week. No problem."

After handshakes and hugs, and a few more photographs of Spud posing with Cracker "just for safety," the writer and photographer were gone. Dirk left for work and Ox and Ruby got back to work.

"What the heck is a carbon print for crying out loud?" Spud said.

"Imprint, or footprint. It's a measurement of your impact on the environment, based on how much energy you use," I said. "How are you going to have another sculpture ready by next week?"

"No problemo, kid," he said. "We've got a plan. Me, Bobby, Hal, and Trip. Four heads are much better than—"

"Right, right. Four heads are better than one." It was one of Spud's favorite expressions. But in their case, four heads probably equaled one and a half. Maybe two, if they'd all had their coffee. I decided to skip the details on his sculpting, since I already had a massive headache and didn't want to aggravate it. The doctor warned me that I might have a lingering headache for weeks or even months from the concussion. But at least I was out of the hospital and my upfront hazard pay bonus check had been sitting on the kitchen counter when I got home.

Meanwhile, there were more pressing issues than Spud and his art career. Somebody had tried to kill me, for starters, and I strongly believed that it was the same man I'd shared stuffed shrimp with at Elijah's. John could also be behind a planned terrorist attack, the whole reason I was called back to SWEET duty to begin with. And I no longer had a means of transportation. The insurance people made it clear that they wouldn't pay my claim until they were certain that I hadn't blown up my own Beemer. Puhlleeeze.

With Cracker on my heels, I headed upstairs and phoned my old pal Floyd, overseer of auctions and granter of wishes.

"Jersey?" he said. "Thanks for the case of Maker's Mark, although you didn't have to do that. I still would have taken care of my favorite SWEET girl."

"That's good," I said, cradling the phone between my ear and shoulder while I struggled with the lid of a Tylenol bottle, "because I need another car. Got anything in my color?"

He laughed, coughed. "You're messing with me right? That X5 is a sweet set of wheels."

"She certainly was. But she got, uh, car-bombed. There was a big kaboom and parts shot everywhere. There's not even anything left to salvage."

Floyd lit a cigarette and inhaled. "You hurt?"

"Nope, just a lingering headache. I thought you went on the patch."

"I did, but they made my skin break out. Itched like mad."

I finally got a few pills out of the bottle and let Cracker sniff them to prove I wasn't withholding a treat. His nostrils worked for a second before he sauntered off with a sigh. "Try the nicotine gum."

"You're not going to get another phenomenal deal like the BMW, Jersey. That was a chance thing."

I rubbed a temple, wishing my head would stop hurting. "I know, and I'm not even going to be choosy this time. Just send me whatever you've got."

He laughed. "Even the Volvo wagon?"

"Except for that. Actually, I'd even take the Volvo at this point, but I can't afford it. The price tag can't be more than a few thousand. Insurance company won't pay my claim on the X5 until they're sure I didn't blow it up myself."

"Did you?" he said and laugh-coughed.

"You really need to try the gum, Floyd," I said. "You know what? I'll send you a carton of Nicorette this time, since you're all set on bourbon for a while."

"And I'll find you a good, reliable set of wheels. Might even manage something in black—your favorite color. But don't expect too much," he warned before disconnecting.

TWENTY

"*This just won't* do!" said Allyson Cooper, mother of the bride. "We need enough chairs and tables so that every single guest can be seated to eat dinner at the same time."

The wedding planner silently counted to five, hearing the chime of a wedding bell on each beat. It was a trick he'd learned to keep his cool. "There's another truck on the way, Mrs. Cooper. We'll have a total of twenty-eight tables with linen, full-service china, and silver flatware. At six guests per table, we can accommodate one hundred and sixty-eight people, and that doesn't include the furniture on the lanai or the tables around the pool."

She nodded to herself. "Well, just be sure to reserve the prime tables for me and my husband and his staff. And Daryl's parents. Oh, and the mayor and his wife. I find it damned interesting that they'd never give us the time of day, until Butch was appointed secretary of Defense six years ago. Now, they act like we've been best friends for life. The mayor told Butch he wouldn't miss our daughter's wedding for anything, can you believe that? Flying in from LaGuardia, just for the ceremony."

"Yes ma'am. I mean, uh, no ma'am."

"So we'll need four tables reserved for my husband and our guests, and make sure they're in an area that security won't bitch about. They need to be accessible and in view at all times. Be sure to mark them reserved."

"Yes ma'am," the planner said and jotted something down.

"The security detail will also need the rundown on exactly what that ridiculous singer is going to do for her entrance. I've never even heard of the band Feather Heavy, but Janie and Daryl wouldn't hear of using anyone else. The things we do for our children."

"Yes, ma'am." The planner didn't bother to tell the woman that Feather Heavy currently had not just one, but two songs on the top-ten country charts. Fans loved the lead singer, who was into extreme sports. They called her the wild child and raved over her grand entrances. For the wedding, she'd be parachuting to a cordoned spot on the lawn where her band would be waiting. He could have thrown an entire second wedding for the money that Feather Heavy would be paid.

"And there will be a separate dining area for the media, yes? We're only talking about six or so, maybe ten or twelve if any of them bring a guest. Low key. Still, we'll have a writer and photographer from *People* magazine, another from that Washington insider monthly rag and, of course, the local newspapers. Plus our own publicist and the wedding photographers. And some social gossip woman. The lizard lady, maybe?"

"It's Lady Lizzy, ma'am. And yes, we're setting up a separate tent for the media right now."

"Good. That is all."

"Rich people," the planner muttered to himself, as soon as the woman couldn't hear him. It would all be over tomorrow, thank goodness. Another successful union. Then, he and his staff could focus on the next nuptial event. At least the next mother he had to deal with was much more pleasant than Mrs. Cooper. Sidestepping a few electricians who were stringing lights, the wedding planner rubbed a hand over tired eyes. It wasn't an easy job by any means, but landing the Cooper-Hodges wedding and reception meant a slam dunk for his portfolio. Put the word out that you'd coordinated an elaborate event for the secretary of Defense and his wife at a private residence, not to mention an event for nearly two hundred people, and you didn't even have to pitch a new client. They booked you without bothering to get quotes first.

Activity surrounded the wedding planner as he moved across the grounds. Teams worked inside the traditional coastal-style, elevated two-story home, and outside in the expanse of gardens and natural vegetation that led to a scenic sandy beach. Depending on which direction a guest looked, they could view the entrance to the Cape Fear River or an expanse of Atlantic Ocean. And, coordinating a wedding and reception on North Carolina's southernmost cape island was a feather in his nuptial cap, just due to the logistics. The residential island was accessible only by boat or chopper and automobiles weren't permitted. Even the golf carts had to be electric. Just planning the movement of guests from Southport to the island's marina, and then to the home by golf cart, was a challenge. But money could buy most anything, including an upper-class wedding on Bald Head Island.

The actual ceremony would take place on a flower-drenched stage that was designed to take advantage of a glistening ocean backdrop, after which guests would file up a sandy pathway to the back lawn for the reception. The bride and groom had insisted on getting married at the house, since that's where they first met. He was the contractor who built her grandparents' retirement home, and when he first spotted the visiting granddaughter, it was instant attraction. They were engaged shortly after, and the young couple wouldn't hear of exchanging wedding bands anywhere else.

The good news for the wedding planner was that the grandparents were happy to oblige and didn't mind all the strangers filtering through their house with decorations and furniture. The grandfather, a devout Catholic, hadn't even complained about the logistics of having two clergymen—one Roman Catholic priest and one Presbyterian preacher—who would co-perform the wedding ceremony.

The wedding planner just hoped that both holy men would say a prayer for the couple and their happy day, as he'd take all the help he could get. Regardless of the best food, entertainment, and support staff that money could buy, sometimes things just went wrong.

TWENTY-ONE

Waking up with a headache was getting old. I asked Ox to give me one of his tribe's cherished natural cure recipes for a concussion, but the only advice I could squeeze out of him was to rest and drink lots of fluids. I wanted to get back to work but Ashton instructed me to lie low. Other than reporting any unusual sightings or accidental contact with a POI, my assignment was officially over, at least as far as Ashton was concerned. But he didn't need to know what I did with my own time. And I figured it would behoove me to figure out who tried to kill me, and more important, why. As I waited for Captain Pete to show up, I thought about hitting the gym, but quickly realized that attempting to exercise would be idiotic. Just bending over to stretch my calf muscles made me dizzy. Peeling a banana, I decided to go for a facial instead of a workout. Maybe I'd get a hot-stone massage at the spa, too.

"There are plenty of ways to destress besides punching and kicking a heavy bag," I told Cracker and dropped a piece of banana into his ever-ready snout. I took his wagging tail as a sign of agreement.

Spud had left early for his studio and I was on my own for breakfast. Since I hadn't swiped any egg molds from Mama Jean's truck, the fruit would have to do. When Lindsey moved in, Spud started cooking breakfast and we'd all been eating well. But now, after my close call with a car bomb, everyone decided that it wasn't safe for Lindsey to continue living at the Block. She packed her one giant piece of rolling luggage and moved back to her father's place. I got the impression that Louise still occupied the spare bedroom and Lindsey slept on the sofa, but I forced myself not to inquire. It wasn't my business. What is that old saying? Something about loving something and setting it free . . . if it comes back, then great, but if it doesn't, then it was a stupid idea to begin with. Or something like that. If Ox and I were meant to be together, we would. The spirits would see to it. And my stomach couldn't take worrying about it any further.

I finished the banana and nursed a cup of coffee, hoping caffeine might help alleviate the pressure in my head, when it dawned on me that Spud might not be safe, either. I could be a walking target. The safety of the patrons at my bar was compromised, too. Ashton had me on round-the-clock surveillance and, as far as we could determine, nobody at Sunny Point knew me by any name other than Jill Burns. But if John—or whoever planted the car bomb—was cunning enough to blow up my Beemer, he could very well track me to the Block. Living on my boat was the only reasonable thing for me to do. It is big enough to comfortably accommodate four people overnight and even has a small dishwasher, washing machine, and dryer onboard. Plus I'd be mobile and could dock at different marinas as needed.

I started packing a duffel bag when my kitchen door buzzed. The security monitor displayed Captain Pete, who—to my delight—was carrying a big box of doughnuts.

"Cripes, it's only ten in the morning," he said in greeting, "and it's already sweltering hot. I just saw a dog chasing a cat and they were both walkin'."

I fixed him a glass of ice water, dug in to a lemon-filled—my favorite—and asked him to give me the rundown on Southport. He grew up there and knows the town's idiosyncrasies as well as its waterways. We talked our way through six doughnuts and a pot of coffee and I decided that I should have enlisted Pete's help much sooner.

"They're right secretive at Sunny Point, so I don't know much about it. No more so than any of the locals know," he said, letting Cracker lick the sugar off his fingers. "I hear tell there've been more rumblings than usual, lately, in Southport."

"Rumblings?"

Pete leaned back and stretched. "Big rumbling booms, loud enough to rattle the windowpanes and skew the pictures on your walls. They happen on a purt regular basis, every two or three months. Sometimes, you might get two or three in the same week."

"What causes them?"

He chuckled. "Officials claim that what residents are hearing is the continental shelf shifting, which lets methane gas escape and explode in the ocean. That's what the newspaper reports."

"What do you think?"

"Sheeeit," he said, drawing out the four-letter word. "Locals have always said it's Sunny Point blowing something up. Doing tests, maybe. Or getting rid of old stuff. But my whole point is that they're real secretive. For good reason, I suppose."

"But you're on the water all the time. You must go right by there."

"True, but you can't get near Sunny Point in a boat. There's a large area of restricted waters surrounding the place, patrolled by the Coast Guard. You travel the shipping channel on the river just going by and they come over the radio right quick. Tell you to keep moving and don't enter the restricted waters."

"Okay, so when container ships are loaded up with their cargo at Sunny Point, how do they get to the ocean?"

"You ain't been out on your boat much lately, have you?"

I rubbed my temples, thinking that I might be on my boat more than I wanted to in the upcoming weeks. "Been working too much when I'm supposed to be retired. Humor me."

He reached into a shirt pocked and produced a Goody's aspirin powder for me. "Well, they have wharfs just off the shipping channel. Once a ship is loaded, it runs southwest on the Cape Fear, along the shipping channel. Same route commercial and pleasure boats take. About eight nautical miles along, the ship passes Bald Head Island and heads into open water."

"Open water meaning the Atlantic Ocean, right?"

"Ain't the Pacific, Jersey. You sure you weren't brain-damaged? Yes, the Atlantic. From there, a container ship can go anywhere. In the case of Sunny Point cargo, most ships are probably headed for the Middle East."

"And these boats are packed with all kinds of hazardous cargo and explosives," I mused aloud. "How many containers are on one ship?"

Pete looked upward to think. "I reckon an average cargo ship is about three hundred meters long and might could hold four or five thousand forty-foot containers. Same size boxes you see on an eighteen-wheeler, going down the highway. 'Course, some cargo ships are much smaller and others are much bigger."

I'd seen the cargo ships and knew exactly what Pete was describing. They are giants. More curious was the fact that John had purposely directed me to think about the incoming shipments when being "helpful" by giving me the printed schedule. But he'd dismissed the outgoing schedules as unreliable.

"How many men are on board?"

"Ships are so automated now that they operate with small crews. Maybe eight or ten men on an average cargo ship."

I bid good-bye to Captain Pete, grateful now more than ever that he'd taught me how to operate my boat. I still wasn't adept at backing into slips but would have to take my chances. I finished packing, stuffed Mama Jean's autopsy report and my other MOTSU paperwork into a briefcase, rounded up some food and weapons, left a note reminding Spud to feed the dog, and let Ox know that I'd be taking off for a few days. He understood it was for the safety of others and didn't try to dissuade me. To the contrary, he'd already figured out my next move before I had, and simply handed over the keys to his truck.

Once on the road, I spotted my government tail immediately and lost them just as quickly before heading to the day spa, where I parked Ox's truck and went in for my facial. Afterward, I took a cab to the Cape Fear Marina.

TWENTY-TWO

Ashton was fuming when I called him from *Incognito* and he let me know it. "You purposely evaded our coverage"—his word for surveillance—"which by the way, was there for your protection."

"I didn't mean to, really. I wasn't even paying attention."

He did the throat clearing thing, his way of silently counting to ten. "Where are you?"

"Just enjoying a few days on the water, Ash. You did pull me from the assignment and told me to rest and recuperate after my concussion," I said into the bulky—and untraceable—satellite phone that Soup installed on my boat.

"I don't care where you are, I expect to hear from you every day by oh-nine-hundred and again by twenty-one-hundred hours. No exceptions."

I had tied up outside Fishy Fishy but left the generator running to keep the cabin cool and the water pumps on. The leather sofa perfectly accommodated my stretched-out body, and the flat-screen plasma television was tuned to a digital music station. Nursing my first beer since the car explosion, it occurred to me that my headache had finally dissipated. "Sure," I agreed. "I'll call you twice a day. What shall we talk about?"

"Don't press it, Agent Barnes."

"No, sir."

Satisfied I wasn't in immediate danger, Ashton calmed enough to have a real conversation. The search of John's place yielded nothing except books on topics from surveillance to hand-to-hand combat, my former handler told me, which wasn't unusual considering John's occupation. He'd come up clean. To top that off, the investigation into Mama Jean's strangulation hadn't churned up any suspects. Numerous people visited her residence—including John, by his own admission—but nobody with an apparent motive. There was no blood, no murder weapon, and not even a missing button that might have been ripped off during a struggle. Nothing. The neighbors weren't helpful, either. No unusual observations and no ideas on who might want to harm Mama Jean. The murder simply didn't make sense, everyone said.

Ashton was difficult to read over the phone, but he obviously didn't share my distrust of John. Either that, or he was frustrated by the lack of pointers, as he liked to call them. Arrows of logic, clues, observations, or pieces of the puzzle that pointed to the truth. Once the pointers sent his team in the right direction, it was a simple matter of digging. Disturbingly, nobody knew where to dig.

He cleared his throat. "Some shrimpers found a body this morning, just out from Holden Beach. A male, probably late forties, obvious homicide. Dumped after he was dead and weighted down with two cinder blocks to keep him on the bottom."

"Ick."

"I never did understand your hang-up about dead bodies, considering your impressive combat skills." Something buzzed and clicked in the background.

"Sorry, Ash, but you won't be able to trace this call. And the dead-body thing probably has something to do with my grandfather chopping the head off a yard chicken and making me watch while the body continued to run without a head. Don't remember a damn thing about kindergarten or first grade, but I remember the chickens. Chickens totally freak me out, too. Chickens and dead bodies."

He started to clear his throat but sighed instead. "It would seem that an undertow carried the body into the shrimp boat's trawling area and the starboard-side dredge snagged it. When the crew pulled up their haul and dumped it on deck, a body rolled out along with all the shrimp."

"How did he die?"

"Haven't identified him yet, but the medical examiner says he was strangled."

"Just like Mama Jean," I said, unable to stop myself from glancing at the water's surface surrounding *Incognito.* Creepy. "Could they be related?"

"Maybe, maybe not. Strangulation is one of the leading ways to murder somebody."

"But?" Ashton wouldn't have brought it up if not relevant.

"The body contained a very unique tattoo over the left bicep. A flaming skull with a beret."

I drank some beer, enjoying the coolness at the back of my throat. "The beret may indicate he was an army ranger."

"Right. And John's brother, the twin who died in combat, was an army ranger. The entire unit was killed at the same time, except for one man."

"I know," I said, before I realized it. Between enlisting help from Soup and my partner Rita, both of whom are magnificent researchers, I'd already read a detailed account of the attack that took the twin's life. But Ashton didn't need to know that, especially since he'd already reprimanded me for investigating instead of observing. The concussion must have caused my stupid neurons to multiply. "I mean, really? They all died except one?"

He did the clear-the-throat thing again. "We're checking to see if any photographs of the soldiers' bodies were taken for identification purposes. See if the same tattoo shows up."

"Anything else on the dead guy?" I wondered if the shrimpers processed their haul of shrimp—the same catch that mingled with a dead, bloated body. Of course they would have. Money is money. I might never eat another steamed shrimp again.

"Funny you ask. A security card—the kind you swipe through a reader—was found inside a shoe. Traced it to a self-storage facility near Supply, North Carolina. Got some people there now, along with a bomb squad just in case."

We talked some more, probably just long enough for Ashton to realize that he really couldn't lock on to my location, and he abruptly ended the conversation with a reminder that I was off the case. And a demand to be careful, along with some sort of a threat about losing my government pension due to insubordination. He may have also said something about a fine line, and me walking it, but I'd tuned him out by then.

Gently lapping water always puts me in a utopian mood. I climbed the ladder to the covered flybridge to read my three newspapers and enjoy both my beer and the heightened breezes. An occasional stray seagull squawked, the sun played hide-and-seek with puffy clouds, and happy people had begun streaming into Fishy Fishy in search of lunch. When grilling smells drifted my way, I decided to join them.

TWENTY-THREE

It was going to be a most productive day, John thought, as he broke the seal on a short container loaded with C-4 explosive. Once inside, he was thrilled to find that this box had a damaged seam in the wall, which created an outlet of sorts. Perfect to run a receiver's soft wire antenna so it would hang outside the box—a receiver that attached to a pocket-sized detonator. Small enough to go unnoticed in his pants pocket, but plenty big enough to do the job.

Working quickly, John double-checked the container's contents against a bill of lading, just as he'd done with several others to ensure the government wasn't getting ripped off by suppliers. Spot-checking outgoing inventory had been a regular part of his duties for years. Only today, he worked solo. Random counts were always performed by two people, but the other uniform hadn't so much as flinched when John sent him on an emergency errand. Heart racing, John scribbled check marks on the clipboard and worked his way back to the damaged spot in the container wall. He saw that the wood pallets of product were perfectly spaced apart, and smiled. He would not have to rearrange anything to install the detonator, or run the small antenna wire—his insurance—to the exterior of the box. He'd secured the best electronics available, but would not take the chance that the remote-control signal might not penetrate the shell of the metal. The result of years of waiting and planning, this mission was too important to screw up with an oversight. Even the weather forecast was cooperating, as though the man upstairs had blessed tomorrow's big event.

"Ready to load this one, boss?" an AJAT worker called through the container's open rear doors. He saw John kneeling, tying a shoelace in the cramped quarters.

"Came up one pallet short but I think it's my math," John told him. "I didn't get nearly enough sleep last night, but, hey. She was worth it."

The man grinned.

John stood up, wiped the sweat from his face. "I'll do a recount, to be sure. Give me five minutes."

"Got it," the man said, and relayed the information to the crane operator via two-way radio.

John finished the installation in less than two minutes. He exited the sweltering container, shut the doors, and applied a special security seal, coded to indicate that the container had been randomly examined. With a hand motion, he gave the okay for loading. Even though he knew exactly where the container would be set, he watched with the anxiety of an all-or-nothing gambler waiting for photo-finish race results. Though his face remained impassive beneath dark shades, John's sigh of satisfaction would have been audible to anyone listening. It was perfectly set, so that the detonator's antenna wasn't blocked in by other containers. How ironic that small amounts of RDX, the main ingredient in C-4, were also used to make commercial fireworks. Thoroughly proud of himself, John reveled in the knowledge that he was going to put on a spectacular show that would be seen from miles and miles away.

Finally, he would atone for his twin's death. The military sent his brother into a battle zone and the military should have outfitted him properly. It would have cost less than a tank full of gas per soldier to provide stronger helmets and body armor. But in their haste, the policymakers didn't take into account the safety of their soldiers. They simply hadn't cared.

John's meticulously packaged explosive charge and the detonator would easily trigger an explosion of the nearest carton of C-4. That explosion would almost instantaneously blow the entire container load of C-4. The rest would be an unprecedented event. High-charge ammunitions for the M1A1 Abrams main battle tank, firing into the crowd, killing those who'd escaped the wrath of flaming, flying metal. A destroyed residence, or maybe twelve or twenty homes. An indeterminable number of secondary explosions. The prettiest, loudest, brightest, and most deadly fireworks display ever seen from the shores of Southport. All launched from a pocket-sized detonator built in his root cellar.

The U.S. military, main manufacturer of the putty-like material, praised C-4's stability. It was relatively safe, everyone knew, since it needed both heat and pressure to blow. They were right about its characteristics. John had experimented with bar soap–sized bricks of the material and learned for himself that the claim was true: a bullet fired directly into C-4 didn't do anything. Once, he'd shaved off pieces and set them on fire, only to watch them slowly burn, like a tiny campfire. By tomorrow night, though, the world would be talking about C-4 and wondering if it was really as safe as first thought. Nobody would know what triggered the original explosion on the container ship. No evidence would remain. No crewmen to tell their tales, either. Details of the most fabulous explosion ever on water would belong to him, and only him.

Midnight would be here before he knew it, John thought, consulting his diver's watch. He finished his shift as usual and went home to rest, so he'd be fresh and physically strong. One more detail needed tending to.

TWENTY-FOUR

Peggy Lee delighted in the solace she found in the laboratory. Even though it was an extension of the company, she worked solo and had come to think of it as her personal place. After all, Chuck had built it specifically for the first phase of Project Antisis, and she was the head chemist. She was the *only* chemist on the project, aside from him, and his involvement was merely oversight. She had the IQ to make it happen and he knew it. He loved her for her brains and her ability to reason and think things through—not for something as insubstantial as big breasts or shiny hair. Looks faded with time. Skin sagged and eyelids drooped. But the ability to implement a project that would change the world . . . that was substantial. That was an accomplishment to last forever.

Elbow deep into purified gel from the leafy shiff bush, Peggy Lee's thoughts strayed to her wedding. Of course there wasn't yet a ring or a date, but she knew it was coming. If she had any friends, she would have jumped at the chance to be in one of their weddings as a bridesmaid, just to get some ideas. She would have been happy just to attend someone else's wedding. It would be sort of like relishing in the foreplay, creating savory anticipation for the real deal.

She found the small vial she'd dropped into the vat, retrieved it, and washed her hands and arms. Automatically, she dipped her fingers into a pile of waxy substance, residual from manufacturing the original purified gel. Made up of pureed fibers, seeds, and the guts of the plant, Peggy Lee had discovered that it made a wonderful moisturizer. It even had a pleasant smell. Of course, she used very little of the real wild leafy shiff bush, since she'd found a way to manufacture a chemically identical, synthetic version. But, perhaps she'd talk Chuck into marketing the plant by-product as a high-end cosmetic or at the least, a hand lotion.

Her daydreams strayed back to Llewellyn's Bridal Shoppe, and the mother and daughter she'd seen shopping there. Peggy Lee wasn't a nosy person by nature, she thought, but she remembered everything she'd heard that day, right down to the street location and date of the wedding. Even if they were checking a guest list and she couldn't get in, she could certainly watch the outdoor ceremony from the beach. After all, anybody could go to Bald Head Island as long as they had a boat, or didn't mind taking the ferry. It's not like only the rich people were allowed.

Although, it would be nice to join the ranks of the wealthy, Peggy Lee thought, smiling at her stainless-steel vats and tables of shiny equipment. Soon, she could have anything, including an oceanfront house on an island and her very own yacht. Very soon. The chemist decided to lock up the lab and head home early so she could pick out something to wear to the wedding. She knew the bride's name was Janie, and wondered if Janie would have used her as a bridesmaid, had they been old friends. Probably not. But Peggy Lee would enjoy the wedding, just the same, because it would be her turn next.

TWENTY-FIVE

John awakened at precisely midnight, drank a protein shake, and headed for his root cellar to collect scuba-diving gear and tools. He was pleased to find the marina quiet. The few live-aboards appeared to be asleep and their boats were dark, shades pulled. He smeared on camouflage grease streaks and motored quietly out of the slip.

The familiar waterways whispered encouragement as John navigated his twin-engine offshore fishing boat beneath a sliver of moonlight, without flipping on his navigation lights. Outfitted in a solid black wet suit, he felt powerful, invisible, unstoppable. John arrived at the allocated rendezvous spot three minutes before two o'clock in the morning. Equipped with his own diving gear, Fred waited in a jon boat. Another of John's hired men, Fred had been so startled by the photograph of his dead team member, he knew better than to make John angry by being late. The boss was getting out of control. But he paid well, and Fred needed the money. They tied off to a cypress tree trunk in the small alcove, and—carrying an assortment of supplies including a battery-powered scuba propulsion unit—waded into the Cape Fear River.

John, gripping the handhold on one side of the encased propeller, and Fred, doing likewise on the other, slid rapidly through the water as one and—despite all the extra weight they carried—arrived at their first destination in less than seventeen minutes. John surfaced briefly to ensure he found the correct green buoy that marked the navigable portion of the channel, then followed the chain straight down, thirty-five feet, to where it was weighted at the bottom. The buoys were usually handled by buoy tenders—boats equipped with a crane—but John planned to relocate them the easy way. He watched while Fred cut the chain loose from its anchored block of concrete, and floated the buoy closer to shore. In this stretch of shipping channel, water depth ranged between thirty and forty feet. Even though boats would now be directed into water a bit more shallow—twenty-six or twenty-seven feet perhaps—it was a slight enough change so that the container-ship captain would simply mutter to himself, rather than complain to the Army Corps of Engineers.

Satisfied with the buoy's new location, John gave the thumbs-up sign. Fred attached the chain to a tie-down screw—the kind used to secure mobile homes—and using a pole, worked the giant screw into the bottom of the channel. Winds were predicted to be light and there weren't any offshore storms to create rough currents, so their jury-rig would hold the hot tub–sized buoy in place long enough to serve its purpose. Like the soft wire antenna he'd run to the exterior of the C-4 container, directing the cargo ship closer to the shores of Bald Head Island was an insurance policy.

Working as a team, the men moved two additional channel markers. It was a strenuous task and their lungs absorbed much more oxygen than if they'd been pleasure diving. After securing the third marker, Fred pointed to his watch, indicating that his tank had run low. John pointed at the last tie-down screw, wanting Fred to make sure it was secure. When Fred kicked his way back to the bottom, his headlamp caught a sweeping flash of fishing net. He spun to avoid it, but John—seizing upon the unexpected opportunity—pulled the netting around his partner and yanked the regulator from his mouth. Fred's eyes went wide beneath his mask when John jerked the man's head backward and used an S hook to attach his long braided ponytail to a wad of the netting. A scream came out with a muted bellow of bubbles.

His light shining on the other man's face, John waited for Fred to die. Head arched back and lashing about, Fred struggled to find his regulator, but it had become tangled in the netting, too. He felt for the diving knife attached to his leg, only to realize that, in his haste to be on time, he'd strapped on an empty sheath. During the last seconds of his life, it dawned on the diver that John meant to kill him one way or the other. Just like the man he'd strangled and photographed, as a message to the others. But Fred didn't understand why. He was a simple body for hire. He didn't know or care what John was up to. He just wanted his money, Fred thought, his body suddenly light and prickly as puzzlement overcame panic in his oxygen-starved brain. Reflexively, he sucked in a breath of cloudy brackish water, shut his eyes tight, and tried to think of something pleasant as he died. Nothing came to mind.

TWENTY-SIX

"*I can't do* this. What was I thinking?" Janie paced in the spare bedroom that had been converted to a dressing room, unconcerned about the loose snap on her gown. "I don't even really know Daryl. I mean, who is he?"

"For God's sake, Janie," her mother said, attempting to corral the girl so a waiting seamstress could mend the snap. "Of course you know Daryl. You love him, remember?"

The girl shook her head. "I'm not sure I'm cut out to do the wife thing."

"You are and you will. Now, stop being a brat and let this woman fix your gown! A crowd is already here and the ceremony starts in half an hour."

Janie stood in place to let the seamstress put a needle and thread to the tiny snap at the back of her waist. "But it doesn't feel right, Mom. It's like all of a sudden, I feel sick or something."

Her mother removed a gold pill case and fished around until she found a small pink round one. "Take this. It will calm your nerves.

You're experiencing the prewedding jitters, or whatever they're called. Everybody does. It's normal." The woman didn't know Daryl all that well, either. But she knew that he came from an upper-class family and the man owned his own business. Her daughter could have done much worse. And with help from her husband, her son-in-law would grow into a hugely successful land developer. Janie would live in a beautiful home and have everything the girl deserved.

Janie swallowed the pill, sucked in a deep breath, and straightened her spine. "You're probably right. I'm okay. I'm fine, really. Just a little nervous, I guess."

A bridesmaid in a sleeveless coral-toned satin gown poked her head in the door. "Everything okay in here? You need anything, Janie?"

"We're all set," the mother answered for her daughter. "Is the rest of the wedding party dressed and ready?"

"Yes, ma'am," the maid of honor said and ducked out of the room. Janie's mom didn't look happy, and she wasn't going to stick around to find out why. They just needed to get Janie through the ceremony and on to the fun part of this day—the reception and drinking and dancing to Feather Heavy.

Outside, the wedding planner surveyed the grounds, relieved to see that everything was moving along as scheduled. Guests mingled, security was in place, the decorations were perfect, a pianist happily pounded out background music, the band's crew had finished setting up, and he couldn't have ordered better weather if he'd written the forecast himself.

From a distance, Joe watched the activity through binoculars. The old Bald Head Island lighthouse was in relatively good condition, probably since there were periodic tours through the landmark. He'd broken in and climbed to the very top, the area where the original lantern used to burn with oil that was later changed to an electric light, and took a few minutes to catch his breath. He wasn't in as good shape as he used to be, but that didn't matter. His orders today were simple. Watch for a specific ship—he'd written the name down—coming through the channel, and push a button at the exact moment it cruised by the target house. Joe didn't understand why he had to wait for a specific container ship, but then he didn't really care. John had been quite specific on when to detonate the bomb he'd planted at the wedding, and if the man said he had to wait for a ship, then he'd wait. He just wanted his money. Hot, Joe drank a bottle of water and settled in to get comfortable. As he monitored the river, he couldn't help wonder who the bride and groom were. And wonder if anyone would die as a result of his actions: raising an antenna and pushing a button. He didn't let his conscience bother him, though. Money was money, and if he hadn't taken the job, another man would have.

Chila Turner, lead singer of Feather Heavy, despised weddings. She hated all the billowing white fabric, the ugly bridesmaid dresses, and all the stupid rituals, such as throwing the bridal bouquet. Besides that, exchanging vows was simply stupid. Nobody really meant it when they agreed to stay together until death. Death was much too far away.

She hated weddings so much that she told her booking agent she'd never perform at one, even if there would be VIPs present. But the woman was relentless and convinced her to take the job. The *People* magazine exposure would be great, she said, and the money was absurdly good for such an easy gig. What cinched the deal, though, was when Chila learned that she could parachute in as soon as the happy couple said, "I do." Special permits were required from local authorities, but that was her agent's problem. Her job was to fling herself out of an airplane and wow some fans. The sound man had fitted her with a special high-frequency, long-range wireless microphone, so she could actually talk to the crowd, after her chute deployed and she floated down. She might even sing a few lines, she thought. She'd made countless jumps and could land on a dime. Or, in this case, fifty thousand dollars. It would be one of her more memorable entrances to a performance. It was going to be a blast.

TWENTY-SEVEN

I lounged on *Incognito,* unable to fully enjoy the delicious feeling of seclusion. A sense that something bad was about to happen—and happen soon—nagged at me, and on top of that, I couldn't shake the feeling that somebody was watching me. I'd moved my boat several times and even had Soup sweep the decks and cabin for a GPS tracking device. He assured me that *Incognito* was clean. I chalked it up to being paranoid—a bad thing—rather than merely cautious—a good thing. I called the Block wanting some reassurance from Ox. Or maybe I just wanted to hear his voice. Probably both.

"He hasn't been in for a few days, Jersey," Ruby practically yelled into the phone. "Ever since you took off on vacation. But everything's fine around here. Except your daddy keeps trying to make off with the fixtures."

"What?"

"I caught him and Bobby dragging out a booth seat. Said it was for his new sculpture."

"Good grief."

"Don't worry. We put the booth seat back and we're keeping an eye on him. We've tightened all the screws and bolts on everything."

"How's Lindsey doing?"

"Happy as a clam. Making friends and jumping around like rock star over that Derma-Zing thing. Her commercial is already airing on TV. Nationwide, they say."

I nibbled a slice of apple and listened to melodic clanging sounds from a nearby sailboat. "You think Ox might be at home?"

"Not my turn to keep up with that man," Ruby said. "Listen, we're busy so I've got to skedaddle."

Great, I thought, sulking. I'm trying to stay alive and my best friend is spending quality time with his ex wife. They were probably doing the tourist thing . . . sightseeing and shopping. And if Louise had her way, looking at real estate. No longer hungry, I tossed the remaining chunks of apple overboard and watched them bob on the water's surface. A fish came to investigate and picked at the fruit until it sank.

I pulled out a notepad and scribbled lines of scattered thoughts about MOTSU, Mama Jean, and John. There had to be a simple connection. Something obvious I'd overlooked. I went back over the copy of Mama Jean's autopsy report that Ashton had sent me, for the third time. Nothing. Earlier, I'd asked Soup to keep tabs on Lady Lizzy's personal calendar and was just about to call him for an update when the satellite phone beeped.

"Hello?" I said, unsure if the beeps meant an incoming call.

"I've got something for you."

"Soup? I didn't realize people could call me on this thing. How'd you get the phone number? Oh, wait. You set it up," I said. "Anyway, what *is* my phone number?"

He slurped something. "Lady Lizzy had a nail and hair appointment this morning."

"So?"

"She has her nails done every other Monday. She has a standing hair appointment the first Tuesday of each month. Today was not her regular appointment day for either one."

"I'm listening."

"I called the salon, pretending to be her assistant. Told them I was confirming an appointment. They said she'd already been in and left. They did a wash and set on her."

I rolled my head in slow circles to stretch my neck. A mere hint of concussion headache lingered. "Maybe she has a hot date."

"Not according to the nail place. Lizzy told them she was attending a big event tonight. Wouldn't say what, but according to the nail guy, she was all atwitter. His exact words. And I'd imagine that Lady Lizzy wouldn't get all atwitter unless it was a big deal."

Two jet skis zipped by the marina, faster than they should have, and *Incognito* rocked slightly from the wakes. "Any thoughts on where she's going?"

"Guess you're going to have to get that direct from Lizzy's atwittering mouth."

"You have a—"

Soup rattled off Lady Lizzy's cell phone number. And then he gave me another useful morsel—of the cosmetic surgery variety—in case I may need it for persuasion purposes.

"Thanks, I—"

He cut me off again. "Yeah, yeah. You owe me. You always owe me." He hung up.

When I reached the gossip columnist, she was baffled. "I don't recall giving you this number, Miss Barnes!"

"You didn't. But you *did* hold out on me, Lady Lizzy. We had a deal, remember?"

"Yes, and I e-mailed you my calendar of happenings as agreed!"

"I hear there's a big shindig tonight."

Traffic noises sounded in the background. "Well, ah, yes. There's a wedding tonight, but I didn't think it's anything you'd be interested in."

I kept quiet, to let her imagine that I knew much more than I really did.

"Okay, okay. Lots of heavy-hitters attending. But, look. It's too late for you to get any bodyguard work out of it now."

I usually don't resort to threats but in this case, I didn't have time to be my usual sweet and cunning self. "Here's the deal, Elizabeth. You're going to tell me everything about tonight's event. VIPs, location, everything. And don't even ask, because I'm not going to tell you why I need it. If you're a good girl and cooperate, then I won't leak it that your last vacation—the one to help vaccinate Third World children—was really a trip to Thailand for a breast lift and eye job."

She gasped.

"You remember the trip, right? It's the alleged missionary work you wrote a column about. You told readers how rewarding it is to help make a difference in the world."

Her voice lost its endless supply of exclamation points as she pulled off the road and gave me the rundown on the wedding. Of particular interest was the Bald Head Island location and the fact that the bride's father was also the United States secretary of Defense. The news made goose bumps pop out on my skin. Ignoring a lone seagull that begged for food from its perch on an outrigger, I called Ashton, who should have already known about the Sec Def's presence in North Carolina.

"Is there a container ship going out of Sunny Point tonight?" I said after he verified that I was not under the influence of coercion with his silly secret questions.

He cleared his throat. "Jersey, I'm not going to tell you again. You are off—"

"Ashton, please. I don't care if you load up my file with demerits or play the threaten-to-withhold-my-pension card. Is there a boat going out?"

He put me on hold and came back in seconds. "Scheduled to depart at seventeen hundred hours."

I told him about the wedding, the VIPs, and my theory that there was something on the container ship scheduled to blow up as it passed the wedding party. John had access to the container loads of munitions and, if he sought revenge for his brother's death, who better to go after than the Sec Def?

"Give me something concrete, Jersey. I can't stop a shipment based on a hunch from a single agent who is recovering from a concussion. There are people on the receiving end of the shipment who need those supplies."

"Can't you prevaricate?" I said. "Stall until your explosives people examine every container?"

"Do you know how long that would take? Not going to happen. For some reason, you're convinced our bad guy is John, when he keeps coming up clean." He paused to sneeze, a deviation from his usual throat clearing when dealing with me. "One, we've just decoded some intel that may discredit our earlier information, so the whole Sunny Point thing might have been a false alarm to begin with. Two, we've thoroughly vetted John Mason. We've searched his house and his property. We've spoken with his superiors. Nothing."

"But—"

"You've obviously stumbled into something. The close call in your car. Mama Jean and the body from the shrimp boat—both with similar markings on their necks. Rest assured that we're staying with it until we figure out what's going on."

"So you won't—"

"They'd have my ass if I intercept a munitions shipment based on a damn hunch. Get some rest, Jersey."

I tried again. "The container ship—"

"Is moving out as scheduled. Security inside MOTSU is so damn tight right now, a mosquito couldn't get through without a security clearance."

He hung up before I could say anything else and I wanted to throw my fancy satellite phone in the air and shoot it like a clay pigeon. I had to get to the wedding, but then what? I picked up Mama Jean's autopsy photographs and studied the purplish markings on both sides of her neck. What had Ashton just said about the other body, the floater? That it had the same markings on the neck as Mama Jean.

"Holy crap," I said to the seagull, which had moved to perch on the bow rail. A vivid memory of John Mason fighting in the parking lot at Elijah's restaurant replayed in my head. He had grabbed the remaining drunk with one huge hand and all but lifted the fisherman off the ground. It was his left hand with the stubby ring finger—the one that got mangled in a corn chopper. The neck bruises seen in Mama Jean's death photos perfectly matched my recall of the one-handed choke hold John had on the fisherman: thumb on the left side of the throat, up under the jaw, and the other thick fingers on the right, all exerting enough inward pressure to asphyxiate somebody. But the ring finger was too short to leave a bruise. There were only four marks instead of five, as would be left from a normal hand. John was the killer and the photographs would prove it.

I redialed Ashton's private number, but he didn't answer. Frantically, I called the main number, gave my identification code, and asked for Ashton. They said he was unavailable. My handler had blown me off. It would be fruitless to keep trying.

My next call was to Ox's cell phone. "Look, I know you're busy with Louise and I'm sorry to bother you," I rushed when he answered on the first ring, "but I have a quick question. If you planned to blow up a container ship that was loaded with munitions, how would you do it? Obviously with a detonator of some sort, planted in one of the containers. But would it be on a timer, or what?"

"Does it need to blow at a specific time? Or anytime the ship is out in open seas?"

"A specific time. At the exact time it passes by a house."

"I'd use command detonation, then, like what was used on your car. The remote would need to be within signal range to the receiver, or detonator, and the user would need to have a visual on both the boat and the house."

"How far of a range, generally speaking?"

"Depends on the equipment. The remote could easily be a kilometer away from the receiver. Or more. What location are we talking about?"

"Bald Head Island and the shipping channel."

"Remote detonation could take place from the beach or a building with an unobstructed view. Even from the air in a chopper or small plane. Keep in mind that if a container ship of munitions blows, it could take out an untold number of houses and nearby people, including the person who detonated it. That's a lot of juice, Jersey."

"Well, maybe John Mason is a die-for-the-cause kind of guy." I disconnected and dialed JJ. I needed a sharpshooter, I told her, and explained that the job could be dangerous. Or to be more accurate, deadly.

"Aren't they all?" she said. "What type of rifle do I need?"

"One that will shoot somebody."

"C'mon, Jersey. Help me out a little bit here."

"We're going to Bald Head for an outdoor wedding. You'll have to figure out where the bad guy has hunkered down. He'll be someplace where he can watch the shipping channel and see the house. If

I'm right, he's going to send a wireless signal that will detonate a bomb on a passing container ship. The ship, by the way, is loaded with forty-foot box loads of explosives and ammunition. Hundreds of them. Thousands, actually."

"Aren't you retired?" JJ said.

"All you have to do is find the bad guy and shoot him before he has a chance to push the button."

She laughed. "Remind me to never retire."

I told JJ to watch for me at the Southport Marina. She said that she and her .416 Barrett rifle would be waiting with bated breath.

TWENTY-EIGHT

"Ready to crash a wedding?" I said, angling *Incognito* close enough to the fuel dock for the Barnes Agency's newest partner to pull off her heeled sandals and jump aboard.

JJ smiled. "Sure. Maybe I'll catch the bouquet."

Gorgeous in a flowing sundress and floppy hat, she certainly didn't look deadly, even though I knew her bag contained a sniper rifle and a few other lethal toys. And I knew for a fact that she had no desire to get married, caught flower bouquet or not.

"What would you do with it if you were to catch it?" I asked.

"Give it to you, so you'll be ready when Ox proposes."

"Yeah, right." Neither Rita nor JJ knew I'd been to bed with Ox. But everyone thinks we'd be perfect together, as a couple. Of course, that was before Louise blew into town and started building a nest at Ox's place.

"Sizzling duds, by the way," she said. "When Ox sees you in that dress, he just might come up with a proposal, if you know what I mean."

My dress was black and satiny and sleeveless with white piping around the waist. Respectably knee length, but invitingly low cut. If we were going to disrupt a wedding, at least we'd look good doing it. Plus, it's the only dress I had in the stateroom closet and it perfectly concealed my backup weapon—a Sig-Sauer P232—in a thigh holster. The Glock, a much bigger and heavier piece, would have to stay in the boat. It was either that, or walk bowlegged.

"Ox is busy with his ex-wife, who's apparently in town for an extended stay. So he's obviously not going to see me in this dress, at least not today."

"You never know," JJ said.

As I pushed the throttle forward to pull away from the dock, Ox stepped aboard with one long stride. Like JJ and me, he was dressed for an outdoor summer wedding in lightweight slacks and a short-sleeved white silk tee.

"You know how I hate to miss a good party-crashing," he said and I wondered if he'd been close enough to hear any of our conversation. JJ's face registered guilt when I gave her a look. She must've called him, although I couldn't say I was mad about it. He climbed to the flybridge. I stood at the console and when he moved behind me, the back of my neck tingled. He radiated a physical energy that reached through the empty space between our bodies. I thought about throwing myself into his arms, but asked him to take the wheel instead. As we cruised to the Bald Head Island marina at twenty-five knots, I gave him an update, admiring his relaxed and capable stance at the helm of *Incognito.*

"Nice dress," he said when I finished with the briefing. "You look beautiful."

"Thanks," I said, noticing his recent haircut. "You look pretty good yourself."

"Want me to run the boat so you two kids can go below and play?" JJ said.

"Hey, I'd be game," I quipped, "but Ox has been busy playing house with somebody else."

I knew the comment sounded petty and I immediately felt small for saying it. But I felt even worse when Ox didn't say anything to correct my assumption.

A reception tent was set up in the marina's parking area and, using fake press passes JJ brought, we pretended to be photographers taking pictures for Lady Lizzy. After a list was consulted, the three of us and our bags of gear were whisked via electric golf cart to the site of the wedding, a lovely home on the southwestern point of the island. We backtracked a few houses, cut through to the beach, and walked back along the water's edge, deciding on a plan of action.

"If our man must see the house from his vantage point," JJ said when we reached the wedding area, "it makes sense that I'll be able to find his location from the house."

"Might could use the sundeck," Ox suggested. We looked up from the beach to spot a wooden platform built over one section of the roof, on the third story. Stairs zigzagged down from the deck to a second-floor balcony. Enclosed with a decorative wrought-iron fence, the sundeck held a variety of large tropical plants in clay pots. There were also lounge chairs, small tables, and a mini refrigerator.

JJ's eyes swept the deck, checked out the rest of the house, and ended up back on the deck. "Probably the best place to station myself, considering that I don't know who I'm looking for or where they'll be."

"Take a camera and tripod, in case anybody asks what you're doing up there," I suggested.

She stuck out a hip. "Well, duh."

"You don't have to be snippy just because I'll be down here, mingling with the guests and eating caviar-covered brie cheese while you're up there, boiling in this heat."

We tuned our miniature two-way radios to the same channel. Ox left to scout the area, JJ headed off to infiltrate the sundeck, and I strolled up a pathway from the sandy beach to the rear lawn. I flashed a press pass to get by a guard and only had to wait ten minutes before I saw movement on the roof deck. JJ had made it and, from what I could tell through the plants, was fishing around in the small refrigerator.

In the half-hour to follow, the property became a jovial, bustling get-together in a whirl of activity, handshakes, and hugs. Air thick with the smells of perfumed people, cooking food, and fresh flowers—the flowers were everywhere—blew over the grounds while servers circulated with trays of mint lemonade. A circle of well-manicured guests surrounded the secretary of Defense and another enveloped the mayor of New York City.

I was pretending to take some photographs when Lady Lizzy strolled up. "Why, hello, Jersey," she said, without the usual exclamation point.

"What, no *dahling* this time?"

Tiny droplets of sweat popped through heavy makeup on her upper lip. She dabbed at them with a cocktail napkin. "Blackmail disagrees with me."

"But I'm here for a very good reason, if that makes you feel any better. Oh, and if anyone asks, I'm one of your photographers."

She eyed my camera. "My photographers use much more sophisticated equipment than that."

"Yeah, well. They probably have their cameras powered on, too."

Fanning her face with a program, she flounced off.

Ten minutes before the wedding ceremony was to start, servers collected empty drink cups and ushers appeared to escort people down to the beach area. Rows of folding, white resin chairs formed a semicircle around a decorated stage, the first three rows marked RESERVED for family and VIPs. A fancy public address system with elevated speakers ensured that everyone would be able to hear just fine. Press pass hanging around my neck, I positioned myself close to the water, as though I planned to shoot photographs of the wedding party as they walked down the makeshift aisle.

"JJ," I whispered into my radio.

"Go ahead," she answered.

"Anything yet?"

"Negative. Not a damn thing, and I've been scouring every back lawn, rooftop, and beach walker I can see, and I can see pretty much everything. With these binoculars, I could count the hairs on a gnat's ass at five hundred meters."

"Ox? You see anyone?"

"Negative," came his reply.

The assembled crowd instantly hushed when the wedding march blared from the speakers and the bridal procession began with a young flower girl throwing handfuls of rose petals on the sand. I pretended to snap a few photographs before returning my attention to the water. As scheduled, a squarish spec came into view and, as it grew larger, it began to take the form of a ship.

I moved farther away from the stage and took some more faux photos. "JJ, do you see the boat coming southbound through the channel?"

She came back after several seconds. "Affirmative. It's the container ship, with two Coast Guard escorts."

"Dammit," I muttered to myself. The wedding progressed with two men in robes officiating. A sniffling bridesmaid dabbed at tears. Carrying a wailing baby, an apologetic mother inched her way out of the crowd. One of the priests said something funny and everyone laughed. About a mile away, the container ship passed Oak Island and continued our way. It was time to get everybody inland and my mind vacillated about the best way to do so. I'd probably need to take the microphone from the dueling priests.

"JJ," Ox's voice came over the radio.

"Go ahead."

"Get a visual on the top of the lighthouse that we passed coming in. The lantern room." Old Baldy is an octagonal lighthouse built of bricks and plaster that has been inoperative since the early 1900s. I knew JJ had already checked it out, but maybe our mark wasn't yet in place.

I was studying the tower when I noticed a woman staring at me with an odd expression. She nudged her companion and whispered something to him, after which he stared at me, too. I fiddled with my camera, as though changing the settings, and snapped a few more pretend photographs. Satisfied, the couple returned their attention to the bride and groom. The container ship grew steadily bigger.

"Male Caucasian, baseball cap, mirrored sunglasses," JJ said. "Holding a small box . . . just pulled a retractable antenna out of it. Looks like the receiver my neighbor's kid uses when he's playing with his radio-controlled dune buggy."

I took another photograph. "Ox?"

"Shouldn't be anyone in there, unless he's a maintenance person from the foundation that owns the lighthouse."

"He look like maintenance?" I asked and took another picture.

"Nope," came JJ's reply.

The bride slid a ring on her man's outstretched finger. The mother hurried back to her seat with a now-quiet baby. A parade of five pelicans sailed by, skimming the water in search of dinner.

"What's he doing?" I asked.

"Just standing there," JJ said. "Appears to be watching the house. No opticals."

He wouldn't need binoculars. He could see just fine when the ship passed by the house.

"Rangefinder says I'm 882 meters away from him," she continued. "Virtually no wind. Clean shot. I'm good to go."

"Ox?" I questioned.

"Your call, Barnes."

"Take him out, JJ. Do it now. Head shot."

The audience of nearly two hundred happy people clapped and whistled when the newly wedded couple embraced. A display of low-level fireworks went off behind them and the crowd clapped louder. Just when the groom kissed his bride, JJ's Barrett went off and it sounded like a bottle rocket being fired from a minicannon.

A surprised crowd looked around to see where the sound came from, unsure of what they'd heard. But with fireworks still popping and sounds echoing off the water, they went back to watching the newlyweds, who obliviously continued to kiss. When the couple stopped to wave to the crowd, everyone stood and the noise level inched up another notch. The secretary of Defense joined his daughter and son-in-law, taking a microphone from its stand on the podium.

He held up a hand to quiet the guests. "My wife and I want to thank all of you for coming to join our family on this most special, most memorable day," he said.

The container ship grew big as it glided by, flanked by the Coast Guard patrol boats. After a few seconds of nothing exploding, my body went slack with relief. Adrenaline draining from my system, I hustled to the house to find JJ. Gear bag slung over her shoulder and camera and tripod in hand, she met me in the backyard. "I'm ready for a drink. How about you?"

We got Ox on the radio. He was on a golf cart and said he'd pick us up in front of the house.

"So much for my drink," JJ said, "and free drinks are the best kind. They've got the premium stuff, too."

We heard the father droning on, as though he were at a political rally. "My job deals with protecting the freedoms that all Americans enjoy, such as the freedom to cherish family and friends on a beautiful day like this," the father continued. "And now, we invite everyone to stay for the reception and dinner." He pointed to the sky, where a skydiver dropped from a small prop plane. "Look up and let's give a big welcome to Chila, lead singer of Feather Heavy—my daughter's favorite band!"

"My God," JJ said. "They got Feather Heavy to perform?"

There were *oohs* and *ahs* and, when the bright yellow chute popped open, the younger people went wild. A screech of static sounded through the band's speakers on the lawn, and the singer's recognizable voice came through. "Congratulations, Janie and Daryl, this is Chila dropping in from above, and I have to say that, even from up here, you guys look beautiful!"

Janie squealed with delight.

"Join me on the back lawn, won't you?" Chila said. "My band is ready and waiting, so let's get started!" A thumping drum beat started and people began filtering to the lawn, where the band started to play as they watched their singer descend. Chila appeared to be right on target for a cordoned-off landing area.

JJ had managed to secure a shot of 1800 Silver tequila in a real glass and we were walking to the front of the house to meet Ox when another piercing screech of feedback sounded. The kind that makes people cringe. Then it happened. The ship blew with a deafening rumble. It started with a sharp crack that hurt my eardrums and in the microsecond of silence that followed—as we spun toward the source of the sound—the air-sucking stillness erupted into a violent explosion and blinding fireball. A wave of hot wind knocked us to the ground and sounds of windows shattering filled my ears. We scrambled upright and ran to the beach as a series of secondary explosions lit up the waterway and spit fiery chunks of steel and shrapnel into the air at lightning speed. Had the container ship not cleared the island and reached the mouth of the ocean, we'd be dead. The bride and groom and all their guests would be dead. The lighthouse and numerous residential houses would be flattened. Stunned, we stood mesmerized by the show, gusts of searing heat engulfing our bodies, surging water rolling way past the high-water mark. Ox found us and led us away from the shore.

"It was the damn jumper," JJ shouted over the noise. "Chila did it."

I rubbed my eyes, to rid them of the green and white spots in my vision. "That makes no sense."

"Her special, long-distance wireless microphone must have been on the same frequency as the bomber's receiver. Chila flipped on her microphone pack to the crowd as she floated down. *That's* what set off the detonator on the ship. The first time she spoke, it didn't do anything. But as she came closer in, her signal was strong enough to reach the ship."

"Let's get out of here, ladies," Ox said and I realized he was right. Everyone else had run away from the explosions, fearing for their safety. Not toward the beach like we had. The vessel was a good distance away, but not far enough when you considered the cargo on board.

Another thundering explosion rocked us and an instant later, something whizzed by my head. A palm tree exploded behind us.

"Anti-tank missiles," Ox yelled. "The fire is setting them off. Let's go!"

We dropped to the sand and belly crawled our way to the street—not a graceful task in a dress and sandals—as a few more missiles whizzed overhead. Once in the road, we hiked to the marina, boarded *Incognito,* and headed up the shipping channel toward Wilmington. Police and rescue boats flew by us in the other direction and we could see an orange medical chopper in the distance. There was no way any of the container ship crew survived. Or those on the Coast Guard boats. The recovery efforts would not be pretty.

TWENTY-NINE

Other than the dead man in the Bald Head Island lighthouse and a heart attack victim who was eating a grilled hamburger on his lanai two houses down from the wedding, the only casualties were the crews on the container ship and Coast Guard boats. Still, thirteen people were dead as a result of the explosion, not to mention the damage done to nearby houses and the shipping channel. Luckily, Chila had been blown onto the roof of a pool house and survived with only a sprained ankle. The media couldn't get enough of her, especially since she was the only one talking. Officials wouldn't comment on the disaster, understandable since they didn't have a clue what caused it. The camera operator who was videotaping the wedding had enough foresight to point his digital video camera at the exploding ship before he ran, and the footage was now airing on every major network.

From start to finish, it took six minutes for the container ship to sink, although the underwater explosions continued for another ten minutes. Shore damage was extensive and the Army Corps of

Engineers worked around the clock to clear the channel. Under heavy security, teams of specialists worked to recover bodies, the sunken vessel, and its scattered contents. And MOTSU was crawling with uniforms, including a special investigative team from the Department of Defense. They didn't know details, but Ashton had been obligated to suggest that an attempt to kill the Sec Def had been curtailed.

"Tell me about the dead man in the lighthouse," Ashton said. We sat at a corner table in the Block. I picked up on at least two of his people, pretending to be customers. One drank coffee and read the newspaper. Another younger one listened to an iPod, acting like he was waiting for a friend. I didn't necessarily mind that people were following my every move and possibly listening to my conversations. It made me feel important, even though the bride's father now had a private security detail that put mine to shame.

"I thought the fellow in the lighthouse was probably John."

"Negative."

Crap. John was still out there, madder than ever, and probably planning to take out his anger on me. I drank some Coors Light from the bottle. "Then I don't know who the man was."

"Shot through the head with something big and fast. We'll probably never find the slug. Was Joan Jackson on the island, by chance?"

I took another swallow. Ashton should know better than to even ask such a question.

"Okay, then." He did a mini cough that wasn't quite his annoyed clearing-the-throat sound. "Let's try it this way. Tell me everything you know about the incident."

I could have started with, "I told you so," but that would only serve to piss him off. "As you know, I suspected that a detonator had been planted on one of the containers in the outgoing shipment. Since the exact timing of when the ship would pass by the target house couldn't have been known, we determined that the device would have to be command detonated."

"We?"

"Just a term I like to use. Me and my alter ego. My *hunches,"* I couldn't resist adding. *The same hunches that weren't viable enough for you to stop the outgoing ship to begin with,* I thought.

Ashton did the throat-clearing ritual. "Go on."

"So we attended the wedding to take a look around. The container ship was passing by just as we saw a man up in the tower, watching the house and holding a remote-control device. Fortunately, somebody shot him, and the ship passed by without incident. Saving a few hundred lives, by the way."

He cleared his throat again, defensive when he should have been thankful. "Unfortunately," I continued, "that's when the singer from Feather Heavy made her grand entrance by parachuting in. She was equipped with a long-range wireless microphone. It was tuned to the same frequency as the receiver on the ship. There was a big bang and you know the rest."

He let forth a string of cuss words. "The country singer did it?"

"Freaky, huh?" I said. "But it's the only explanation that makes sense."

I drank my beer while Ashton made a brief phone call, hung up, and cussed some more. When he calmed, he revealed that the key card found on the floater—the body that the shrimp boat pulled in—opened a storage unit registered to Mama Jean. It held the makings for explosives, detonators, and some nifty electronics. Most likely, the storage unit was where my car bomb had been built.

"Well, Mama Jean couldn't have blown up my car," I mused. "She was already dead. My money is still on John Mason. Especially since the autopsy photographs will prove he choked her."

Ashton didn't comment on Mason and it occurred to me that

there was something about the security worker my handler knew that I didn't. He was holding out on me.

"Don't know what the connection is, but we found a diver tangled in netting at the bottom of the channel," Ashton said. "A channel marker was drifting away in the current and when divers went down to investigate, they found him. No key card on this body, but his prints are all over the storage unit."

"He's dead?"

Ashton sighed. "Of course he's dead."

I shivered at the thought of his bloated, dead body sharing the same waters as my boat. "Ick."

"Three channel markers were tampered with, apparently to route the ship even closer to the target home. Chances are, there was a second man. Would be nearly impossible for one man to do it alone."

"Mason."

Ashton shook his head in disagreement. "I'd think it was the man in the tower, but now that they're both dead, we may never know. As far as John goes, he's as upset by the explosion as everyone else. I spoke with him earlier this morning. He's worried that his job is in jeopardy, because something like this happens, people get fired."

I wanted to scream, but finished the Coors instead before speaking. "Have forensics take a look at the photographs of the choke marks on Mama Jean's neck. The same ones you found on the shrimp boat's body's neck. They'll match John's left hand. A piece of his ring finger is missing. As I already said, it proves he's their killer."

"We'll take another look, Jersey, but I think you're grasping at straws."

I asked my handler if I was still receiving a paycheck. I'd remain on the payroll until his crew pulled out of Southport, he said, and reminded me once again that I was officially off the case. He also told me not to attempt to evade the surveillance.

"No argument from me, boss."

"Good work, Barnes," he said and stood to leave. "And pass along my regards to Joan Jackson."

I retrieved another beer from behind the bar and returned to the table to drink and contemplate. Why was Ashton so vehemently protecting Mason? It was almost as if he knew the man. I'd barely gotten the screw cap off when Lindsey plopped down across from me.

She power-chugged a glass of water. "Man, is it hot today. Seems hotter here than in California. And the people wear more clothes, you know? Like there's a dress code or something. Weird."

I laughed at her assessment, which was probably true. Skimpy is the fashion of choice on the West Coast. Or maybe they just prefer to be more comfortable. "How are you liking your job?"

"It's okay. I mean, I like the money. But seating people and running food is kind of boring. And some of your customers are weird. Like that guy over there?" She pointed to the young fellow with the iPod. "He hasn't ordered anything but a glass of tea, and he's been sitting there for an hour."

The same amount of time I'd been in the bar. "Go over there and tell him that if he's going to pretend to be listening to music, he should at least make sure the earphone cord is plugged into the unit."

I nodded at the kid's shirt pocket, which held the iPod. The cord had fallen out, and was hanging straight down. Lindsey laughed. "What a doofus. Is he an agent or something?"

"Yep. Bring him another tea and a bowl of peanuts when you go."

I watched Lindsey deliver the tea. The guy realized she was right about the earphone, blushed, and gave me a stupid little wave as though we were playing a game of hide-and-seek, and he'd been found. I wondered if I'd ever been that green, when I first went to work for Ashton.

Lindsey returned and said she wanted to ask me about something.

Hoping like crazy it wouldn't be a sex talk, I led her outside to the riverwalk. We continued along the path for a few blocks and stopped at a shaded bench that overlooks the river. The iPod kid followed at a distance. It took some prompting, but finally Lindsey blurted it out.

"I think I could be pregnant."

Crap. It was going to be a sex talk. My mother never spoke to me about sex or boys and the bulk of my early education came from television movies. "Why?" I finally said. It was all I could think of on such short notice.

"Well, my period is late. And my stomach kind of hurts. Like nausea, maybe."

I've never been pregnant, but the symptoms sounded right on target. "So you've been having sex? I didn't think you had a serious boyfriend."

"I don't. I hate boys. And I'm still a virgin, I guess."

I closed my eyes to enjoy the feeling of sunshine on my face for a few seconds, while I decided how to plow on. I took the direct approach. "Lindsey, either you have had sexual intercourse, or you haven't. You're either a virgin or you aren't. There's no such thing as maybe when it comes to that."

"We kind of played around a little, before I broke it off with him. My boyfriend in California, I'm talking about. That's like all he ever wanted to do was get his hands under my clothes, you know? He kept pressuring me to go all the way. I never did. But he . . . you know . . . well. We, like, fooled around a little bit."

"But you never actually had intercourse, right?"

"Right," she said in a small voice.

We people-watched in silence and it struck me again how much of Ox was in Lindsey. Both physical features and characteristics, such as being content to appreciate a good silence without trying to fill the gaps in conversation.

"Okay, then," I said after some time. "I'd say it's virtually impossible for you to be pregnant. Sometimes your period is just late. The nausea could be from bad food. But just to be on the safe side, let's get you to the doctor and find out what's going on."

"Okay. Can we go today?"

She must have been fretting over the late period for days. "I'll make a phone call and see when they can work you in."

"Thanks, Jerz," she said with a hug. "You won't tell Dad?"

"About this conversation? No. But he has a right to know that you're going to the doctor."

Her face fell.

"We'll tell him that it's just for a checkup, okay?"

She brightened. "Deal."

Since it wasn't an emergency, the receptionist at Daisy Obstetrics & Gynecology asked if she could work Lindsey in later in the week. I told her that would be fine. At least I had something scheduled on my to-do list, other than worry about a madman with a penchant for explosives.

THIRTY

Forgetting about discipline, John Mason threw a lamp against the wall. The faux Tiffany shade burst into pieces, but that didn't make him feel any better. The Jill Burns bitch was like a golden child, untouchable, mocking. Somehow, somebody got to the man he'd sent to Bald Head Island and picked him off, disrupting the entire plan. It had to have been her. Loyal to the end, Joe must have struggled to activate the detonator, even while dying, and managed to do so before he went unconscious. It's the only thing John could figure. But the fact that the container ship eventually blew up was of little consolation. It missed the mark.

Years and years of waiting for precisely the right opportunity, hours and hours of creating a strategy, suddenly worthless. A brilliant plan of action, wasted. He should have done the damn job himself. He would have known better than to take up position in such a visible place. People gazed at lighthouses all the time. They took lighthouse pictures and collected lighthouse figurines. The idiot deserved to die. John scooped up the mangled lamp and threw it at another wall. He should have done the job himself, he thought again. Joe didn't know that he would kill himself, along with the entire wedding party. But John wouldn't have minded doing the job, even knowing that one push of a button would sign his own death certificate. At least he would have died happy, blissful in the knowledge that he'd accomplished the mission.

He dropped to the ground and grunted out fifty push-ups to calm himself before going out to the root cellar. John would miss his house, he thought, especially the huge yard and all the trees. But mostly, he'd miss his secret place. An hour later, the dirt cellar was stripped bare, except for the bricks lining the walls. He carried bags of supplies and gear to the trunk of his car and planned to dispose of most of it later, at the landfill.

Back inside, he packed a canvas duffel bag: clothes, razor, soap, toothbrush, weapons, and banded stacks of twenty and fifty dollar bills. Surveying the house, John did a mental check to make sure nothing important or telling was left behind. Earlier that morning, he'd listed the property for sale and told the real estate agent to give all the furniture and his clothes to a charity. He lived sparsely to begin with, and now, he wouldn't need material things.

Deflated, John fell into a chair and rolled himself up to a small wood desk that would soon be in another's house, a poor family perhaps who needed it for their child's schoolwork, and scripted a resignation letter. Addressed to his AJAT supervisor, he stated that the stress of the recent situation was bearing on him so he decided it was time to retire. As one of the people who oversaw the loading of the sunken container ship, he felt a certain responsibility, he wrote, even though nobody knew what caused the explosion. It could have been a freak accident, caused by a careless crew member and a discarded cigar, or faulty wiring, or any number of causes. What made up his mind, John continued writing, was that he had put in enough time with the company to become fully vested in the 401(k) plan and collect retirement benefits when he turned sixty-five. He no longer felt as though he could be an effective security contractor. John signed the letter and wrote a forwarding address and phone number at the bottom. They belonged to a furnished apartment in Charlotte, North Carolina. He'd paid the six-month lease in advance, in cash, even though he never planned to use it. He wasn't going to bother hooking up an answering machine to the phone line. The military police—and everyone else in line behind them—would want to question him further, John knew. Over the next months, they would question every Sunny Point employee and contractor, and every supplier whose products moved through the facility. But he was low on the totem pole, in the overall scheme of things. And they couldn't question him if they couldn't find him. Even if they were to locate him, there was no way they could pin anything on him. Of that, John was certain. Even Mama Jean's warehouse rental would point to the dead men, but not him. She'd rented it with plans to open a small café and had started collecting used restaurant equipment. When she changed her mind, he helped her out by selling the equipment, but he'd kept the garage-sized storage space. He paid a year's rent in advance by mail, with a money order and he never visited the place without first putting on gloves. He'd even disabled the storage facility's one security camera, and the on-site manager hadn't bothered to repair it. John's tracks weren't just covered, they were nonexistent.

Nonetheless, the failure of his mission overwhelmingly frustrated him. A spent man, John made up his mind to leave the whole godforsaken country behind. He hated America's leaders and the weak people who elected them. He no longer cared to live on U.S. soil and couldn't wait to get out of Dodge. His twin brother would have to understand that he'd tried. He'd done his best to avenge the senseless death, but it wasn't good enough. Somebody outsmarted him. Before he boarded his other boat, a thirty-eight-foot sailboat, and navigated to the Caribbean Islands, he planned to track down the bitch, and kill her.

THIRTY-ONE

Living on Incognito felt like a vacation, except for the fact that I was always looking over my shoulder. Not only was a dangerous lunatic most likely after me, but I continued to get the impression that I was being followed. Probably Ashton's surveillance. If so, I hoped it was an agent with street smarts. Somebody who could take out John Mason before he got to me.

Ashton had threatened to freeze my future retirement money if I didn't follow his orders, which included keeping my government-issued cell phone charged up and powered on so they could locate me through the built-in GPS tracking device. And I had to periodically report in. Overall though, if I didn't think too much about my handler, green agents with iPods stuck in their ears, or John, I could enjoy my leisurely time on the water.

I was eating a late breakfast of honey-soaked buttermilk biscuits and fresh cantaloupe, reading a juicy novel, when the boat's satellite phone beeped.

"Hello?"

"Jersey, you've got to quit playing on that boat of yours and get home. Spud has done it again."

"Dirk? How did you get this phone number? What *is* this phone number?"

"Your daddy and his pals went to the outdoor firing range—get this—to shoot up their alligator. It's on fire."

"The alligator?"

"The clubhouse. Fire engines are already here."

"Anybody hurt?"

"No, but that could change at any second if you don't get over here and shut him up."

"The alligator?"

"Very funny." Dirk told me which firing range my father was in the process of destroying and hung up without laughing.

Incognito was already tied up at the marina, so all I had to do was lock her up and figure out a way to get myself to the shooting range. Luckily one of the dockhands was in a benevolent mood and let me borrow his Honda CBR 1000 motorcycle. It was a crotch rocket, the kind that is ferociously fast and versatile, but designed so that you have to practically lie on your chest to grip the forward, low-placed handlebars. In shorts and athletic shoes, I sped through traffic, unwittingly giving everyone I passed a nice view of my jacked-up backside, and made it to the shooting range in ten minutes.

Two fire engines were on hand and several men in full gear struggled to keep two high-pressure streams of water pointed at the rustic clubhouse. But the mood appeared light. No lives were in danger and only the shell of the wood-shingle building was on fire. Strangely, though, it only burned in patches. Fifty yards away, something moved beneath a giant fire-retardant tarp, and wisps of caustic black smoke escaped from the edges. I angled my bike through the men to find Dirk holding a shotgun, my father, Bobby, and several grinning firefighters.

"Remember the giant animatronic alligator that spilled all over the road, along with the mannequins?" Dirk said without preamble.

I nodded.

"That's the alligator under the blanket. Spud and Bobby attached the tail back to the body. Brought it here in Bobby's van to shoot holes in it with this." He held up the shotgun. I didn't tell Dirk that it was my .12 gauge Benelli Super Sport, but I did glare at my father long enough to make him flinch. I made a mental note to take away his key to my gun cabinet.

"Oh, for crying out loud," Spud said. "This place is a shooting range. And since Sally the art-magazine lady went so wild over the Chrysler sculpture, we figured we'd shoot up the gator, too."

A fireman laughed out loud and a coworker elbowed him. The thing beneath the blanket continued to move and hiss, but it seemed to be slowing down. The firefighters patiently waited for it to die a slow, mechanical death.

"When they started shooting, something activated the animatronic battery pack. Sparks from their ammo hitting metal must've caught the gator's vinyl skin covering on fire," Dirk continued. "From what I can ascertain from the only witness"—he looked at Bobby—"a section of the tail exploded, spewing pieces of the flaming gator skin into the clubhouse. As you can see, the pieces stuck, and set the building on fire."

"Aw, it's not my fault," Spud whined, mermaid walking cane in the air. "The mini golf course should have disabled all their animals before they sold 'em. We didn't know the stupid alligator could come alive out of the blue, for crying out loud."

Looking at my lieutenant friend, I tried to keep a straight face. "Has Spud done anything illegal? Aside from burning down a building, I mean?" The flames were now extinguished, but blackened spots on the exterior of the clubhouse continued to sputter and smoke.

"I'm not sure if it's illegal to shoot a fake alligator, or not," Dirk deadpanned, and the beginnings of a grin appeared on his mouth. "But surely your daddy was trespassing."

"We weren't trespassing, for crying out loud," Spud said, voice rising to a near-screech. "I'm a member of this gun club!"

"Then you should have known that it was closed today," Dirk countered. "The clubhouse was locked up tight. There aren't any cars here. The big sign on the gate says CLOSED."

"That's why we did it, you fool! Because the range wasn't open today. Nobody would try to stop us."

Our mini circle stared at the blanket as the gator let out a squeaky groan and finally stilled.

"We are gathered here today to mourn the passing of a loved one . . ." a firefighter said and they all laughed.

Dirk pretended to be angry and scolded my father. "First, you cause a traffic jam and several near-accidents. And now you almost burn down a two-thousand-square-foot clubhouse. I think you ought to reconsider the art career."

A silver-haired woman rushed up and threw her arms around my father. "But he's a sculptor at heart, don't you see? You can't blame him for trying to create another masterpiece!" It was Fran Cutter, the woman he'd nearly killed with a mannequin in the road.

"Fran, what are you doing here?" I asked.

She fluffed her hair. "Why, I'm his girlfriend, sweetie. I've come to bail him out, if they take him to jail."

I looked at Spud. "She's your girlfriend?"

The walking cane shrugged. "Was cheaper than fixing her scooter."

THIRTY-TWO

Anchored in the Cape Fear River on the west side of Carolina Beach, I'd cooked dinner for myself and it was divine. The relatively secluded spot offered some privacy and a first-row seat to view all the wildlife and critters that lived along the banks of the river. Following directions on the light-in-the-bag briquettes, I'd fired up a small charcoal grill and cooked a fresh grouper filet, skin side down. Just for kicks, I cut a sweet potato in half and threw it on there, too. Tending to the smoking grill while relaxing on *Incognito*'s aft deck was delightful, and when I tasted the results, it dawned on me that I could actually cook. I'd even squeezed on fresh lemon juice, drizzled some olive oil, and chopped sweet basil leaves. Give me a set of egg molds and steamer bin or put me in front of a charcoal grill and I could rock on with the best of chefs. Unselfconscious in my favorite skimpy bikini and enjoying the solitude, I ate slowly, relaxed and perfectly content.

Body swaying to the lazy tunes of Van Morrison, I was sipping a glass of brandy for dessert, watching the lower sky change colors as an orange sun kissed the water, when a chill surged through my body. Internal alarm bells vibrating, I grabbed my Glock, chambered a round, and turned off the music to listen to my surroundings.

Hearing nothing unusual, I climbed to the flybridge for a 360 view, when movement in the water grabbed my attention. Aiming at something I couldn't see on the portside, I waited, thinking it could be some playful marine life or a pair of rowdy ducks. With an abrupt expulsion of water, two men surfaced, entangled, fighting. One in full scuba gear and the other bare-chested with only a mask and snorkel, they wrangled, treading water, in water too deep to stand up. I could only watch, gun aimed between them, unsure of who they were or what they fought over.

They ripped the masks off each other's faces and when the bare-chested one spit out his snorkel, I realized it was Ox. The other well-muscled figure was John Mason, his face smeared with camouflage grease. I shimmied to the lower deck and took aim, but couldn't lock in on a clean shot. Ox's fist connected squarely with John's nose and blood squirted before John lunged, shoving Ox underwater. In full-out hand-to-hand combat, they worked their way to shore with a series of grunts and splashes. Rolling on the sand, Ox stabbed John in the leg with a knife at the exact same moment that John pulled what looked like a garage door opener out of a zippered dry bag that was secured around his waist. Bloodied teeth showing through a smile, he pushed a button. As it occurred to me that my boat was about to blow up, both men dove back into the water—John heading away from *Incognito* and Ox swimming toward it. Still gripping my gun, I jumped overboard and swam for shore, praying that Ox would get away from the boat in time. I moved inland and took cover behind the thick trunk of an oak tree, squatting, listening for movement, hoping that John would come back onshore and give me the opportunity to kill him. My surroundings remained quiet for what seemed like ten long painstaking minutes—in real time perhaps thirty seconds—until Ox's form surfaced, clutching what looked like a plastic lunch box. As soon as he was in shallow enough water to get a good foothold, using both hands, he heaved the thing out over the open water. With a muffled pop and hiss, it exploded just before it hit the water, and sent a mushroom ball of water high into the air.

I ran to meet Ox at the water's edge. Dripping wet and breathing heavy, he reached out to touch my face. "You okay, Barnes?"

I nodded. "I'm fine. Are you hurt?"

"Don't think so."

Gun still in a ready position, I surveyed the thick brush and trees. We were on an undeveloped section of the river and John could easily circle back through the woods. I almost hoped he would.

"He's gone," Ox said. "Didn't want to stick around for the explosion. Looks like he put a forty-five or fifty second delay on it, to give himself enough time to get away."

Ox had thrown the bomb in the same direction that John went. "You think the explosion got him?"

"No."

"Where was it?" I asked.

"Attached to the prop shaft, below the engine room."

"How did you—" I started to ask how my best friend had known about the bomb, and then I knew. The feeling of being watched ever since I started living on my boat was real. "You've been following me."

Wiping the water from his body with bare hands, he breathed deep to catch his breath. "Of course I've been keeping an eye on you, and everything around you. From my Carolina Skiff. Center console makes it a bitch to sleep in, but you're worth it."

"Ruby said you took time off from the Block." I couldn't keep my eyes off his bare chest and slippery stomach. And thick biceps, still pumped from exertion. "I thought you were spending time with your ex."

"Louise flew home to California."

I searched his eyes for emotion. "Are you okay with that?"

"I'm very okay with that, Barnes." He took my hands, placed them around the back of his neck, and waited for me to pull him close. After a moment, I did.

I could have stayed right there on the sandy strip of beach, in his arms, damp skin pressed against damp skin, for hours. But Ox was thinking more clearly than I and smartly suggested that we get back to the Block. Now that John knew my boat, there was no reason for me to continue living aboard *Incognito.*

With Ox leading the way in a single-engine inshore fishing boat, I stayed in his wake all the way to the Cape Fear Marina, keeping the Glock within easy reach just in case. Shaking out my jumpy muscles, I backed into my regular slip while Ox tied off his boat at the dry-storage loading dock. His truck waited in the parking lot and, after changing into dry clothes and securing *Incognito,* he drove me to the Block.

I tried to thank him for once again saving my life but he interrupted by telling me that I'd saved his life, too. Five years ago, when he showed up in Wilmington, a broken man. I didn't know what to say to that and we rode for several miles, deep in our own thoughts. I wanted to ask what happened with Louise, but decided Ox would tell me when the time was right.

"Your new vehicle was delivered," he said, when we were almost at the Block. "Ruby signed for it."

"Excellent. What did I get?"

He looked at me and grinned. "You don't know?"

"Floyd didn't say. But he promised to send me something in my favorite color—black. After being without a car, I'm happy with anything. As long as it's not that gross station wagon."

"Well, he did keep his word on the color." Ox smoothly avoided a car that pulled out in front of us, and watching his calm, capable, and masculine profile, my thoughts wandered to our encounter in bed. I craved more of the same and wondered if the desire was reciprocal.

"What did I get?"

"Better if it's a surprise," Ox told me, turning in to the Block's parking lot, right next to a black hearse. Undertakers were dining at the Block? Their vehicle could be bad for business. I asked Ox if he knew who the meat wagon belonged to. He smiled.

"Nuh-uh. No way. Tell me that thing is not my new car."

He handed over a set of keys and his smile grew bigger.

"You're screwing with me, right?" I scanned the lot for other, unfamiliar cars. "It's really that Buick Lucerne over there, right?"

Smiling, Ox headed inside the Block, leaving me in the parking lot, staring stupidly at the hearse. The doors unlocked when I pushed the button on the key fob. Just to be sure, I stuck the key in the ignition and turned it. The hearse cranked right up.

"Oh, crap." I sprinted to the nearest phone I could find and dialed Floyd.

"What were you thinking?" I yelled into the handset before he'd finished answering. "This thing is a limo for dead people and you know how I can't stand to be near dead people!"

"Is there anyone back there right now?" he asked.

"I don't know. I didn't look."

"Probably not," Floyd said. "But if you do find a body in there, let me know and I'll give our mechanic a good talking to. He should have caught something like that before the hearse went out."

"This isn't funny, Floyd. I can't drive a meat wagon. You're going to have to take it back and send me something else."

I heard foil crunching and then chewing. Probably the nicotine gum. "It's a late model. Perfect condition. Leather seats, a kick-ass sound system, power everything. *And* it only cost you a grand."

I thought about that, and my declining checking account. "Only one thousand dollars? Why so cheap?"

Floyd explained that the hearse was confiscated from a crematory in New Jersey that was really a money-laundering and drug-running operation, and profits were indirectly ending up in the pockets of a known terrorist. The business wasn't cremating bodies nor did it have the equipment to do so. And the hearse sported numerous modifications. In Floyd's words, it was "tricked out." The saved street locations on the hearse's navigation system, in fact, busted the case wide open and led agents to a commendable takedown.

"Well," I said, trying to envision myself behind the wheel of a hearse, "the whole dead-body thing still creeps me out."

"Best we can tell, the vehicle was purchased new, right off the assembly line. It was probably never in service as a hearse, so it never transported any bodies." I heard Floyd ripping into another piece of gum. "At least none that were on their way to a legitimate funeral, anyway."

That news made me feel a tiny bit better. That, and the one-thousand-dollar price tag. "But if the car is uh, tricked out, and has low mileage, why is it so cheap? And at that price, why didn't somebody snatch it up, then turn around and sell it to a funeral home for a big profit?"

"Vehicle can't go to the general public, not even a funeral home. It's a condition of sale. In addition to the modifications I told you about, the hearse has compartments for weapons and several nifty places to stash drugs. Oh, by the way, you'll need to fill up when the needle reaches the halfway mark or you'll run out of gas. Fuel tank was modified with a holding compartment, as well."

"Still," I said, "for that price, you'd think *somebody* would've snatched it off the auction block."

Floyd did a laugh-snort. "Who the hell wants to drive around town in a hearse?"

THIRTY-THREE

"This is rad!" Lindsey declared, when I picked her up from school in the hearse, which Spud had nicknamed the corpse caddy. Strange what a teenager perceives as cool. She fiddled with the XM radio, jumping from station to station as we drove to Daisy Obstetrics & Gynecology for her doctor's appointment. Music thumped out of five rear speakers that were probably worth more than the thousand dollars I'd paid for the vehicle.

"So what do all your friends think about Derma-Zing," I said, to keep her mind off the fact that she might be pregnant. We'd find out soon enough.

"Derma-Zing is amazing!" she said through a practiced smile. It was the tagline for all the advertisements. "Seriously, I'm having so much fun with it. Everybody at school thinks I'm this huge star, so making friends hasn't been a problem at all. It's like, I'm in demand or something. And designs are so popular now at school, the principal banned them."

For some reason, other drivers always wanted to see who was

behind the wheel of the hearse. A nosy woman in a passing car stared hard at my tinted window, trying to see through it. Ignoring her, I glanced at Lindsey. "Why ban Derma-Zing?"

"You know. Some students will put a cuss word in their design, or a skull and crossbones, or they write their boyfriend's name. The principal said it's distracting, so now, if a teacher spots a design on you, you can get detention."

"Seriously?"

"It's no biggie. The ban actually made more girls want to buy Derma-Zing. We just put the designs where our clothes cover them up. Everybody who's anybody uses it."

I inched the volume down so I wouldn't have to talk so loud. "Is it still available only through the Web site?"

"Nope," she near-shouted, turning the volume back up when Feather Heavy's brand-new song "Blown Away" came on. "Most sales are still over the Internet, but now Derma-Zing is in department stores. There's a starter kit with three colors and a deluxe kit with seven colors. My picture is on the front of the starter kit box. How cool is that?"

"That's pretty neat," I said, wondering if the word "neat" was like, so *out.* "Are you getting paid extra for that?"

She shook her head. "One contract price for the initial marketing blitz. But Spud says that we'll negotiate up for the next contract. He's my agent."

A sculptor and now an agent for a teenage model. Since barreling his way back into my life, my father never ceased to amaze me. I found a double pull-through parking space at the doctor's office and inserted the corpse caddy, drawing more curious looks. A woman pulling out of the lot actually stopped to wait and see who would emerge from the hearse. I made it a point to wave at her. Lindsey made some sort of sign with her hand and I didn't know if it was friendly or insulting. My knowledge of street sign language is limited to the peace sign and the middle finger.

"You're not pregnant, Lindsey," Dr. Pam Warner said, after she examined the girl and we'd been seated in the doctor's office. Pam has been my doctor for years and is a personal friend. "I am concerned about the nausea, though, especially if it continues. We may want to run some tests, maybe take a look at your eggs and fallopian tubes, but for now we'll wait and see how you feel in a week or two."

"What do my eggs have to do with anything?"

"Well, it's pretty interesting, really. A woman's entire supply of ova, or eggs, is formed in the fetal stage of life. So you were born with all of your eggs already stored in your ovaries."

Lindsey leaned forward. "Wow. They didn't teach us that in health class, when we went over the reproductive system."

Dr. Warner nodded. "It's true. Maybe a million eggs or more, each resting in its own little sac. When your hormones kicked in during puberty, the ova began to mature. Then you ovulate—that's when an egg is released and you have a menstrual cycle. An average woman may only use about four hundred of her ova and the rest are absorbed back into the body."

"Yeah, I remember the part about ovulation," Lindsey said. "One egg goes every month. So what's going on with me? I started my period when I was twelve and I've never been late."

"We're not sure, but right now, I'd say it's nothing to worry about. For some reason, you didn't ovulate like you usually do. But it's not that uncommon for a young girl to skip periods, especially athletes and people who are really physically active. Even stress can cause a missed menstrual cycle. Are you having any problems at home or at school, Lindsey?"

The girl shook her head. "I just moved here, but I love Wilmington, and it's excellent to spend time with my dad. I got a modeling job for Derma-Zing and I've made a bunch of friends. Everything's great."

I nodded in agreement. "I'd have to say that Lindsey is a happy, really well-adjusted kid." I asked what we needed to do about Lindsey's symptoms.

"Nothing right now. As long as the nausea stops and she doesn't have any other symptoms, we'll just wait for her cycle to resume. If she goes longer than two or three months, we'll do additional testing to see what's going on."

"I feel pretty good," Lindsey said. "I mean, my stomach is still a little queasy, but it's not as bad as it was."

Pam Warner spent another ten minutes talking to us. Noticing a photograph of two girls on the desk, Lindsey asked the doctor if she wanted a Derma-Zing kit for her daughters. She pulled an unopened kit from her handbag, explaining that she got them for free.

"Lord, yes, I'll take one," Dr. Warner said. "My girls have gone crazy over this stuff. You've just saved me twenty dollars."

Lindsey showed off her television smile. "Eighteen ninety-nine for the deluxe kit, plus tax, of course."

Pam thanked Lindsey and we thanked the doctor. Outside, we climbed into the corpse caddy and, heading to the grocery store, drew more stares.

"You'll get used to it, Jerz," Lindsey said. "Pretend you're a celebrity in a stretch limo. It's fun."

Yeah, right. I'd have rather been driving the Volvo station wagon. And I still wasn't convinced that the casket carrier hadn't toted dead people before the money launderers bought it. Or maybe after. Yuck.

THIRTY-FOUR

Angry that my cell phone had been turned off, Ashton explained that causing his agents to lose track of me had endangered my safety. I'm not sure that a stringy kid with an iPod stuck in his ear would have been able to do anything but watch as *Incognito* blew up with me on board, but in any event, I claimed that the powered-off cell phone was a simple oversight. Ashton still refused to believe the man Ox wrestled with in the water was John, but then I had seen the diver with my own eyes.

Media continued to swarm around the site of the container ship explosion and speculation ran thick, but at the Block, things had returned to normal. At least as normal as they could be with Spud—the resident artist—repeatedly trying to confiscate a commercial blender and Lindsey—the resident celebrity—signing autographs for customers. And, of course, John Mason, who was still on the loose. Security measures at the bar were quietly upped and Ashton assured me that neither John nor any other suspect would be able to get within half a mile of the historic building. I asked what other suspects Ashton was referring to but he had no answer.

It was another beautiful but sticky-hot day, the kind that would draw lunch orders of cold salads, sandwiches, and iced-down drinks. Lindsey and Ox were meeting with Holloman and his advertising agency rep at the Block and I'd been invited to join them, along with Spud, who was decked out in his "agent" gear: fedora hat made of straw with a white feather stuck in the band, unlit cigar, diamond pinky ring, and his fancy redwood walking cane with a giant sperm whale tooth for the handle. That was in addition to the plaid shorts, penny loafers, and black knee-high socks. Geriatric pimp was the occupation that came to mind when I saw the getup, but Lindsey didn't seem to notice her agent's unusual attire.

"Before we get into the new contract negotiation," Holloman said, "I want to thank you, Jersey, for your great idea about marketing Derma-Zing to college coeds. We're in the process of obtaining licensing rights for the top fifty universities with athletic programs and we'll have Derma-Zing kits on the shelves of college bookstores within weeks. Each will have three tubes—the school's colors—and stencils of their mascot and logo."

"I'm surprised your company moved so quickly, but that's great. I hope it sells well for you."

His eyes gleamed. "Oh, I'm certain that it will. And it was all your idea. Simply brilliant."

Lindsey finished applying a smiley face to the back of her hand. "Will I get to model for the colleges, too?"

"Well, that's one thing we addressed in your new contract. We'll add a few new faces to the new Derma-Zing products, but we still want to use you to target the high school girls. And we'd like to do one shoot of you with the college girls, too."

"That's super," she said, adding a few sun flare marks to her design, turning the smiley face into a sunburst.

"No it ain't super, for crying out loud," Spud said, tapping the cane's giant tooth on the tabletop. "Have you read this contract, doodlebug?"

"How could I have read it?" she said. "We just got it and you've had it the whole time."

Holloman drank some black coffee. "What's the problem?"

"Cleavage is the problem, for crying out loud. You're not going to plaster her cleavage all over for the world to see. It says right here that clothing for the shoot will include bikini bathing suits with push-up tops, miniskirts, and tank tops. What's that about? I've seen those Victoria's Secret ads with the push-up things."

The ad agency gal jumped in. "That's standard attire for this type of ad campaign, but let me assure you that there will be no vulgarity or nudity."

"Damn right there won't," Spud said. "She's not going to be prancing around in a bikini."

My mouth twisted with amusement at the irony of Spud acting like a protective grandfather over someone who wasn't even a blood relative. He'd never been protective over me, but then how could he? He wasn't there to make me change an outfit before going out, or scare a boy into bringing me home on time after a movie date.

"Well," the woman explained, "to reach the college market, we have to spruce things up a bit. Take it to the next level. Coeds out having fun, partying, showing off their Derma-Zing designs."

"Like those wild girls you see on late-night TV? They can't keep their tops on."

"No, no, nothing like that," the ad agency woman said. "If it will make you feel better, you can modify the wording on that part of the contract. Limit the girl's skin exposure. No cleavage. No bare navel shots."

Spud gave Lindsey the once-over. "Ain't nobody going to be drooling over doodlebug's body."

"Hello, people?" Lindsey said. "I'm sitting right here. And I think I should make the decision about what to show or not to show. Right, Dad?"

"No swimsuits, no low-cut tops, no short shorts or miniskirts," Ox said. "And no missing school to travel. They either do the photo and video shoots in Wilmington, like before, or we don't do them at all."

Lindsey rolled her eyes and Spud started crossing out lines on the contract.

Holloman's arms shot out to his sides. "We're happy to shoot here again. The town of Wilmington is surprisingly accommodating. And, we're not going to degrade our models, Mr. Oxendine. Trust me. We don't have to. This product sells itself. We're filling so many orders that we can barely keep up with demand. My company manufactures Derma-Zing, but the plant I contract with to package and distribute the product had to hire additional staff."

"If a business grows too fast, won't that cause problems?" Lindsey said. "I took a business class last year, an honors class."

Holloman shook his head. "No, it's perfect! My goal is to expose as many teenagers to Derma-Zing as possible, and sales have already exceeded my expectations. But now, I want to take the advertising to the next level, while the product is hot. We're even looking into Europe and Japan. In trial markets, the Japanese girls have gone nuts over Derma-Zing. They love western fads. Even do their cute little designs using a string of American words that don't make sense."

He continued on his rant for several minutes while his ad agency gal took notes and Spud finished amending Lindsey's contract. Holloman's enthusiasm bordered on maniacal, especially for someone who was president and owner of a large corporation. And to top that off, Cracker didn't much like him and the dog has excellent instincts. I met Ox's eyes over the table and could tell he thought the exact same thing about Holloman. It would be easy enough to sever ties with the man and let him find a new high school spokesperson.

But Lindsey had kept her grades up as promised, and her first paycheck had cleared with no problems. It was excellent money for a sixteen-year-old to earn, and Holloman appeared to be a legitimate businessman. Still, something seemed off.

The six of us met for another hour, going over the revised contract and discussing exactly what Lindsey's responsibilities would be. When everything was settled and Ox had signed the contract, Holloman returned to his normal, more relaxed self and asked if he could buy everyone a drink.

"Not for me," Spud said. "I've gotta get to my studio to finish *Nature's Wrath* so the magazine can get their pictures. That's the name of my new sculpture. And speaking of the arts magazine, the lady wants to interview you, Lindsey. I told her about you and Derma-Zing, and how it's really nothing but artwork, with kids using their bodies as the canvas. So the magazine wants to do a story on it."

"Exactly!" Holloman said, revving up again, his eyes looking a bit crazed. "Derma-Zing isn't just a product, it's a *movement.* An artistic statement. Great work, Spud. I'll let my secretary know to expect a call from the magazine. Perfect. Perfect."

I wondered if perhaps Holloman was bipolar. His demeanor had flip-flopped between polished professional and hopped-up Derma-Zing fanatic.

Lindsey kissed Spud on the cheek. "Thanks, Spud. That'll be fun. And, no thanks on the beverage, Doc. I'm meeting some friends."

"Glad that you're feeling better, Lindsey," Holloman said. "Those stomach bugs can be pesky."

With a wave, Lindsey disappeared. Ox and I declined Holloman's offer for a drink, too, and once the man and his ad person were out of the bar, we treated ourselves. We both wanted a beer; we just didn't want to drink it with him.

"What is up with that guy?" I said, enjoying the welcoming chill as a swallow of Amstel Light flowed down my gullet.

Ox shook his head. "Something bothers me about this whole Derma thing, but I can't quite figure it out. I don't know if it's because Lindsey suddenly seems so grown up, and it makes me realize I've missed a lot of her life since the divorce. Or, if it's because Holloman is a nut bag."

"Maybe both?"

"Maybe. But Lindsey is having so much fun with the modeling, I hate to take it away from her. The spirits brought her to live with me, and I don't want to do something that will chase her back to California."

"I see your point, but I think every young woman needs—and wants—a strong, caring parent in her life. I know I did."

Ox looked at me, his thoughts unreadable.

"Lindsey might get mad if she doesn't get her way," I said. "But ultimately, she's going to appreciate that you care enough to be involved and watch out for her."

He thought about that. "For now anyway, I'll let her do the modeling, as long as her grades don't drop." We clinked Amstel bottles to Lindsey's newfound fame and her next paycheck, which would fatten her college savings account even further, but as we drank, my thoughts were disquieted.

I'd done a quick background and credit check on Holloman's company, but decided to look further, just for my own peace of mind.

THIRTY-FIVE

As Ashton and I walked through Airlie Gardens, sixty-plus acres of walking trails and landscaped, blooming grounds on the east side of Wilmington, I couldn't remember ever being so infuriated. He led me to a small, ornate gazebo and we sat on the bench inside. A marker told me the structure was actually a chapel. I didn't feel closer to God, but it did offer some shade. My body was damp with perspiration and if I was hot, I knew Ashton had to be suffering in his slacks and long sleeves. But the gardens were guaranteed privacy. I poured some bottled water onto a paper towel, wiped the sweat from my face, and waited for my handler to tell me why he'd knowingly endangered my life.

"John Mason was an agent for us back in the late 1990s. We recruited him from the law enforcement pool and, after he completed training, we put him to work in North Carolina for SBI, undercover, to root out what we thought was a cover-up of incoming weapons on charter fishing boats. SBI came up clean and I transferred

John to MOTSU in December of 2001, in a cooperative effort with Homeland Security after nine-eleven."

I drank my remaining water and watched a hand-holding couple walk by. "He left SBI for MOTSU when his twin brother died."

"Affirmative. But the timing was coincidental."

I waited.

Ashton pulled a handkerchief from a pants pocket and wiped his face. "Almost immediately he wanted something better, more exciting, more dangerous. I chose to keep him in place at Sunny Point, but the more time that went by, the more persistent he became in putting in for transfers. Eventually, I let him go, after we realized he wasn't agency material. But he'd been doing a fine job as far as MOTSU was concerned when he went to work for AJAT Security. Has been working at Sunny Point since. Well, until he resigned, that is."

"How was he recruited?" I asked.

"That's not relevant," Ashton said, making me think that it could be very relevant. I'd have to enlist Soup's help to get all the details, since my handler wouldn't divulge them. Soup had broken into the SWEET system before, back when I was an active agent. I knew he could do it again.

"Have you been keeping tabs on him?"

"Of course, but nothing to the level that we would for an agent of your caliber," Ashton answered. "John always got his reports in on time, he did exactly what we asked him to do, and we never had any problems with him."

A black and purple butterfly landed on my knee, fluttered its wings briefly, and flew off. "Then why didn't you grant his request to transfer to fieldwork, or whatever it is that he wanted?"

"A good agent is eager for action, Jersey." Ashton wiped the area on his forehead where the hair had begun to recede. "But a great agent tempers that desire with caution. Maybe it was due to the death of his brother, but John asked for the most dangerous stuff we could throw at him. Actually told another operative that he didn't care if he lived or died." He studied my eyes. "That's the type of man who will not only get himself killed, but endanger others as well. I couldn't chance it."

"But you let him stay at the ammo dump?"

Ashton's forehead moved up briefly. "Private citizen, just like you. And there was no reason not to. As I said, he'd done a fine job."

The saving grace breeze died down to nothing and we got up to walk back toward his car.

"Dammit, Ash, you should have told me about John Mason before you put me on the roach coach. At the least, I think I deserved to know he is a former agent once you knew I'd had contact with him." No wonder his background checks came out clean. It was the background that SWEET invented for the man, up until the point that he'd gone to work for AJAT Security.

"There was no reason to suspect him. We've had another agent working at MOTSU, undercover, for the entire time. Still there, in fact. Says that John was well adjusted, showed up for work on time, and did his job."

Yeah, right. Well adjusted enough to want to kill people with explosives.

"Tell me about the incident on your boat, full details," Ashton said.

I told him everything, right down to what I'd eaten for dinner, and how Ox had been keeping an eye on me without my knowledge.

"Oxendine is good," Ashton mused. "We didn't know he was watching you, either."

"Good thing he was." Ox's people originally survived by melding into an environment of swampland and riverbanks, and it seemed as though he had inherited those skills. We reached the car and I climbed in, automatically aiming the air-conditioning jets at my face.

We sat in the car, air blasting. "You're positive of the ID?" Ashton said.

I didn't bother to respond.

"Did you see the hand?"

I sighed. "He wore gloves. The kind divers wear so they don't get cut up by coral and such."

"And you said his face was smeared with greasepaint?" Ashton persisted.

"Yes."

"But you're still sure the man in the water was John Mason."

"Yes, Ashton, I'm positive," I said flatly. "By the way, where is John now?"

"We've been unable to pick him up," Ashton said. "His house has been listed for sale and as you know, he turned in a resignation letter to AJAT. But he isn't living at the forwarding address he left."

"And you're still in doubt as to who is after me?"

He shifted into gear and pulled out. "Don't make this personal, Jersey."

"It's very personal to me, Ashton. It's my life you seem to be taking so lightly." There had to be a good reason why he refused to accept the fact that John Mason was a SWEET agent turned bad. I needed to find out what it was.

THIRTY-SIX

When Chuck walked into the lab, Peggy Lee dropped the sandwich she held and ran to meet him. She was even more ecstatic than usual to see her boyfriend—she had wonderful news. Peggy Lee was quite sure that she'd never before experienced a miracle, but knew that her current situation qualified.

"I'm so happy to see you," she said, snuggling into his arms. "I've got something great to tell you."

He laughed and let her kiss him. "You've met your weekly quotas?"

"Of course," she told him. "Don't I always? But it's something else."

He went to the refrigerator, where she kept cold drinks for him, and took out a can of seltzer water. "So what's made you so happy? You're almost glowing."

Peggy Lee had thought about this moment and gone over and over it in her head. She'd rehearsed the words she'd use, how she would say it, and visualized how his eyes would light up with delight when he heard. But now, in the pressure of the moment, she forgot her monologue and went with the short version.

"I'm pregnant," she said, almost jumping up and down.

Chuck stopped in mid drink and, frowning, set his can down on a table, next to a row of glass vials. It was not the reaction she anticipated, and her enthusiasm level dissolved into confusion.

"How did this happen?" he asked.

"I don't know," she said, wringing her hands. "Obviously it happened because we had sex. But I don't know how I got pregnant. I've been sterile my whole life."

Sitting on an oversized rolling desk chair, Chuck wondered whether the woman had tricked him into believing that she'd been born with defective eggs. Had she planned to get pregnant all along, hoping for child support, or better yet, a quick marriage proposal? Studying her hurt face for a full half a minute, he determined that she couldn't have lied to him. She didn't have a shrewd bone in her body. Brainy and book smart, sure. But way too naïve to have deceived him.

Chuck finished his seltzer water and motioned her to sit on his lap. "Come here, Peggy Lee."

She did, and tried not to cry.

"You surprised me, is all. You being pregnant is the last thing I'd ever have expected, especially after you told me you can't have children," he soothed. "Had I known there was even a chance, you'd have gone on the pill."

"But, don't you see? This is . . . well, it's a miracle. The fact that a baby is actually growing inside me, right now. The doctors said I'd never be able to conceive."

Last week, when she woke up to throw up for the second morning in a row, she'd gone to a walk-in clinic, thinking she had a virus. And when that doctor told her she was pregnant, she immediately made an appointment with Daisy Obstetrics & Gynecology to confirm the diagnosis. The doctor who examined her quickly agreed that she was indeed with child, and after reviewing Peggy Lee's medical history, was as astounded as she'd been. A fertility specialist, he ordered some special tests and he planned to personally oversee every stage of the pregnancy, he'd told her. Once the baby was born, he was going to submit an article to the American Medical Association's journal.

Chuck took Peggy's face in his hand and gently angled it so she had to look at him. "I'm happy that you're able to get pregnant, Peggy, if that's what it takes to make you feel more secure about being a woman. But a baby simply doesn't fit into my plans right now. Or your plans. *Our* plans."

Struggling to keep in the tears, she could only nod.

"We'll make an appointment for you to get it taken care of, first thing next week. All right?"

Getting off his lap, she flashed back to just days ago, when she'd watched from the beach on Bald Head Island as the young couple exchanged their vows with plans to spend a lifetime together. It was the same day the specialist confirmed her pregnancy, and witnessing the wedding ceremony, she'd felt her cheeks grow wet with tears of joy. She wondered if the bride, Janie, hoped to have a child with her new husband. And when the explosion happened just minutes later, knocking her to the sand, she'd instinctively put her arms around a still-flat belly to protect her baby. She didn't want to abort it. She didn't want to lose Chuck, either. Miserable, she stared into space, wondering why nothing could ever go right in her life.

"All right?" he repeated, louder.

Peggy Lee nodded.

He stood. "Good, then, let's get to work. I've got a lot of information for you, and believe it or not, we have to up production again. We're almost there, Peggy. The initial phase of Project Antisis is almost there."

The chemist barely listened as her boss told her to alter the formula, tripling the amount of active ingredient. She should have protested, citing the negative side effects it would cause. She should have told him that a reformulation at this point might compromise the project. But lost deep inside herself, she didn't bother.

THIRTY-SEVEN

"Spud, you can't keep depositing your trash at the Block," I told my father. He'd paid a towing company with a flatbed to haul his burnt alligator sculpture to my bar and deposit it outside, next to the impaled Chrysler. "I'm sure we're violating a city ordinance of one sort or another."

"You can't violate any rules with art, for crying out loud," he said and his walking cane punched the ground with each syllable. "Besides, a photographer is coming to get photos of my new sculpture for the cover story. And Sally the magazine lady is coming again to interview Lindsey about Derma-Zing."

I asked Spud what he planned to do with the gator afterward and he said something about selling it to the highest bidder. Ever the optimist.

"Hey, glad to find you both here," Dirk said, walking up. "I'm pleased to announce that the department is not going to press any charges against you, Spud, for the gun club fire. Nobody could find anything on the books to address the incident, other than disorderly conduct, and I talked the chief out of that one."

"Thanks, Dirk," I said since my father didn't.

"You're welcome."

We sat at the end of the bar. Ox served me and Spud a draught, gave Dirk an ice water, and delivered a basket of grouper bites with hush puppies. Dirk loaded the fish with Tabasco and dug in. "Owner of the shooting range is fine with that, as long as you pay to repair the clubhouse. Damages come to"—he pulled a sheet of paper from his breast pocket—"twelve thousand, four hundred dollars."

Spud's mouth worked for a minute before any sound came out. "What? Are they insane? Twelve thousand dollars?"

"Twelve thousand and four hundred," Dirk repeated, enjoying the moment. "The building had wood shingle siding. If the firefighters hadn't arrived so quickly, you'd have burned it to the ground."

Spud's mouth worked some more.

I tried not to laugh. "Spud, how much was the repair bill for Fran's Vespa scooter?"

"Almost six hundred dollars, for crying out loud. The Vespa dealer said the whole front fender and tire had to be replaced. And he claimed that my mannequin's arm scratched the little windshield, too."

"Well," I said, "you got out of that one by dating Fran, so she'd pay the bill."

"Woman's loaded," Spud reasoned. "She can afford it."

"My point is, maybe you should go talk to the owner of the range. It's a woman, right? Ask her out. Maybe your dating charms will work a second time."

Ox smiled at me from behind the bar. Dirk ate his fish. Spud's face grew red. Sally, the magazine lady, walked in and spotted my father. Rushing over, she greeted him warmly and asked if his sunburn hurt.

"He's not sunburned," Dirk said. "He's just red from the heat.

Spud has been outside putting the finishing touches on . . . what's your new sculpture called?"

"Nature's Wrath," Spud muttered.

"It's striking, Spud," Sally said. "I don't love it as much as the other one, *Road Rage,* but it certainly does make a statement."

Spud's color, starting as his forehead, inched its way back to normal. "Thanks."

The local contracted photographer arrived shortly after Sally and the three of them went outside to gaze at the alligator. I caught a glimpse of Spud posing between the two heaps of scrap when Ruby called my name. Somebody was looking for Spud, she said, and the visitor had come through the side door so he hadn't seen see the trio.

"I'm his daughter," I told the man. "Can I help you?"

Dressed in casual business attire, he looked to be in his fifties, and like everyone else entering the Block, his clothes stuck to his body. Overhead, all the fans spun at full blast.

"I'm here from the insurance agency to look at Mr. Barnes' Chrysler LHS." He handed over a business card that declared him to be a senior insurance adjuster. "It's my understanding that the other adjustor wasn't quite sure what to make of the vehicle, so the case was assigned to me. Once I see the vehicle, we can get your father paid."

Smiling, I led the man outside.

Dirk followed me. "Oh, this is going to be good."

"Got to see this," Ox agreed. Ruby came, too, along with a few regulars who'd been keeping up with Spud's blooming art career.

The insurance adjuster introduced himself to Spud and did a double take at the mannequin-eating blackened alligator before turning his attention to the car. He felt some of the bullet holes and slowly walked around the crushed heap, touching the giant forked prongs that had impaled the Chrysler's belly. An astounded expression overcame his features. "Amazing," he said to himself. "I never would have believed this if I didn't see it with my own eyes."

"It *is* utterly amazing, isn't it?" Sally said to the man. "I think the piece is really incredible. It belongs in a gallery, that's for sure."

Eyes jumping back and forth from Sally to the insurance adjuster, Spud's mouth started working again, but the sounds that came out weren't forming words.

"Excuse me?" the adjuster said. "What are you talking about Miss—?"

She stuck out her hand. "Sally Stillwell, *Eclectic Arts & Leisure* magazine."

He shook it. "Al Hughes from Action Auto Insurance Company."

"You're an art enthusiast?" Sally said.

"No," he said. "But if I was, I certainly wouldn't want to see a totaled passenger vehicle sitting in a gallery."

Flustered, Spud stepped between the two of them. "Er, uh, Sally, if you'll just go inside, we can finish talking where it's cooler. Lindsey should be here soon, for the Zerma-Ding interview. I mean Derma-Zingerview. Oh, for crying out loud. Just go inside and wait, would you?"

"Of course, Spud. But first I want to finish my conversation with this rude man." She turned to the adjuster. "You don't have to be so insulting, just because you don't like the sculpture."

Al Hughes snorted out a laugh and pointed at Spud's car. "You call that thing a *sculpture*?"

Sally took a step toward the man. "For your information, *Road Rage* could easily bring in twelve or fifteen thousand dollars, maybe more, from a serious collector. I can already envision it sitting outside a museum of modern art. Once my article prints and word gets out about the group of law enforcement officers who created it under Spud's direction, there's no telling who might buy it!"

The adjuster cocked his head at the mention of a dollar amount. "You mean to tell me that this . . . this . . . impaled, shot-up, twisted wreck of a Chrysler could be sold to somebody as *art* for fifteen thousand dollars?"

"Of course! Why are you so shocked?"

Al Hughes jotted something down inside a folder. "Because I am an insurance adjuster. I'm here to inspect the vehicle so my company can pay Mr. Barnes's claim. As I understand it, his car was run over by a garbage truck while parked outside this bar, and then it was used for cover during a violent shootout. Now that I've seen it, we'll haul the heap to a salvage yard and pay the estimated market value. Forty-three hundred dollars and some change."

Sally told the photographer to stop taking pictures. "I was under the impression that the sculpture was Spud's vision, created from scratch."

Sally and Al studied each other for a split second. In unison, they turned to look at Spud.

"Oh, for crying out loud! It's the car from hell!" my father said and stomped into the Block without explaining himself.

Ox convinced everyone to sit around the same table and, once drinks and hush puppies were served, Sally and Al were laughing it up like old friends. Decked out in some of her new clothes, Lindsey joined the group and patiently waited for the magazine writer to stop flirting long enough to conduct the promised interview.

Food and drinks tend to flow much more freely when those doing the eating and drinking know it's free, and even Dirk decided that he was off duty for the rest of the day so he could partake in a bourbon and Coke. The photographer stuck around, too, and called his girlfriend to join him. When Spud's fan club—Bobby, Hal, Trip, and Fran—showed up, we moved an empty table to connect with the two already pushed together. Cracker happily sauntered from human to human, collecting bites of hush puppy and shelled peanuts. After the third round of drinks and much prompting from Sally, Spud finally spilled the real story about his car. Dirk and Bobby filled in the details.

"Well Spud, I feel as though I've been duped," Sally said, brushing a peanut shell from Al's pants leg. "You've deceived me and my magazine."

"You're the one who saw the stupid car and said it was a sculpture, for crying out loud. You're the art expert."

She sipped on her chardonnay. "True, but you didn't correct my assumption. And now, I've got an upcoming magazine with no cover story and we're on deadline."

Spud coughed up the piece of food he was in the process of swallowing. "You're bumping me off the cover?"

She nodded, sipped. "I can't, in good conscience, put an artist on the cover who is a fraud."

"He's not a fraud, sweetie," Fran said. "He has a studio and everything."

"A studio that, by his own admission, he just rented two weeks ago."

The conversation went back and forth like this for another ten minutes. Ignoring the two women, everyone else ate and drank and made it a point to be merry. Except for Spud, who'd removed a paper menu from its plastic slip and busied himself scribbling numbers on the back side of it. Sally declared again that she would not have Spud on the cover of her publication and that her decision was final. Grinning, Lindsey pulled out a Magic Marker–sized tube of Derma-Zing and began applying a grapevine to her forearm. As Sally watched, Lindsey used a different color to draw tiny daisies where the grapes should be. Smartly, the teen remained silent and waited for Sally to come up with the idea.

"Derma-Zing will be the cover!" Sally said, touching Al on the knee. She instructed the photographer that his assignment had changed and told him to get the girl. Within minutes, two portable lights with umbrella-looking canopies were erected on tripods and he began snapping shots of Lindsey and her arm from different angles.

Spud finished scribbling on the paper and slunk in his chair. "Seventeen thousand dollars! That stupid car is going to cost me almost seventeen thousand bucks."

The rest of us were wise enough not to ask, but Bobby had to know the details. Arms flying overhead, Spud rattled off a list of expenditures: supplies for the new sculpture including the possessed alligator, his studio rental, business cards, repairs to the shooting range clubhouse, and the cost of taking Fran out to dinner, twice.

"If it will make you feel any better, Mr. Barnes, you'll be receiving a settlement check shortly." Al produced a calculator and calculated. "Forty-three hundred and thirty-two dollars."

"That won't even buy me a decent new car," Spud muttered.

"You don't really need a new car," Lindsey theorized, "since you can't see to drive and they took away your license. Right?" Nobody else at the table could have gotten away with voicing it.

"They took away your driver's license?" Fran said, rubbing Spud's back. "Poor thing. They wanted to take mine, too, but one of the ladies in my bridge club forged a report from the eye doctor so I could get it renewed."

"I didn't hear that," Dirk said, and drank.

"I'm the proud holder of a valid driver's license," Fran continued, "and I'll give you a ride anytime."

Spud's spine straightened and he turned on his girlfriend. "That's why you mowed down my mannequin and got her hand stuck in your wheel! Because you didn't see her! And you gave me a repair bill for nearly a thousand damn dollars."

"But you didn't have to pay it, remember?" Fran smiled and the skin around her sparkling eyes crinkled. "You took me out to dinner, instead."

Al Hughes thanked Ox for the hospitality and stood. "This has been a most interesting afternoon, folks, but I've got to get going. About your uh, car-sculpture, Mr. Barnes, a tow truck will be here tomorrow to haul it to the salvage yard. But if you'd like, you're welcome to buy it back from the insurance company for six hundred and seventy-five dollars. That's the salvage value. If you want to do so, I need to know now, before it's hauled off."

Fran raised her hand, as though at an auction. "I'll take it, for seven hundred dollars even."

Al's shoulders went up. "What the heck. Sold, for seven hundred dollars."

Excited, Fran kissed Spud, telling him that he'd just sold his very first sculpture. A real sculpture!

Just to make a point, Sally argued that a sale didn't qualify something as art.

Al closed his notebook. "The car is Miss Cutter's now, Sally. She can call it the *Mobile Mona Lisa* for all I care."

Not offended, Sally laughed. After exchanging phone numbers with her, the insurance adjuster left. Lindsey got her interview. And, with Fran fawning over him, Spud got drunk.

THIRTY-EIGHT

I recognized the number on the caller ID and wondered what Lady Lizzy wanted with me. "Hello?"

"Dahling!" she drawled, sounding like her normal exclamatory self. "I was wondering if your agency could accept some bodyguard work on short notice."

Surely she knew that I didn't really offer personal bodyguard services. Heck, if anyone needed a bodyguard right now, *I* did. "I don't think so, Lady Lizzy, but I can recommend someone. How short of a notice are we talking?"

"For an event tonight!"

I doubted I could get anyone that quickly, I told her, but Lizzy plowed on. She'd received a nasty letter, she explained, in which the writer threatened to cut her—as in, literally slice her with a knife—at tonight's "Slasher Soiree." A private party and advance viewing of a new horror movie, the event would draw a few hundred people.

"I get threats and crazy e-mails all the time!" the gossip columnist said. "But this one seems serious. He demanded a retraction of something I insinuated about his girlfriend, and when I didn't do it, I got this letter about the party tonight. And I can't *not* go!"

"You obviously know the identity of this person. Have you contacted the police?"

"I certainly have! They sent an officer to talk to the man and he claimed he didn't know anything about it. But I'm scared. This creep has me shaking so badly, I can't put on my own mascara."

In her world that amounted to a crisis. I could ask JJ or Rita to babysit Lizzy, but that would be the equivalent of asking them to detail my car, an especially punishing task since I now drive a hearse. Ox and I had already planned to spend the evening together, away from the Block, to talk. On the other hand, I did owe Lady Lizzy a favor, sort of. I had to strong-arm the information out of her, but it did lead to saving many lives. It wouldn't be too horrible for me to babysit Lizzy for a few hours, if I could talk Ox into going. We'd get to preview a horror flick, have a drink, and then we could go somewhere quiet to talk.

"Tell you what, Lizzy. As a *personal favor* to you, I will go to the party and bring a friend. We'll keep an eye on things." If anyone knew the rules of the favor game, she did. Business favors were tokens to be accumulated and redeemed. And I might need her help again someday.

"Fabulous! I'll put you and a plus one on the guest list." She gave me the address and asked if I could be there at six for the cocktail hour.

A small crowd had already gathered at St. Thomas Preservation Hall on Dock Street when Ox and I arrived. Film-screening parties are always an eclectic mix, from gaffers wearing fashionably ripped blue jeans to gem-studded celebs. I used the occasion as an excuse to deck out in a provocatively low-cut dress with just enough flare in the skirt to conceal a thigh holster. My spiked heels weren't ideal bodyguard attire, but they looked damn good. Ox wore a pair of slacks with a white silk tee and lightweight summer blazer that nicely covered his Kimber .45 automatic. I'm sure there was a knife somewhere on his body, too. Seeing him, people stared a bit longer than was polite, probably thinking he was somebody important that they should recognize.

I sipped my virgin drink—a juice concoction served in a martini glass and called a "slashertini"—while we studied the photograph of the alleged stalker. I'd also gotten a copy of the official complaint. A recent gossip column apparently included a photograph of the guy's girlfriend kissing somebody else. According to Lizzy, the column wasn't even about them. They were nobodies. The girlfriend just happened to be in the background when Lizzy's photographer snapped a shot of a movie producer.

"Something tells me this guy is for real," Ox said, scanning the crowd. "And a bit unglued."

"So you think we'll see some action tonight?" I teased, tossing out the double entendre.

"I feel certain of it."

For the next half hour, we mingled and studied the partygoers, never straying too far from Lady Lizzy. Keeping an eye on our surroundings rather than each other, we spoke in low voices about possible additions to the Block's menu, Spud's new girlfriend, and Lindsey's new school friends. We'd just touched on Louise's abrupt departure—a topic I'd been waiting to hear about—when Ox nodded in the direction of a lone man, weaving through the people, trying to blend in. On a direct path to intercept Lady Lizzy, he moved with purpose and, as he got closer, we made a positive ID. I headed for Lizzy while Ox went to stop the guy.

"He's here," I whispered in her ear. "Just act natural. We've got it under control."

"Dahling!" she exclaimed and gave me the double air-kiss. "So wonderful you could be here!"

"You don't have to go overboard," I said under my breath.

Twelve or fifteen feet away, the guy yanked his arm out of Ox's grip and continued toward Lizzy. When Ox stopped him for the second time, a switchblade popped open in each hand.

Lady Lizzy sucked in air with a sharp, "Oh!"

Seeing the activity, nearby people backed away to leave a wide berth, but nobody got overly alarmed. These were, after all, movie people.

"Sheesh," I said. "I didn't think anybody even carried switchblades anymore. What a putz."

Ox disarmed the guy before he had a chance to swing the knives, and put him in an arm lock before the switchblades clattered to the floor. Anyone not watching very closely missed it. I found a disposable zip strip hand restraint in my handbag. Ox secured the guy's wrists behind his back.

"Dude," I said to the panting man. "Your girlfriend has obviously moved on. Get over it already."

He spit in my face.

"Shouldn't have done that," Ox said.

I threw a fist into the stalker's solar plexus and, as he bent over, followed it up with a knee to his groin. He slowly buckled with a groan.

Ox wiped the spittle off my chin with a damp napkin and handed me a fresh slashertini, one made with real alcohol. "Guess we're done here," he said. "You want to hang around for the movie?"

Telling him no, I dialed Dirk's mobile. "Few days ago, Lady Lizzy filed a complaint against somebody who threatened her," I said into the phone.

"I haven't read it, but whatcha got?"

"He just tried to stab her with switchblades."

"Switchblades? Nobody carries a switchblade anymore."

"That's what I said. Anyway, Ox took the knives away from the bad boy. Can you send a cruiser by to pick him up? No blue lights, please. We're at a film-screening party."

"Sure thing," Dirk said and asked for the address.

Ox subjected himself to the double air-kiss from Lady Lizzy—only with him, she actually planted her lips firmly on his cheeks—and we made our escape in Ox's truck. I motioned for our tail to follow and then, just for fun, powered off my government-issue phone so that Ox could lose the guy. We were rid of the coverage within two minutes. Had Ox been driving my old Mercedes, it wouldn't have taken that long.

The muggy day grew pleasant as the clock rolled into dusk and we crossed the bridge to Wrightsville Beach. Sand massaging our bare feet, we walked for a mile, taking in the ocean smells and sounds, waving at other beachgoers. We stopped at a vacant beach rental and sat on their wooden walkover steps, facing the ocean. Ox ran his fingertips lightly along the inside of my arm, caressing, deep in his own thoughts. After a time, I took his hand between mine and put it to my mouth, kissing each of his fingers, one by one. A low sound escaped his mouth.

"I can't stop thinking about our night together," I said.

He pulled me to him and crushed his mouth against mine, just for an instant, before backing off to a more leisurely, seductive kiss. "Me, either."

My body didn't want to interrupt the moment, but my mind had to know. "You were about to tell me before when Lady Lizzy's stalker showed up. What happened with Louise?"

He stared at the breaking waves, water and sky melding together as the sun set. "Nothing that should interfere with us," he said. "But you have to know, don't you?"

I nodded. I couldn't give myself to him until I knew for certain that he was 100 percent available. Settling for anything less was not an option. Not with him.

"For a time after Lindsey was born, Louise was the perfect woman. We were the perfect couple, very much in love, selfless, devoted to our little family," he said. "The higher up I moved in the military ranks, the more time and focus my career required. But I was there as Lindsey grew up. I stayed faithful to my wife. I provided for my family. I thought everything was the way it should be, but somewhere along the way, Louise became unhappy. Maybe she felt stifled, or maybe she got tired of the military life and all of its restrictions. I don't know. I honestly thought everything was good with us."

Staring at the ocean, he continued. "When she handed me divorce papers the day I took early retirement, it blew me away. I never had any idea how miserable she was. And when I realized that she waited until I retired so she'd get half my pension, it floored me. How many nights had she shared my bed, wishing she were elsewhere? Why couldn't she have told me something was wrong, so we could fix it?"

"I remember," I said. "You were devastated when you first came to Wilmington. Wandering, trying to decide where to go and what to do."

He smiled. "And you kept me in Wilmington. Gave me the opportunity to sort it all out and get on with my life."

"Where do the two of you stand now? What happened while she was here?"

Looking at his eyes, barely illuminated by a pole light, I could read his mind: *Don't ask if you don't want the answer.* Ox would never lie to me. And I should be a big enough person not to ask—or not to let the answer bother me.

He sighed, rubbed a hand over his face. "We just talked for the first few days she was here, catching up on each other's lives, being cordial. Then one night she made Lindsey's favorite dinner and we went down memory lane with our daughter, sitting around the table, laughing like we used to. After dinner, Lindsey went to the movies with my next-door neighbors and Louise opened a bottle of wine. Told me she wondered what it would be like if we were still together. Asked if she'd made a mistake by divorcing me."

I knew what was coming next and my shoulders tightened. I shouldn't have asked. I wanted to stop him from talking—to tell him it didn't matter—but I just sat there, focusing on the sound of the ocean and thinking about the forces of the universe that seemingly guided our lives.

"We slept together, Jersey. But it clarified everything. It was mechanical. We went though the motions without a real connection. I didn't feel anything. All the anger and resentment was gone. All the old passion and love was gone, too. Louise realized that I've gotten on with my life. And I realized that the woman I married no longer exists." He took my hand, searching my eyes for acceptance. "My past with her is a closed chapter, and I'm good with that. Except for Lindsey, whom I thank God for every day, there is absolutely nothing left of my relationship with Louise."

"Is she going to marry the live-in?"

"That's for her to figure out."

We stood to walk back to the truck and Ox moved to kiss me again. I resisted, my head a jumble of conflicting thoughts: relief, excitement, betrayal.

"If you didn't mean so much to me," I said, "and if our night together wasn't so intense, it wouldn't matter."

Midway back, he took my hand. It felt right and good and I wanted to throw myself at him and tell him none of it mattered, after all. But stubbornly, or perhaps stupidly, I couldn't wrap my brain around the fact that he would allow himself to sleep with his ex—unless he thought there might be a chance of reconciliation.

And if that were true, his night with me hadn't been as special as I'd thought.

"Please don't over-think this, Jersey," he said, when we'd reached the parking area and he opened the door for me. "My heart has belonged to you for a very long time."

THIRTY-NINE

A woman in a smock smiled at Peggy Lee when she walked into the clinic, as though the appointment were for something pleasant, such as a massage. Unable to smile back despite the Valium she'd swallowed earlier, Peggy signed in and sat down to wait. She buried her face in a gossip magazine but curiosity made her sneak peeks at the others in the waiting room: a mother with a young teenager, another woman about Peggy Lee's age who was well into her pregnancy, and a fidgety man. She'd barely skimmed the fashion section when she heard her name.

Ready to get the abortion over with, she followed the nurse through a door and was surprised to find herself in a small consultation room rather than an examination room.

"Hi, Peggy. I'm here to counsel you and answer any questions you have, before we take you in to see the doctor, okay? Basically, we just want to make sure that you've considered all of the options available to you, and that you're sure this is the right decision."

Peggy Lee started to cry.

"This type of visit can be upsetting for some women," the nurse said. "Why don't you tell me exactly what you're feeling, so we can talk about it?"

Without a word, Peggy Lee grabbed her purse and ran from the room to the first exit door she found. It took a few minutes to locate her car and once she did, she sat in the driver's seat and stared at the building until her tears dried. Suddenly angry at Chuck, she slammed the car into gear and drove to the nearest shopping mall, where she wandered through a department store until she came across the baby section. Why wasn't he excited about their baby? Peggy Lee wondered, fingering the miniature booties and caps. Why couldn't he see the miracle for what it was?

A saleswoman approached. "Are you looking for a gift today?"

"I'm pregnant," Peggy Lee announced and the lead ball in her stomach dissipated. Her miracle baby wasn't something to be ashamed of or fret about! The life should be celebrated, regardless of Chuck's initial reaction. He'd eventually come around. Until he did, she'd just let him think that she had an abortion.

"Oh, how wonderful," the clerk said and asked Peggy Lee what she needed.

"Everything."

Peggy Lee selected a bassinet, crib, bedding, and stroller. Sifting through cushy soft blankets and tiny sleep sets, the chemist realized that she had indeed experienced a miracle. Her eggs that refused to mature were now suddenly doing their thing. The fertility specialist from Daisy Obstetrics & Gynecology had called her in person to relay the test results, and asked if she'd been taking any new trial drugs. Peggy Lee assured the doctor that she hadn't, and he reaffirmed his opinion that the reversal of her lifelong condition was a miracle. She loved the word *miracle* and repeated it in her head, trying to decide on a boy's and a girl's name that started with the letter *M*.

Daydreaming of the time when she'd hold her baby as it sucked in its first breaths of air, Peggy Lee selected a fancy polka-dot diaper bag, bottles, wipes, clothes, and a spinning mobile made of stuffed animals to hang over the crib. Her bill came to more than seven thousand dollars, but Peggy Lee's credit was perfect. She opened a charge account with the department store and saved 10 percent on the total.

"If you're going to have a baby shower, you can register here before you go," the clerk said. "You choose what you want in advance and that way, your friends can shop for your gift without worrying it's something you already have."

Peggy Lee knew there'd be no baby shower and she certainly didn't have any friends. Nonetheless, she completed the registration form, telling the saleswoman to choose the registry items for her. She signed the charge slip and learned that her entire order would be delivered to her apartment later in the week, but she walked out of store with one shopping bag. She planned to look at the whimsical mobile every morning, so the delicate wonder that grew inside her could see the fuzzy animals through her eyes.

FORTY

Lindsey continued to work two or three days a week at the Block. She loved talking to the Block's regulars, eating the fresh catch of the day for dinner, and playing poker with Spud afterward. But today, Ox told me that Lindsey didn't feel well when he picked her up from school, even though she insisted on working her regular three-hour shift. He had a right to be concerned. Lindsey looked horrible.

"I'm fine, really," she fibbed, when I asked her what was going on. "It's just the stomach thing again. I'm fine to work my shift."

I brought the girl upstairs to my kitchen and took her temperature. It was elevated, but not alarmingly so. Her breathing and pulse were normal, but she obviously felt lousy. I forced her to tell me what hurt.

"It feels like really bad cramps, you know? Like when you're having your period and you feel all bloated and stuff?"

I nodded.

"Well, it's like that, but worse. I thought maybe my period had finally come, but it hasn't. And my head hurts a little, too."

I asked what she'd done at school, and what she'd eaten for lunch. She'd had a normal day and ate a turkey sandwich with mustard for lunch. "But what's weird," she added, "is that the same thing is going on with Cindy. She's in my art class and she was kind of freaked out today. Anyway, she told me that her stomach was killing her *and* that her period is late." Lindsey lowered her voice. "But she's still a virgin, too."

I brought Lindsey some ice water and made her take a couple of Tylenol. "Does Cindy's mother know?"

"Yeah, she's going to the doctor."

Two girls out of the hundreds who attended the high school did not make a pattern, but still, it was an odd coincidence. I wondered if other girls were experiencing the same symptoms, but time would answer that question. Meanwhile, Lindsey was going back to see Dr. Pam Warner. This time when I called the practice, they agreed to work Lindsey in right away if I could have her there before five o'clock. Due to the efforts of Holloman's newly hired public relations firm, Lindsey was supposed to do an interview with a North Carolina magazine at six o'clock, but I made her call and cancel. Lindsey agreed that the most important thing in her life was family and school, and that her modeling efforts were simply a way to earn college money. She'd already decided that she wanted to be a television sports announcer, not a model. Certainly, Holloman would understand that people sometimes got sick. When I told Ox I was taking Lindsey back to the doctor, he decided to go along.

Just for kicks, we took the hearse and Lindsey had a ball riding in the back. She dumped ice and canned Pepsis in the insulated compartment, and brought a DVD of music videos to watch on the flat-screen television.

"It's rad back here!" she called through the modified electric sliding window, that lowered just like those in some limousines. "Need some A/C, though. Crank it up, would you?"

Ox glanced my way from the driver's seat. "You sure she's sick?"

We made it to the medical complex in plenty of time and Lindsey saw Dr. Warner again. I went into the examination room with Lindsey while Ox stayed in the waiting room. Pam took Lindsey's temperature—which had risen slightly since I'd checked it—and drew some blood, which a nurse carried out to test. When the doctor pressed on the girl's abdomen, Lindsey flinched.

"Take it easy, would you, Doc? That really hurt."

Dr. Warner pressed again, on the other side, and got the same results. When Lindsey sat up, the woman quizzed her on her symptoms and verified that she hadn't been menstruating. She asked about drug usage and Lindsey told her that she didn't do *any* drugs—not even prescription. Pam asked me to step outside for a minute.

"Would you mind going back to the waiting room for a few minutes? I'll call you back in when we're ready," she said in a quiet voice. "I feel sure she's telling the truth, but sometimes young girls won't admit things in front of a parent or guardian. Sex, drug usage, habits. I'd just like to quiz her again, by myself."

I felt sure that Lindsey was telling the truth, too, but didn't argue with my doctor friend. Ox had stepped outdoors to make some phone calls, so I found a table of magazines and sat down in the waiting room.

"Are you pregnant, too?" a woman asked. She wasn't showing, but sat with her hands protectively folded over her stomach.

"Nope, not me. I'm waiting for someone." I opened the magazine, but like an overly friendly passenger on an airplane, she wanted to talk.

"I am," she announced. "I was never supposed to get pregnant because I had defective eggs. I was born with them. But all of a sudden, bam! I'm having a baby now and my doctor says it's a true miracle."

"Congratulations. You must be very excited," I said, hoping to get back to my magazine.

She laughed, nervous and fleeting. "Probably more information than you wanted, but I am excited. I'm so excited, I can't tell you how much. I'm a chemist and have spent years researching a fertility drug."

I smiled at her. "The drug worked, then."

"No, it never did."

Now she had my attention.

She did the nervous laugh again, seemingly unsure of herself. "It's a long story. But I'm just happy to be having a baby. I'm Peggy Lee, by the way."

"Jersey."

"I've never known anyone with that name," she said. "Thank you, Jersey. You're the only person to congratulate me, other than a sales clerk in the department store. And she was earning a commission."

The comment struck me as strange, but we didn't talk further because I was summoned back to the exam room. Dressed, Lindsey sat on the doctor's round stool, studying a chart on the wall.

"To be honest," Dr. Warner said, "I'm stumped. I thought that Lindsey may have some type of bacterial infection, but her white blood cell count is normal. The tenderness has me concerned, though. I'm going to schedule a vaginal ultrasound and a few other imaging tests. Is that agreeable?"

"Sounds like a lot of fuss over a simple stomachache," Lindsey said.

Pam laughed. "Don't worry, the tests won't hurt. They'll just give me a better picture of what's going on inside your body. It's like a puzzle, and I need some more pieces to figure out the big picture."

Lindsey shrugged. "Whatever you think, I guess."

"Additional tests are fine," I said. "If nothing else, for peace of mind."

Ox's forehead creased with worry when I relayed the information during the return drive, but Lindsey had returned to her energetic, happy self, jamming to music videos in the rear of the corpse caddy.

"It may just be normal female stuff," I told him. "The tests are nothing invasive, okay? The doctor just wants to figure out what's causing Lindsey's symptoms."

"If anything happens to her . . ."

I squeezed his hand. "Nothing's going to happen to her."

He nodded.

FORTY-ONE

Chuck was spending more time than normal in Wilmington lately and Peggy Lee realized the exhilaration she always felt upon seeing him had become slack, like an overly stretched piece of elastic. The desire to see him remained strong—she loved him, after all—but now that there was a secret between them, her devotion to the man had faltered. She planned to tell him about the baby but she had to wait until she was too far along for a safe abortion. Otherwise, he'd try to change her mind.

"Peggy Lee," he said, going to the refrigerator for his customary seltzer water. "You're glowing. Glad to see the pumped-up production and extra hours haven't worn you down."

"Not at all," she said, although she had started to grow weary of the excessive overtime. She'd rather have been out shopping, or reading books on baby care. When her work with Project Antisis ended, she planned to join a mom's club and socialize with other parents. Maybe she'd even make a friend.

"There's no seltzer water." Chuck slammed the refrigerator door and cold air shot out with a hiss.

"Oh, sorry," she said. "I forgot to get some more. But there's Coke and ginger ale in there. And plain water."

"You know I don't drink soda. And that cheap bottled water you buy tastes like it came out of the sewer."

"What's the big deal?" she said, suddenly in the mood to challenge him. "Just go buy some seltzer water. There's a store two blocks down the road. For that matter, why don't you get us something to eat while you're out? I skipped lunch and I'm starving."

Perplexed, Chuck studied the employee. She'd never spoken back to him. To the contrary, she always agreed with everything he said. And in the past, she'd gone out of her way to please him. She had even started checking him into the hotel before he arrived, to save him time. She'd put drinks in the mini fridge and fresh fruit on the desk. But this was a different person. Who did she think she was, demanding that he bring in food? Maybe she *was* working too many hours and hadn't gotten enough sleep. Chuck thought about hiring a lab assistant for her, but immediately knew it was a bad idea. He couldn't take the chance. Secrecy was vital to the success of the project.

"Peggy, Peggy," Chuck said. "You're right, the water is no big deal. My flight got delayed and it's put me in a bad mood."

"Are you going out for food? I've still got at least another two hours here before I can quit for the day. And to be honest, room service is getting old." Peggy used to love the routine. She'd work all day, then drive to Chuck's fancy hotel, where she'd take a bubble bath while he checked e-mail and returned phone calls. She'd come out wrapped in a big towel and climb into his lap, teasing him, until he stopped working and carried her to the bed. They'd make love—he always taught her new things to do to him—and then they'd order room service and watch a movie while they ate dinner in bed. But for some reason, she wasn't up for the bubble bath or eating while staring at a television.

Chuck felt like telling his chemist to go and get her own food, if she was hungry. But he held his tongue. Everyone was entitled to a bad day, now and then, he supposed. And he needed Peggy Lee, more than she knew. She was the only person he had entrusted with the formula, and he couldn't chance having her quit on him. Or worse, talking to somebody about what she'd been working on.

"Peggy, I know you're working very hard and I appreciate everything you do, really. I'm happy to go and buy you a fast-food hamburger. But I won't eat that crap," he added without meaning to. "Why don't I bring you a sandwich and then I'll go grab a bite to eat by myself while you finish up here."

Peggy Lee finished filling a container, sealed it, and peeled off the double-layer latex gloves. Now that she had her miracle, she wasn't taking any chances. Come to think of it, she didn't want to eat fast food, either. It wouldn't be good for the baby.

"I've got a great idea," she said. "I can make up the time tomorrow, so why don't I quit early today? I'll change clothes and we can both get something to eat, together. At a real restaurant. Won't that be fun?"

Chuck didn't like this new Peggy, he decided. If he didn't know better, he'd think she was still knocked up, the way she'd started acting hormonal. He most certainly didn't want to be seen in public with the homely woman. She didn't even bother to color her hair or buy fashionable clothes, much less wear lipstick or eye makeup. His live-in girlfriend wouldn't be caught dead without makeup and nice clothes. But something told Chuck it would be best not to rock Peggy's boat. Maybe they wouldn't see anyone he knew.

He took her shoulders and kissed her pale mouth. "That is a

great idea. Why don't you get changed and meet me at the hotel. I'll take you out for a delicious meal. We'll find someplace romantic," *and dark,* Chuck thought. Low light was a good thing. "Do you have a dress you can wear?"

FORTY-TWO

When he learned that *Incognito* didn't blow up, John Mason put a fist through the stateroom's locker door. Furious with himself for damaging his sailboat, he hit the teakwood slats again, bloodying his knuckles. It had been easy to learn that Jill Burns was really Jersey Barnes. But trying to terminate the bitch who had ruined his life's mission had infuriated him. He should just sail off as planned. Start a life somewhere outside the United States, away from the country that had gobbled up his brother's life as though he were a piece of ripe fruit. Something held him back, though, especially now that he knew everything there was to know about Jersey Barnes.

The night they'd eaten dinner at Elijah's restaurant, John remembered that a waitress knew Jersey and asked if she'd been out on the water lately. He went back to the restaurant and made sure he sat in that waitress's section. Because of his looks and build, he stood out and, just as John figured, the server instantly recognized him. Hoping his assumption that Jersey owned a boat was correct, he told the waitress that he planned to buy his girlfriend a gift but couldn't remember the name of her boat. *Incognito,* the woman promptly answered, as though it were a *Jeopardy!* television show question, adding that *Incognito* was a small yacht, not a boat. John gulped down the rest of his lunch, headed for the nearest Internet café, and logged on to BoatInfoWorld, where he entered the name of the vessel. Numerous other Web sites provided the same information but he knew this one from memory. A screen popped up giving him information about the boat, including its home port, owner, mailing address, and Coast Guard documentation number. John didn't have much use for the government, but federally funded agencies sure did make it easy to gather information about citizens. Almost everything about a person was out there and easily accessed, if you knew where to look for it.

Even though her boat was documented to the Barnes Agency, simple legwork revealed the rest of the story: Jersey Barnes owned the agency as well as a restaurant called the Block, where she lived. Surprisingly, she was a former SWEET agent, just like him. He'd even secured her personal cell phone number. Some text messages would be fun, he decided. Since he couldn't leave town until he got some form of satisfaction, some semblance of revenge for his twin's senseless death, John figured he may as well enjoy the hunt.

Explosives hadn't worked on Jersey, so the only sensible thing to do was take a different approach. He already had something in mind, something that would leave Jersey Barnes thinking about him for hours, maybe days, while she died.

Meanwhile, he would have a little fun. Using a prepaid phone, he composed the first of several messages and saved it to the draft file for future use:

Jill Burns is a nice name. Jersey Barnes is better.

FORTY-THREE

Chuck had to admit that Peggy cleaned up pretty well. When she'd spotted his invitation to a charity mixer at the Wilmington Hilton lying on the hotel room dresser, Peggy wanted to go. It was a fund-raiser to benefit North Carolina beauty pageants, hosted by an organization that promoted all the great student causes, including teen pregnancy prevention. Chuck had donated graciously, offering additional scholarship award money to pageant contestants, provided the Derma-Zing logo received priority placement. He would be in town anyway to install some upgraded lab equipment, so he agreed to attend the mixer. But he hadn't planned on going with his chemist. Taking her out to dinner had seemingly opened the door to more demands.

She had grown tired of always staying in the hotel room when he was in town, Peggy complained, and demanded to know if he was embarrassed to take her out. What could he do—tell her the truth? He thought about skipping the event altogether, but they were expecting him. Besides, he wanted to see for himself how many of the young girls in attendance sported designs. Not that he was concerned about sales. Almost four million girls ages fourteen to twenty had already used, or were currently using the product. The Derma-Zing Web site gained thousands of new hits daily and the college program had successfully launched. But additional PR never hurt. Especially when his designs were on beautiful, hip role models.

Chuck gave Peggy a salon gift certificate to get herself fixed up and had some clothes and shoes delivered to her apartment. It made her feel pampered, she said over and over again as she thanked him. Showing off a new haircut and style, and wearing a slinky white cocktail dress, Peggy was now presentable. Almost pretty. She hadn't quite gotten the hang of walking in the heels, but the dress showed off her slim figure and shapely breasts.

Before they left his hotel room for the mixer, Chuck made Peggy promise not to discuss her work in the lab, for obvious reasons. Confidentiality was imperative, he told her, and in a few more months, when he sold off the Derma-Zing branch of his company, she'd be a wealthy woman. He made sure to periodically dangle the money carrot, and so far it had worked to keep her motivation up. That, and the fact that Peggy thought their personal relationship held promise. The gullible idiot actually believed he was in love with her. Chuck planned to fuel the fantasy, right up until the chemist had served her purpose.

Walking into the hotel, Peggy grabbed his arm—only slightly wobbling on her heels—and stretched to kiss his cheek. "Oh, Chuck. This is fabulous. I'm so glad we've started going out, to do things together."

Chuck almost scolded her for kissing him in public when a thought bloomed. On the off chance that Project Antisis were to be discovered, he could pin everything on his chemist. She would make the perfect scapegoat. She worked solo and had zero social life. He could claim to know nothing of her past research with fertility drugs.

He'd simply made a bad judgment call by dating an employee, and everyone who saw them together could vouch for the fact that Peggy was enamored with him. All he'd have to do is explain that Peggy was so screwed up in the head because he broke up with her. She was a terrific insurance policy.

He rubbed her back. "You look very pretty, Peggy. And I'm glad you're having a good time. Just remember what I said about not talking work to anyone, understand?"

"Okay."

Chuck rarely drank alcohol, but tonight would be an exception. He found a bar and ordered a screwdriver for himself and a glass of wine for Peggy. When he passed it to her, she declined.

"I thought you wanted to have fun tonight, Peggy," he said. "Lighten up a little."

Not wanting to disobey him, she took the glass of wine and pretended to sip. As soon as he wasn't looking, she quickly poured some of the liquid out, into a discarded lowball glass. The doctor told her it would be best to completely abstain from alcohol and she eagerly agreed. She wasn't even going to take aspirin or acetaminophen.

Hanging prominently above the stage where a live band pumped out music he didn't recognize, a large Derma-Zing banner was illuminated by two spotlights. Chuck didn't recognize anyone in attendance, but the coordinator made it a point to introduce him and ignite conversations. The party was what he expected: average hors d'oeuvres, loud music, a few local newspaper photographers snapping human interest pictures, smiling businesspeople and professionals who'd come to network, parents of aspiring Miss North Carolina contestants, and lots of pretty girls—most of whom wore delicate ankle or wrist designs. Eyes scanning the ballroom, he spotted one of his spokesmodels strutting his way.

FORTY-FOUR

"Hiya, Doc!" Lindsey, said, reaching Holloman first. I'd driven her and a friend to the Wilmington Hilton, where Derma-Zing had sponsored a charity event.

"Why, hello ladies." He bumped Lindsey's fist when she held it out. "What are you doing here?"

"I'm a local celebrity now. I get invited to all these things. Besides, your PR lady told me I need to start making more public appearances, even though you don't pay me for all the extra time."

He laughed. "You've been reimbursed quite nicely for your time so far. By the way, how are you feeling?"

The girl shrugged. "Okay, I guess. My stomach still hurts, so the doctor is going to run some tests."

"Really? What tests?"

"Nothing major, Dr. Holloman," I intervened. Lindsey's medical history was none of his business. "We didn't realize you were in town."

He pointed to the Derma-Zing banner. "My company is a sponsor,

Jersey. We support all types of charitable causes in communities nationwide."

"You mean your company ECH Chemical Engineering & Consulting, in Roanoke?"

The comment caught him off guard and I sensed his memory backtracking to recall if he'd ever mentioned Derma-Zing's parent company in front of me. "Why, yes, that's right," he said.

I turned my attention to the woman standing next to Holloman, nervously fidgeting with her wineglass. Since Holloman hadn't bothered, I introduced myself and Lindsey, explaining that Lindsey had done the Derma-Zing television commercials.

"Magazine spreads, too," Lindsey said.

The woman looked up and did a half-smile. "Hello, I'm Peggy Lee."

She looked much different tonight, I realized, but Peggy Lee was the woman I'd met in the doctor's office waiting room. The pregnant chemist. Before I could acknowledge that we'd already met, the woman excused herself and hurried off, walking as though her shoes hurt her feet.

Holloman ushered me and Lindsey away from the too-loud music. We found a table and, when I mentioned that I was starved, he graciously left to get a plate of finger foods. As soon as he'd gone, I asked Lindsey if she'd been discussing her doctor visits with Holloman. Sure, she replied. He called almost every day to see how she felt, ever since he heard she'd been sick. That factoid sent a chill along my spine. Why was he so interested in Lindsey's health? From where he stood, she was simply one of several Derma-Zing models, and none were indispensable. I told Lindsey never to discuss anything personal with the man, starting right now. She didn't understand why, but agreed with a shrug and a "whatever."

Holloman returned with a plate of peeled shrimp and freshly cut fruit, each stabbed with a toothpick. He told us to help ourselves.

"Is your father here tonight?" he asked Lindsey.

Lindsey ate a bite of cantaloupe. "Nope. Jersey brought me and a friend. Cindy's outside talking on her cell phone, but she'll be here in a minute."

"That's too bad." He finished his orange juice. Since a lime wedge floated among the ice, I assumed the glass contained vodka, too. Odd, since he'd never had an alcoholic drink during all the times he'd been at my pub. He'd never had Peggy Lee on his arm, either. "I want to tell Mr. Oxendine what a fabulous job you've done for us," Holloman said.

"Thanks," she said, and spotting her friend, excused herself. Talking with Holloman was one thing, but letting her friends see her hanging at a table with the adults was another. That would be totally not cool in Lindsey's world.

When the girl moved out of earshot, Holloman quizzed me about my knowledge of his company. The fact that I knew of ECH bothered him, which made me wonder why it mattered. I find the direct approach works well, especially to shock someone into showing a reaction. I'd done a background check, I told him, and learned that ECH produced quite a few different adhesives for commercial use. Most impressive, I said, was the government contract he'd just secured to manufacture a new sealant material for hazmat suits.

His mouth pursed briefly and something flashed in his eyes. Anger? Surprise? "You're quite thorough for a bar owner, Miss Barnes. That's confidential information, as we're a privately held corporation."

I gave him my bimbette smile, complete with a hair toss. "Really?"

"It's been nice talking, but I should go find my date and circulate." He stood up, leaving the food and his empty glass. "Tell Lindsey I said good-bye, will you?"

I'd been keeping my radar on Peggy Lee and knew she'd gone into the hotel's corridor. I dumped the ice from Holloman's glass, wrapped the glass in a napkin, and dropped it in my handbag. Following Peggy Lee, I caught a flash of white dress as she disappeared into the women's restroom.

I found her standing at the sink, doing a bad job of applying lipstick. Her wineglass sat on the counter. "Peggy Lee, hi, it's Jersey. Remember me from the doctor's office?"

She stared at my reflection in the mirror with nervous eyes.

I handed her a paper towel to blot the lipstick. "What's wrong? You left so quickly, we didn't get a chance to talk."

She realized she was supposed to use the paper towel on her lips, and did so. "Please don't say anything to anyone about the baby, okay?"

I dug in my handbag to find some lipstick of my own and swiped the tube across my lips. "Sure, okay. Your business is your business. But I have to say that I don't think you should be drinking."

"Oh, I'm not." She turned to me, unsure of whether or not to confide in a stranger. I gave her my friendly woman-to-woman smile. "I've been pouring the wine out," she finally said.

"Whatever works," I said, sounding like Lindsey.

"See, Chuck doesn't know I'm pregnant," she explained. "I mean I was all excited when I found out and couldn't wait to tell him. But then his reaction . . . well, he didn't want a baby. He thinks the earth is already overpopulated. As far as he knows, I got an abortion."

"How do you know Charles Holloman? I mean, Chuck."

"I actually work for him."

"You're a chemist, right?"

She nodded. "I've got a lab here in Wilmington. I make a raw material for Chuck."

"What else does your lab do?"

"It's really his lab. But I'm the only chemist there." She bent over to adjust the strap on a shoe. "I only make the one ingredient, and it gets shipped to the production company for—"

"Production company for what?"

Clamming up, Peggy Lee said that Chuck was probably looking for her. I agreed that he was.

"Lindsey is a beautiful girl," Peggy Lee said. "Is she your daughter?"

"She's my best friend's daughter, but to me, she's family."

A vertical crease appeared between her eyes as Peggy Lee headed out of the restroom.

"Don't forget your glass." I handed the wineglass to her, along with a Barnes Agency business card. "Call me anytime you need to talk. And I won't say anything to Chuck about your baby, promise."

She dropped the card into her purse, poured half her wine into the sink, and left with a tentative wave.

My mobile phone buzzed and the display was JJ's number—her signal that the job was done. I headed outside and found her in the valet parking area.

"All set," she said. "You've got full coverage on Holloman's rental car. I'll let you know where he goes and what he does for the rest of the week. He's reserved the car through Sunday. By the way, how'd you know he'd be here?"

"The PR lady told Lindsey she really needed to attend, since Derma-Zing is a main sponsor. Figured Holloman would want to see that his money is being well spent," I said. "What about our equipment?"

"Manager at the rental company will hold the car until I recover the electronics. I made up some private-detective-cheating-spouse story. Told him I needed to check the car for ticket stubs, that sort of thing. Cost you a hundred bucks."

"Good job. Let me round up Lindsey and Cindy, and let's get out of here."

JJ stuck out a hip. "Can't I at least come in and get something to eat? You promised me free chow."

"You look like a cat burglar. Besides, I meant you'd get free food at the Block."

Bored, Lindsey and her friend sat in the hotel lobby, applying a Derma-Zing design to a grinning valet parking attendant. I asked if they were ready.

"Sure," she said. "This party blows."

I'd parked the corpse caddy across the street and once on the road, Lindsey and Cindy cranked up their music in the back. JJ pushed the button to close the sliding divider. "Cripes. Did we used to like that kind of noise?"

"Probably," I said, lifting my dress to remove the Sig and thigh holster. I checked my rear- and side-view mirrors out of habit. The roads were quiet, normal, except for Ashton's coverage, which I'd already spotted earlier in the evening. One of them had stayed with the hearse and the other tried to meld with the partygoers. I ignored them, just like I was supposed to.

My mobile phone chimed, alerting me to a text message. I handed the phone to JJ and asked her to read it.

"Who's Jill?" she said and read the message out loud.

Jill Burns is a nice name. Jersey Barnes is a better one.

So John Mason hadn't left town. And he had done some digging. "My roach coach alias," I said, realizing that not only had the identity of my boat been compromised, but now, he knew the name and whereabouts of both the Barnes Agency and the Block.

Using JJ's phone, I placed a call to Ashton.

FORTY-FIVE

Think you're untouchable? Think again.

The second text message that came from an unknown sender was more sinister than the first. When I alerted Ashton, he wanted to put me in a safe house until the "situation" was over. I refused, logic telling me that a former SWEET agent would be able to track down a safe house. He'd never become a true field agent, but John Mason had made it through the first level of training. If he wanted to find me, he would. My strategy was to be prepared and, as Ox had taught me, hope the spirits were on my side when it happened. Meanwhile, I needed to find out what Edward Charles Holloman was up to.

Rather than force me into a safe house, Ashton put full coverage on me, the Barnes Agency, the Block, and my vacant boat. He read me the riot act about keeping my cell phone powered on and went so far as to suggest a microchip bracelet. I knew the price tag for my protection continued to grow and wondered if Ashton was sorry he'd called me back into service. I didn't fret over the flowing government dollars for too long, though. The background research on Peggy Lee

Cooke and Holloman proved a much more interesting use of my time.

The fingerprint obtained from Holloman's glass revealed that he'd applied for a conceal-carry permit, which meant he had a predisposition to be armed but also held an appreciation for rules. They also told me that Holloman didn't have a criminal record. His parents were killed in an overseas industrial accident, after which Holloman founded his chemical engineering company. What struck me as suspicious, however, were the radical environmental causes that he supported. His company prospered by making all sorts of commercial adhesive products and sat nowhere near the green end of the environmentally friendly scale. Yet he gave hundreds of thousands of dollars to a hardcore cult whose mission was to reduce usage of the earth's natural resources.

While Holloman was an enigma, Peggy Lee was what she appeared to be on the surface: a capable research chemist with few social skills. She didn't pop up in any Internet searches, except for a few trade publication articles in which she was mentioned as conducting fertility research. No marriages, no children. No rap sheet. No social organizations or clubs. She didn't belong to her college alumni association. Even her neighbors at the apartment complex where she lived could recognize her photograph, but didn't know her by name.

My next visit needed to be the lab where Peggy worked, and thanks to the GPS locator JJ put on Holloman's rental car, I knew exactly how to get there.

A nondescript building with no signage, the laboratory was in Wilmington's industrial section and when I found a small Honda with a license tag registered to Peggy Lee Cooke, I knew I was at the correct spot. During the time I waited, sitting in the hearse, a constant stream of trucks traveled the roads. Nondescript delivery trucks, brown UPS trucks, refrigerated trucks, tractor-trailer rigs, and workers in pickups. Two hours, one Pepsi, and one bottled water later, a FedEx van stopped at the lab. Its driver went inside with an empty hand truck. He came out wheeling four large boxes. He went back in to collect another four. He returned a third time to make it a total of ten. Soon after the FedEx van continued on its route, Peggy Lee emerged. Hair in a ponytail and still donning a lab coat, she put on sunglasses and went straight to her car. Based on the time, she was either going for a late lunch or heading out early for the day.

The entrance door was equipped with a dead bolt lock and a standard lever door handle lock. I picked the lever lock in seconds and was pleased to find the dead bolt unengaged. A wall-mounted numerical keypad beeped when I walked in, but the alarm system was not set. Either the chemist was careless, or she planned to return soon.

I found the packaging area, where she put her raw ingredient into cardboard boxes for pickup and backtracked until I found a partially full box. Inside were opaque glass bottles filled with a thick substance. I stashed two of them in my backpack and searched the lab until I came across a desk and computer. I stuck in my earpiece and called Soup. As usual, he was home, clacking away at a keyboard. That's the good thing about computer hackers. They're always there.

"Okay, I'm standing in the lab in front of a computer and I've got the memory stick thingie you gave me. What do I do with it?"

"It *so* turns me on when you talk techie to me," he said.

"C'mon. I've got to hurry."

"Laptop?"

"Desktop." We did some rapid-fire question and answer until Soup told me where to insert the stick and which buttons to push. "Now what?" I asked.

"Now you wait and watch."

The computer screen came to life and the light on his memory stick started flashing. According to Soup, it was copying the hard drive.

He slurped something. "Depending on the file sizes, it could take fifteen or twenty minutes. You may as well go play with something else while you wait. When the blue light on the device stops flashing for more than five seconds, it's done. Just yank it out. Unplug the power cord to the computer, count to six, plug it back in. They'll think it was a power surge." He hung up before I could say that I owed him.

While I waited for Soup's device to do its thing, I rummaged. I sifted through desk drawers, looked through the contents of four refrigerators, and searched the bathroom. Finding nothing of interest other than a bunch of lab-type stuff, I went back to the smallest of the refrigerators and found a ginger ale. The blue light continued to flash as I drank my soda. I waited. My phone buzzed.

"Holloman's on the move and it looks like he's headed to the lab. Aren't you there now?"

"Yep." I disconnected and, standing on a chair, peeked through a small window near the ceiling of the building. Holloman's rental car pulled in, right next to the front door. I sprinted to the door, locked the dead bolt from the inside, ran back to the computer, removed the stick without bothering to see if it was done, unplugged the computer power cord, and shoved it back into the outlet without counting to six. I went inside the bathroom and shut the door. Using the toilet for a step stool, I jimmied open a push-out window above it, and ungracefully hauled myself and my backpack through the opening. Landing in a patch of weeds, I crouched, listening, until I heard the front door open. As soon as it clicked shut, I headed across the street.

Taking a break to smoke cigarettes, two workmen from a screen printing shop watched as I sprinted toward them and made my way to the corpse caddy, which I'd backed in next to a Dumpster. I shook out my hair, adjusted my bra, and climbed into the hearse. Pulling out, I gave them a big smile and wave. Dumbfounded, one just stared after me, but his buddy waved back.

I drove by Soup's place to give him the memory stick.

"Hey, interesting set of wheels you've got there. Is that what retired people drive these days? Casket baskets?"

"How fast can we see what's on there?" I said, ignoring his smirk.

Soup told me he'd get on it right away and call me later.

When I arrived at the Block, the parking lot was jammed and loud music emanated from one corner of my bar. Cutting through the crowd of people, I found Ox and pulled him into the kitchen.

"I don't know what's going on yet, but we need to get Lindsey out of her Derma-Zing contract. I don't think we want her to have any further contact with Holloman or his company."

Ox smiled. "I was going to tell you the exact same thing. I just had a talk with the modeling agency and Lindsey has fulfilled her new contract. But even if she hadn't, I agree that we don't want her involved anymore."

The physical nearness to Ox fired up my nerve endings and my hands migrated toward his body. I picked up a discarded beer carton to give them something else to do, and updated him on Peggy Lee's laboratory. "What do you think about it all?"

Ox removed the cardboard box from my grip, tossed it against a nearby wall, and took both of my hands in his. "I think I'd be destroyed if something happened to either one of the women in my life, Jersey. That would be Lindsey and you, just in case you're wondering."

We would have stood like that long enough to enjoy the moment if Ruby hadn't hustled by. "You'd better get out there and tell your daddy to quit giving away shrimp and crab leg platters. The hush puppies and chicken fingers were one thing. But all the seafood's gonna add up to a pretty penny."

I let go of Ox's hands. "What is he up to now? And who brought a band in here?"

"Beats me," Ox said. "I just got here."

Ruby let out a jolly belly laugh. "You two didn't set this up?"

We shook our heads. A cook shouted something to another cook and a server hurried by looking stressed.

"Oh, this is priceless!" Ruby said. "Spud and his friends have put on a fund-raiser. Got Wilmington's art council involved and everything. Flier advertises fifty-cent beer, dollar drinks, and free food all night long. Plus no cover charge for the music. They're going to auction off his two sculptures at ten o'clock."

She pulled a folded sheet of paper from her apron pocket and passed it over.

Incredulous, I scanned the page. "They made a flier? And who authorized free food?"

"Spud said you did. That you were helping him raise enough money to pay for the damage at the shooting range." With a final hearty laugh, Ruby scooted off. "Your daddy is a piece of work."

A stray customer wandered into the kitchen. "Hey, do, uh, you guys know where I can get my raffle ticket for the drawing?"

"What drawing?" Ox said to the girl, who looked like a college student.

"The paper said there'd be dollar raffle tickets for sale, to win a year's worth of free lunches. One a week. I'll spend five dollars to try and win that!"

"Paper?" I said. "You saw this in the *newspaper*?"

"Well, yeah." She held out a five-dollar bill.

People kept piling in and, for the first time ever, Ox began to worry that we might exceed our allowable occupancy per the fire marshal. The band stopped playing promptly at ten and a professional auctioneer took the microphone. Apparently, Fran donated *Road Rage* for the cause, after she bought it from the insurance company. The auctioneer went full-bore, arms and body synchronized with his voice, as he put on a show that could have enticed an accountant to buy a fifty-dollar bill for a hundred dollars. Despite his rhythmic, melodic skills of persuasion, nobody bid on the Chrysler. The alligator brought a single bid of one hundred dollars, but the businessman retracted his offer when he learned that the tail no longer moved. Ever persistent, the auctioneer took a twenty-minute break to allow prospective bidders a chance to look at *Road Rage* and *Nature's Wrath* one more time. During the second round of bidding, not a single person raised their hand. Nobody even lifted their arm to take a drink of their fifty-cent beer. Not surprisingly, the arts council folks had already left. Shrugging, the auctioneer found Spud sulking at the bar and asked for his fee.

Spud's voice came out in a high-pitched squeak. "Fee? You didn't raise any money, for crying out loud! How am I suppose to pay your fee out of the profits when there ain't no profits?"

"Sorry, pal," the auctioneer said. "This is how I earn my living. I can't help it if nobody wanted your sculptures. I did my best. You could glue gold coins to those things and they still wouldn't sell."

"How much does he owe you?" Bobby said.

"Hundred dollars. But considering how things turned out, let's make it fifty and I'll get out of here."

Fran scrawled out a check, signing it with a flourish. The auctioneer pocketed the check and made his exit.

"I ain't gonna be no kept man, Frannie," my father grumbled. "I can pay my own bills."

"Good, because I'm going to stop the music soon so we can get all these people out of here," I said. "I'm sure the band will want to be paid before they go, too."

"Oh, for crying out loud," Spud stuttered. "I was going to pay them out of the profits from selling the sculptures."

Bobby and Hal and Trip pretended they had to go to the urinal and smartly sauntered away, not wanting to be near Spud when he started looking to borrow cash.

Fran rubbed my father's back. "I'll pay the band tonight, sweetie, and you can pay me back later."

Spud grumbled his thanks. Since his poker buddies had collected eighty-eight dollars from raffle ticket sales, I let the band go ahead and give away the advertised prize of free lunch for a year. Ox put the eighty-eight bills in the register before Spud had a chance to pocket them.

By midnight, the Block had mostly cleared out, Spud went to bed, and Cracker was so stuffed from all the dropped food, he wouldn't move. One of the cooks threatened to quit, Dirk stopped by to tell me that I had to move Spud's abandoned vehicle off my property or I'd be fined, and Ox estimated that we'd given away more than nine hundred dollars' worth of food. Only Ruby, a bartender, and the other servers were happy with the evening's outcome. All the free food and cheap beer had filled their pockets with wads of tip money.

FORTY-SIX

"*What is this,* Peggy?" Chuck said, holding up a pamphlet on prenatal diet tips.

Peggy cringed. Her mind spun, trying to come up with a plausible reason she had the publication. "Wh-wha-what were you doing in my purse?"

"I was looking for a pair of reading glasses. I've misplaced mine."

"I don't use reading glasses," she said.

"Dammit, Peggy, answer me. What are you doing with this, unless—" He stopped in midsentence, instantly knowing she'd betrayed him. Ripping the pamphlet in half, he threw it at a trash bin. "You didn't get the abortion."

Instinctively backing away from him, she put her hands over her belly. "I went to the appointment, I swear. But I couldn't go through with it. I *want* this baby."

Chuck shoved her into a chair and stood towering over her. "Why did you lie, Peggy?"

"I told you. I want this baby, and I knew you'd try to make me get rid of it. Besides, I didn't lie. I just never told you that I didn't do it."

Chuck paced the length of the lab to calm down. "Are you still committed to Project Antisis?"

"Of course I am," Peggy Lee said, just to keep his temper in check. She was no longer sure what she believed in, especially now that she'd experienced the bliss of pregnancy. She just knew she'd do anything to protect her miracle baby and keep it safe.

Chuck sat in a chair next to his chemist. "With your help, Peggy, we have pulled off something that will alter the future of the world, do you realize that? Since people don't have enough sense to stop reproducing, we've intervened. We have prevented *several million* potential pregnancies from happening in developed countries." Chuck's eyes had glazed over. "Do you realize how beneficial to the preservation of the earth that is? Do you?"

Peggy Lee could only nod.

"That's several million fewer greedy, hungry, careless humans. Several million fewer plastic toys and multimillion fewer disposable diapers in landfills. We've impacted everything from water usage to polluting plastics to oil-gobbling cars on the road. We've made a dent, Peggy, a huge dent. We've made a difference. We have helped the people of this earth."

Wide-eyed, Peggy Lee nodded again.

Chuck took a deep breath, eyes closed, face to the ceiling and paused that way before speaking again. "Isis was the goddess of fertility. You and I, Peggy, and a lot more environmentalists just like us, realize the benefit of being *anti* Isis. Project Antisis will be the savior of the earth, and Derma-Zing is just the beginning."

Chuck went to the refrigerator and removed a plastic bottle of spring water, irked that Peggy still hadn't bought more of his favorite canned seltzer water. He returned to the chair and slowly drank. Derma-Zing had already exceeded his most aggressive expectations, Chuck thought. Usage was up to four million girls, and with the new formulation, sterilization could be caused with as little as two applications. Drinking the water, he made the decision to close out phase one of Project Antisis. Not only had his chemist betrayed him, but some users such as the Oxendine girl were demonstrating physical symptoms. It was just a matter of time before medical professionals started talking to each other and began searching for a common element.

Chuck finished the bottle of water with a single tilt of his head and told Peggy Lee that they would immediately stop blending the secret additive into the Derma-Zing adhesive. Meanwhile, he'd list the Derma-Zing company for sale.

Lost in her own thoughts, she nodded again.

Chuck smiled. The single product's huge success would ensure a quick sale, probably to one of the large cosmetic manufacturers. That would be his seed money to start phase two. And so it would go, for as long as Chuck could keep Project Antisis alive.

Meanwhile, there were loose ends to take care of—two of them. He had to dismantle the lab and move production of the Derma-Zing adhesive back to his main facility in Virginia. And he had to keep Peggy Lee quiet, until he decided the best way to eliminate her. Chuck had enough foresight to know that the chemist might start to turn, and he'd bought the jewelry weeks ago, just in case she did. He went to his briefcase and returned with a small gift-wrapped box.

Eyes opened wide, she ripped off the paper and opened the lid to reveal a gold ring with a big diamond in the center of it. "Oh, Chuck!"

"Peggy, I had planned to propose to you after we sold off Derma-Zing, when we could take a break and travel for our honeymoon," he said, trying hard to make the ridiculous lie sound sincere. "But considering the circumstances, I'm going to go ahead and ask you now. Will you marry me, Peggy?"

Unable to speak, she stood and hugged him tight. When she found her voice, Peggy Lee remembered the tiny life that steadily grew inside her. "What about my baby?"

"You'll have the baby—*our* baby—and we will raise him to be a good person, who will take care of his environment."

Tears rolled down Peggy Lee's flushed cheeks. "Oh, yes! Yes I'll marry you, Chuck."

FORTY-SEVEN

Saying the matter was urgent, Dr. Warner called and wanted to talk in person. We met at Le Catalan French Café, which for me was a short walk from the Block. Foamy balls of clouds crept across the sky and we sat outside, facing the riverwalk, to watch them. I ordered the chicken curry salad with fresh bread and she had the quiche of the day. Bypassing the extensive wine-bar menu, we both opted for ice water.

"I've seen three other patients with the same symptoms Lindsey exhibited. After checking with the other physicians at Daisy Obstetrics & Gynecology, we've identified eleven girls going through the same thing," Pam said.

"All from the same high school?"

"No, that's the first thing I checked. Several go to Lindsey's school, but one goes to a private school and one is home schooled. Another is a student at UNC. And one eighteen-year-old lives in Ohio. She was vacationing with her family."

"There must be a common element," I said, when the obvious

plowed into my brain with the force of a jackhammer. "Good God. It's the Derma-Zing."

"Come again?"

"I think it's the Derma-Zing, Pam." I thought of Lindsey's television spots and the help I'd given Holloman by suggesting college-logo stencils, and felt sick. "Did you happen to notice if your three patients wore Derma-Zing designs?"

"That stuff is so popular that we see it on kids all the time. None of the doctors in our practice would bother to note whether or not a patient had a design. No reason to."

I rubbed my temples, my old concussion headache creeping back. "There is now."

Our lunch arrived. Neither of us bothered to pick up a fork.

"My girls love drawing their little designs on each other," Pam said. "They've used the product for a couple of months now and they're fine. But tell me why you think the Derma-Zing is causing Lindsey's symptoms."

I downed some ice water to stop the queasiness in my stomach and told her exactly why. Holloman's odd behavior that could have been an ad for bipolar disorder and his obsessive interest in Derma-Zing, when the product was less than 4 percent of the total net revenue for ECH Chemical Engineering & Consulting. The hardcore environmental causes that he supported. The fact that he'd built a satellite lab in Wilmington, where only one chemical additive was manufactured, by only one employee. And that employee was a loner who'd spent years researching a fertility drug. Plus, the timing worked. Lindsey's health problems became evident just after she became a heavy user of the product.

Pam cut off a corner of her quiche but didn't eat. "You think they are intentionally putting something in Derma-Zing, which is causing—"

"Problems with the girls' reproductive systems," I finished, flashing back to a conversation with Holloman at the Block. "When talking about marketing, Holloman said his goal was to *expose* as many girls to the product as possible. He used that exact word. Expose."

Pam's face went pale. "This sounds like something out of a futuristic horror movie. Do you think he's purposely trying to sterilize young females?"

I was slowly nodding, my cerebrum working, when recall of another conversation caused a chill to shoot up the back of my neck. "His goal is population control. Peggy Lee said that Holloman thinks the world is already overpopulated. Apparently, they've been having sex and she got pregnant."

"Wait a minute," Pam said, thinking. "Is that Peggy Lee Cooke? I think she's been seen at our practice."

"Exactly. That's where I first met her—in your waiting room. Anyway, Holloman told her to get an abortion. He doesn't know she's still carrying his baby."

Our server stopped by to refill water glasses and ask if anything was wrong with the food. We assured her the food was fine, and no, we didn't need any to-go containers.

"Jersey, I called you because you're a personal friend and I'm concerned about Lindsey. I was just trying to clarify in my own mind what the next step should be. Contact all the other area physicians' offices to see if there's a pattern? Notify CDC?"

"All of the above."

"But I still don't have a diagnosis. And we don't have any proof that Derma-Zing is tainted."

"Then you need to get those tests on Lindsey done," I said. "I'll take care of rounding up evidence. We've got to stop him, Pam."

Pam chewed on the lemon slice from her water glass. "Wait a minute. What if it's the chemist? Maybe Holloman doesn't know anything about it."

"They both know about it," I said. "They'd have to."

"I pray to God that you're wrong about all this, Jersey."

"Me, too," I said, but knew I wasn't. "Where's the closest lab that will analyze the product, quickly, without questions?"

"I'd go through your cop friend, to take advantage of the forensics lab they use," she told me. "Plus, I'd use a second lab, so you get two independent results. As soon as I get back to my office, I'll call you with the name of a good one. But let me warn you, analyzing the product for proof of tainting will be hard, if not impossible."

"How so?"

Pam explained that any number of potentially suspect substances could be found in Derma-Zing, but if they weren't known toxins, they wouldn't cause alarm. If the chemist was manufacturing something new, especially an ingredient derived from a plant hormone, discovering its long-term effect could take months or years of trial testing. The bottom line, my doctor friend said, is that Derma-Zing was considered a cosmetic and therefore not regulated by the FDA.

"It's something like a forty-billion-dollar industry. Cosmetic products contain thousands and thousands of chemical ingredients, which aren't screened for safety or FDA tested," she said. "If you read some of the reports that I do, you'd be scared to use deodorant or body lotions, much less wear wrinkle-reducing creams and skin-firming makeup."

Pushing the uneaten quiche around on her plate, she threw out some shocking examples, including cancer-causing chemicals found in children's bubble bath, toxins found in nail polish, and traces of lead found in lipstick.

"Derma-Zing is just like any other unregulated cosmetic product," she said. "They can put anything from beeswax to synthetically manufactured chemicals to exotic plant and berry extracts in there."

"And it's all being absorbed through the skin," I said. "But the difference with Derma-Zing is that they are willfully trying to sterilize an entire generation of young women."

"Possibly," Pam said, her scientific training mandating caution.

Although Lindsey's appointment for the additional tests was a week away, Pam agreed to do them tonight, in her office, after hours. Leaving our uneaten lunches behind, we headed out, spotting a couple of college students with ankle designs.

I was waiting to pick Lindsey up when school let out for the day and we drove straight to the Block. I dragged her upstairs and used nail polish remover and baby oil to get all the Derma-Zing off her body. Afterward, I made her take a shower and scour her skin with an exfoliating body wash. Even though she thought I was overreacting, she was good-natured about it, and promised to tell everyone at school to stop using the product.

"I'm going to feel really silly, though," she said. "I mean, like, here I've been on television telling everybody how great this stuff is, you know? And now, I've got to tell people that it's bad for them?"

"Until we get the proof we need for a national recall, you've got to get your friends and those at your school to stop using it."

"But if I tell somebody it's bad for them, I'm going to sound like an idiot," she complained. "Hey, I know. I'll put the word out that little kids are into Derma-Zing. You know, like twelve- and thirteen-year-olds? Then *nobody* will want to be seen wearing a design. It will be totally uncool. I can even tell them how to get their designs off, with nail polish remover and baby oil."

"Good idea. You do whatever works. Don't talk to anyone from Derma-Zing, not even the PR lady or ad people," I said. "If Holloman calls you, just hang up. And if you see the man, stay away from him, okay? This is a serious situation, Lindsey."

"You are like, so wigged out. And you're not even sure that Derma-Zing is what caused my period to stop."

"Lindsey, I am sure. I just can't prove it yet."

Unconvinced, she shrugged.

I tried a different route. "Here's the thing. If anything bad happens to you, your mother will make you go back to California in a skinny minute and none of us wants that." It was a cheap shot, but at least I got through to her.

"You know I don't want to go back to live with Mom and Albert."

"Then you must promise to do what I've asked, even if you don't necessarily agree."

"Okay," she finally said. "I promise. The whole Derma-Zing thing was getting kind of old, anyway."

When she went downstairs to work her shift, I tried to shove my personal feelings aside and figure out a course of action. The headache I'd acquired at lunch hadn't quite gone away, and it was difficult to think. There was simply no plausible way to alert the millions of Derma-Zing users that they might be poisoning their reproductive systems. At least not yet. We had to get something tangible to take to Ashton, and CDC, and NIH, and anyone else who'd listen. Even the national press wouldn't touch the story until they had substantiating evidence. With help from a chemist, Soup was still trying to make sense of the data copied from the laboratory's computer. The testing facilities wouldn't have conclusive results from the samples for days, maybe weeks. Pam Warner couldn't prove what was causing her young patients' similar symptoms. The immediate answer was to put pressure on the chemist and see what she'd divulge. I'd have to pay her a visit in the morning.

My headache revved up a notch when another text message appeared on my phone:

A slow death will allow you to think about what you've done.

FORTY-EIGHT

Too excited to sleep, Peggy Lee had been fully awake since three o'clock, her mind a swirl of thoughts. Chuck hadn't mentioned a date, but she assumed he'd want to get married quickly, before their baby began to show. Where would the ceremony take place? It would be a small affair, but special nonetheless. Maybe they'd do a short and sweet ceremony on the beach, or maybe Chuck would want to do something wild such as fly to Las Vegas for the weekend.

Hugging her pillow and flipping over, Peggy Lee wondered how much she could spend on a dress. She'd always wanted a delicate, silky, layered, sequined gown, under which she'd wear a lacy garter belt. Regardless of where they did it and what she wore, Peggy Lee was ecstatic. She would soon be the wife of a president of a research company. An established businessman and chemist. Someone who understood the scientific world. Someone with a vision. Flipping to her other side, Peggy Lee readjusted the pillow and conceded that she didn't have to wear an expensive gown. She wouldn't mind getting married in a dress, with Chuck at her side in a nice suit and tie. She knew he would spend lavishly on their honeymoon, even if he hadn't yet sold the Derma-Zing division. Staring at the rotating ceiling-fan blades, she wondered where they'd live. Virginia, of course. But would she move into his current place? She'd never been there, but knew it would be spacious and open and adorned with beautiful upgrades such as granite and tile and oversized picture windows. All the things she'd seen in home and leisure magazines. Feeling the ever-so-slight roundness of her belly, she thought again of her baby and went through a list of baby names. Restless, she sat up and turned on a light to look at the mobile of stuffed animals she planned to hang over the crib. Deciding she'd never be able to sleep, Peggy Lee headed to the shower. Going to the lab early would give her a jump start and she could leave before the evening rush hour to visit a bridal shop.

Few commuters were on the road before sunrise and Peggy Lee made it to her lab more quickly than usual. Strangely, the alarm system was off. She could have sworn she'd set the alarm the prior evening. When the fluorescent lights flickered on and flooded her lab with bluish illumination, Peggy Lee screamed.

Metal tables lay twisted, overturned, and glass vial remains were scattered everywhere. Refrigerator doors stood open, their contents broken. She immediately went to her desk and found the computer on the floor, its casing broken as though it were smashed with a baseball bat. Using a Swiss army knife she'd carried since she was a kid, Peggy Lee removed the hard drive. It took some doing to detach the bent metal cage from the mangled frame and when she did, she couldn't believe what she saw. Several long nails had been driven through the guts of the hard drive, effectively destroying it. Every bit of her work had been saved on there, and whoever had trashed it knew something about computers. But they didn't know about her backup disks, which Chuck insisted she keep at the lab instead of in a secure, off-site lockbox. She threw open the bottom drawer, only to find it empty. On her hands and knees, the chemist searched the floor and every single place the backup disks could conceivably be. Nothing. Her personal hard copy files were missing, too. She prayed that Chuck's set of backups—the second and only other set—were safe and intact. Otherwise, her years of research and documented findings on the wild leafy shiff bush were gone.

Across town, Chuck parked in a convenience store lot and walked the three blocks to Peggy's apartment building, carrying a bag of croissants, champagne, and orange juice. She'd be jubilant over the romantic breakfast in bed and she'd drink her spiked mimosa without thinking twice. While she died, Chuck could plant the telling evidence. By the time he reported her missing days later and the authorities found her, the drug that stopped her heart would be long gone from her system. If he was lucky, it might even cause an embolism. Either way, the death would be ruled natural causes and she had no family or friends to challenge the cause of death.

Whistling, Chuck reached Peggy's dingy apartment door and, careful not to touch the doorknob, inserted his key. Adjusting his backpack of goodies, he slowly opened the door, touching only the key, when his cell phone rang. The caller ID was the laboratory phone number.

"Yes?" he answered, incredulous.

"Chuck!" Peggy Lee cried. "Somebody's been in the lab! Stuff is strewn everywhere!"

Damn his luck! She never got to the lab before seven thirty or eight o'clock in the morning. Silently cursing, he told Peggy to calm down and asked if anything was missing, just for something to say.

"Some files are gone. And the computer is broken. There's glass all over the place. What happened, Chuck? Who could have done this?"

Chuck quietly closed her apartment door. "Probably some kids, getting their kicks by vandalizing buildings. Or it might have been a drug addict looking for money. Who knows?"

"Was the alarm set last night?" she said.

"I don't know, Peggy. I guess. We left together and I haven't been to the lab since. But you were the last one out. Did you forget to arm the system?"

"I must have." She sounded uncertain. "When I came in, it was off. And then I turned the lights on and saw all this mess. What should we do?"

Chuck cursed his luck again. He'd planned to hit a club tonight, someplace with dancing and pretty girls. But now, he'd have to see her for dinner and do the job then. At least he could go ahead and plant the evidence, Chuck thought, so it wouldn't be a completely wasted morning. Holding the cell phone to his ear, he slipped on plastic shoe covers. "Stay calm, Peggy. It's okay. The main thing is that you're safe. I'll call the police and come right over. Meanwhile, you stay put until they get there."

"Okay."

Chuck hung up and cursed out loud as he found her dresser. He'd purposely never gone to her apartment but it was a small one-bedroom, and drab at that. The first thing he did was find her journal, the one she called her depression days journal. She'd mentioned it once, after they'd had sex, telling him she no longer needed to write in it. Flipping through the pages, he smiled as he reads clips she'd written years ago: "I'm a failure and my research proves it . . . I hate to see all the smiling mothers with strollers when I go to the park . . . why am I being punished?"

Pleased to find no entries concerning him or Project Antisis, Chuck stashed the diary inside a folder containing her research files and placed the lot on the floor, beneath her bed. Next, he found the freezer and deposited vials of chemicals and a package of frozen plant matter inside a near-empty ice cream carton. Last, he went to Peggy's tiny bathroom, where he left a self-help book on depression. He'd inserted it into a clear plastic book jacket protector, one he'd removed from a well-used chemistry book that was covered with her prints. When he finished, Chuck put on a baseball cap and mechanic's jersey, and slipped out, pleased to see that it was barely daybreak.

Back at the lab, Peggy Lee stopped in her tracks when she spied a crumpled blue seltzer water can lying in the trash bin. She recycled and knew for a fact that there weren't any aluminum cans in either of the trash cans. Peggy Lee hadn't bought any seltzer water to restock the refrigerator since she'd emptied the garbage last week. What were the odds that the vandal just happened to drink seltzer water and it just happened to be the same brand Chuck drank?

Surveying the damage for a second time, more calm than the first go-around, she realized that everything crucial to Project Antisis was missing or destroyed. But all the expensive lab equipment sat untouched. Not only that, but Chuck quickly said he'd call the police, when he should have been worried about privacy. The only way he could know they wouldn't find anything incriminating is if he was the person who had cleaned out the lab. The person who'd hammered nails through her hard drive to ensure its death.

Not caring that she'd left the lab door wide open, Peggy Lee ran two blocks to the next street and banged on the door of a gemologist's building. Despite the time, she knew he worked odd hours and took it as a good sign that his lights were on. She'd met the Israeli once, when he was out for a walk and she'd ventured outside for some fresh air. His was an Internet-based business and he didn't have a public showroom. He peeked through the door's small security window and buzzed her in.

Peggy Lee shoved her engagement ring at him and asked if the diamond were real. Not wanting to get involved, the gemologist didn't ask questions. The examination took less than twenty seconds.

"Sorry, lady, is no real," he said in his thick accent. "Is no even good-quality glass."

She didn't want to believe him. "But it's so sparkly. Are you sure?"

His arms went up in surrender. "Like I say, is fake. The gold is worth maybe seventy, eighty dollar. But stone is fake."

Sobbing, Peggy Lee stumbled back to the lab. She went straight to the trash bin to make sure she'd really seen the seltzer can and hadn't just imagined it. Its crumpled form looked like a laughing mouth. The prenatal diet pamphlet lay beneath the can, torn in two.

"No, no, no," she said to the garbage, even though her scientifically trained brain screamed the truth inside her skull. Chuck had destroyed the lab. He didn't want their child and he never planned to marry her. It didn't occur to the chemist that her life might be in danger until she was strapped behind the wheel of her Honda. Numbed by the betrayal, Peggy Lee drove until her fuel gauge needle hit red. She pulled in to the first motel she found—a nondescript place in Whiteville—and registered with cash under a fake name.

FORTY-NINE

My doctor friend called me with Lindsey's test results and the news was bad. Telling Ox his daughter might not be able to have children was the hardest thing I've ever done. Especially since I felt responsible. I should have checked further into Holloman's background when Lindsey first got involved with him.

"Pam will explain it all to you in detail," I told Ox, "but Lindsey's ovaries are a mess. Her eggs are damaged and most likely, she'll never be able to get pregnant."

His face was unreadable. "What about her? The rest of her?"

"Pam said that Lindsey is the picture of health. Liver functions, kidney functions, heart and lungs—everything is perfectly normal, except for the ovaries. Depending on whether or not her body is still able to produce a reasonable level of hormones, there is a possibility she'll have to go on a hormone replacement therapy since she's so young. But we don't know yet."

"And you think this was intentionally done to her and the others?"

"Yes," I said and told him why.

I've seen Ox angry before, but now he looked murderous. Had Holloman walked into the Block, Ox may have killed him on the spot. Once he had some time to fully digest the news, we talked some more—mostly about the best way to get the word out. Girls needed to stop using Derma-Zing immediately. Unfortunately, there was no proof that the product had caused Lindsey's condition. My lab samples of the raw material and shelf samples of Derma-Zing were being tested, but as Pam had warned, results might be inconclusive at best.

Ox strolled outside and stood against the railing of the riverwalk, breathing slow and deep, as if drawing strength from the water. After a time, I followed and stood beside him.

"You shouldn't feel responsible, Jersey. Lindsey used Derma-Zing in California before she ever came here, remember?"

"Yes, but still—"

"Thanks to you, Lindsey is off the stuff. What we need to focus on now is getting all the other girls off it." He rubbed a hand over his face. "It rips me apart inside to think that my little girl has been harmed. But Holloman ended up in our bar for a reason."

"What do you mean?"

"We will stop the monster. But imagine if he never came to Wilmington. Lindsey—along with millions of other girls—would continue painting the stuff on their bodies."

"If I could swap my healthy ovaries for her damaged ones, Ox, I'd do it in a heartbeat," I said. "Someday, she'll want to be a mom. And you'll want to be a grandfather."

Standing tall, Ox closed his eyes and breathed in the scent of the river. His face was serene, calm. "I see a grandchild in my future, Jersey. I see two. Lindsey's going to be just fine."

I asked Ox if he wanted me to tell Lindsey about the test results.

"As I said, I see grandkids in my future."

"But—"

"Knowing what's been done to her body isn't going to help

anything." Our eyes locked and I understood that he meant to protect his child. The news that she might never have children of her own could damage Lindsey even more than the Derma-Zing had. I filled my lungs and acknowledged his concern. I understood.

We agreed to visit the chemist at her lab first thing in the morning.

Ox decided to take Lindsey and Spud to the movies but I declined to join them. I had some work to do at the Barnes Agency. And I wasn't sure I could put on a happy face around Lindsey, at least not tonight.

Walking to the corpse caddy, I didn't detect any of Ashton's people watching. Either they were getting much better at blending in to the background, or else somebody had screwed up the scheduling. As I put the wagon into gear and pulled out, something stung the back of my neck. Responsively, I reached to rub the spot and when I did, a metal cuff snapped around my wrist.

"Keep driving." The voice belonged to John Mason.

My body suddenly felt light, floating off the seat, and I realized he'd drugged me. The other half of the cuffs was attached to a latch in the slider window and my arm remained bent over my shoulder, locked in place through the glass divider. My instinct was to let go of the wheel and grab my Glock from my handbag, but my muscles were leaden and uncooperative. It was stupid to carry a weapon in a handbag. I knew better, but hadn't bothered to strap on a shoulder holster since I was just running across town. The hearse straddled the center lane and it took every ounce of my concentration to pull back to the right in time to avoid an oncoming truck.

"I'm going to wreck the car," I said, my tongue thick.

"Turn left here."

I wanted to shove my foot on the accelerator and go for the Glock, but my muscles obeyed John instead of me. I slowed to turn.

"Go to the second light and take a right."

I did. We drove like this for twenty minutes, John giving sparse instructions, and me struggling to keep my eyelids up. Finally, he ordered me to stop in a pancake house parking lot. When he unlocked me and yanked me out of the car, I grabbed my cell phone off the seat—the government-issued one with the tracker—and tucked it beneath the underwire of my bra. The next thing I knew, I was in the back of a van.

John dumped the contents of my handbag on the van floor beside me and fished out the Glock and my personal cell phone. He pocketed the gun and destroyed the phone between his foot and the pavement. Trancelike, I watched him pull the bills from my wallet and take my zip-tie plastic cuffs. Bastard probably wanted his pair of steel cuffs back and planned to restrain me with a pair of my own plastic ones. When John finished going through my belongings, he patted down my body with groping hands and found Ashton's cell phone tucked beneath my bra strap.

"You little bitch."

I threw myself at him, snatched the phone from his hands, and fell to the pavement. With every ounce of mental capacity I could muster, I concentrated on not letting the phone slip out of my fingers while I slid open the battery cover, removed the SIM card, and closed the cover. He jerked me up and backhanded me across the face, sending me back to the ground. The phone flew out of my hands. Wiping the blood from a cut lip, I stuck the SIM card in my mouth, between my gum and cheek.

John searched the empty parking lot until he found the second phone. He stomped on it until nothing remained but mangled parts.

"What do you want with me?" I asked.

I don't think he answered. Moments later, I sensed movement. We were on the road. I'm not sure how much time passed, but when we stopped, whatever drug he'd injected into my system had begun to wear off. Headache pressure behind my eyes felt like dual ice picks stabbing my optical nerves. I looked down to see that my hands were now secured in front of my waist with one of my own disposable zip-tie restraints. He led me through grass and trees and I heard a dog barking in the distance and something nagged at my drunken brain to find a stickpin. I stumbled without meaning to, and when he jerked me to my feet, I remembered why I needed a pin. The disposable cuffs. There was a simple way to get out of them. I fell against his chest, hoping to lift a fountain pen or something else to use, but there was nothing there. Trees grew dense as we walked along uneven ground illuminated only by moonlight. When he yanked me to a stop, I wanted to fight, to deliver a lightning-quick butterfly kick and follow it up with a spinning double-handed fist to his head. I wanted my Glock back. I wanted to kill him. My mind's eye envisioned exactly how I could do it, but my muscles wouldn't cooperate. John lifted a piece of earth out of the ground. It was a door to an underground cellar.

With a shove, he sent me tumbling into the hole.

"I like your spunk, Agent Barnes," he said. "It makes me happy to think that you'll last for a while, while your systems slowly shut down from a lack of water and air. You'll probably suffocate before you die of dehydration. Either way, you'll have plenty of time to ask yourself why you got involved. Why you had to be a nosy bitch and interrupt my mission."

The door dropped. I sensed him packing dirt and pine needles around the edges of the wood door and then everything became blaringly silent. I spit out the phone's smart card and dried the saliva with my shirt. Unfortunately, it was useless without a power source. I stuck it in a pocket.

Reminding myself not to use more oxygen than necessary, I spent half an hour examining every inch of my dirt-and-brick prison, hands still banded together. Hoping that electricity had been run at one time, I searched the crevices between every brick for wire and came up empty. The entire cellar was empty. And dark. In total pitch blackness, using my hands, I determined that it was just me and a dead bug. About eight feet long by four feet wide, the hole was almost deep enough for me to stand. Crouching with my shoulders against the overhead door, I pushed until my leg muscles quivered from exhaustion, and the healing wound on my back fired stabs of pain down my spinal cord. Nothing happened. Not only was there the weight of dirt on top of the door—he must have built it like a giant square planter—but John had also secured it from above. Heart slamming against my chest, I sat down to slow my pulse rate. There had to be something I could use, if nothing else to get the plastic cuffs off. Starting with the sandals on my feet, I mentally worked my way up to the small gold loops in my earlobes, my fuzzy brain thinking that there must be a use for my watch. It contained a battery! And I could use an earring to make a straight pin and get my hands free.

I got an earring off, straightened out the loop, and managed to wedge it downward between the roller-lock tension system and one of the wrist straps. The pin contraption stopped the teeth on the strap from engaging and I was able to loosen the strap enough to get one hand free. I did the same with the other side and, enjoying the accomplishment, rubbed my hands to get the circulation back. With two free hands, I used the corner of a brick to pry the back off my wristwatch and removed the round battery. It was a far cry from a cell phone battery, but it was juice. With the gold posts I broke off my earrings and a part of the watch band, I connected the tiny battery to the metal terminals on the SIM card. Holding it all against the ceiling of my dirt hole and unable to see a thing, I prayed like hell that I had the connections right.

FIFTY

I lost track of time, but took it as a good sign that my lungs still worked. I contemplated digging a hole to the surface, but knew the cellar was old. The dirt had become compacted, almost stone-like. I didn't have any digging tools—other than French-manicured fingernails. And I didn't want to be found dead, fingers raw to the bone from having attempted to dig myself out. How undignified. Not to mention grotesque for the unlucky person who found me.

The only thing left to do, I deduced as I began to grow light-headed, was to carve a good-bye message into the dirt floor with my wristwatch. It might get read or it might not, but at least it would give me something to do. I was trying to decide what to write when I heard dogs. Or I might have imagined them. When the faint barks grew louder and stopped above me, I knew I'd been found and promptly passed out.

When I came to, Ox was lifting me out of the hole, his mouth to mine, forcing air into my lungs. Blinding floodlights made my eyes tear. There were people everywhere. The dogs' handler was trying to round up the animals, I heard Ashton's voice, and two paramedics moved in to get a look at me. When they finished checking my vitals, I felt Ox's hands run over my face and he held my eyelids open with his thumbs. When my eyes focused on him, he smiled.

I sat up. "How long have I been in there?"

"He snatched you between the Block and the Barnes Agency," Ox said. "We found the abandoned hearse. If he brought you straight here from the restaurant parking lot, then you've been underground for seven hours. It's almost morning."

"Good grief. What took you so long?"

"Where's your phone?" Ashton demanded.

"He smashed it." I handed over the smart card, watch battery, and earring contraption.

Laughing, Ox pulled me into a crushing hug. "They only got a blip of a signal, Jersey, but it was enough to narrow your location to John Mason's property. The team scoured the grounds and the house, but found nothing. They increased the search radius to a mile and spread out in a spiderweb grid. But I knew you were somewhere on this property. I could *feel* it. I convinced Ashton to fly in the dogs."

"Thanks, Ash."

Either too angry or too relieved to respond, he only nodded.

"We need to get an IV in her," a paramedic said.

"I'm fine," I told him. "No IV needed. Quart bottle of Gatorade will do."

"Don't you at least want some oxygen?" he asked.

"Can I have a tank to go?" I said. "I'm outta here."

When I awoke later that morning and went downstairs to retrieve the daily newspaper with Cracker leading the way, I found my handler waiting for me. Looking as though he'd had no sleep, he sat at the vacant bar, drinking coffee, even though the Block wasn't open for business until lunch. Cracker ran to greet our visitor. Yawning, I made sure my jammy top was buttoned to a reasonable height. Just because Ashton had authorized the charge for my big boobs didn't mean he had a right to look at them.

"You're going to a safe house," he said.

"What, no 'good morning'?"

He looked at me with tired eyes. "Go pack your things."

"Not even a 'How are you feeling after your night in a dirt hole, Agent Barnes?' " I studied my hands. "My back is sore and my fingernails are trashed, by the way. Maybe the agency can treat me to a mani and a massage?"

"I'm serious, Jersey. Your escorts will be here to take you as soon as I make the call. Go pack."

After he broke in, Ashton had put a pot of coffee on to brew. I went behind the bar and poured myself a cup. "No. But thanks for the offer."

"I'm not asking," he said.

"I don't care whether you're asking or telling. You and I both know that I'd be a sitting duck in a SWEET retreat. You may as well strap a flashing neon target to my forehead." I fished around to find some sugar, poured, stirred, and drank, grateful for life's simple pleasures such as caffeine. "I am much more concerned about the *real* terrorist threat here, Ash. Not some two-bit thug on steroids who gets off by dumping a woman in a root cellar."

"He took out two of my agents on coverage duty."

I felt bad for the deaths of two people I didn't know, but it wasn't my fault that Ashton had underestimated John Mason. I propped opened a side door to let Cracker out. "Did you read my report on Derma-Zing? That's the real terrorist action."

Ashton half-sighed, half-cleared his throat. "We are evaluating the information."

"Excuse me?"

Ashton sucked down a long swallow of coffee. "The scheme sounds far-fetched. But just for the sake of debate, let's say it's true. We've already got a full docket and I'm shorthanded as it is. Another agency would have to handle the investigation."

"Which agency?"

"Probably the FBI along with individual state agencies. If it's truly a problem in Europe and Japan, then Interpol would have to be notified. Back on our side of the water, the CDC would have involvement and the Federal Trade Commission might step in. All the individual state health agencies. I'm really not sure."

"Exactly," I said. "If we don't take care of it, this thing will get shuffled around like a freakin' customer complaint at the DMV office. Meanwhile, Peggy will bolt, along with the evidence we need to take Holloman down. And more important, the evidence we need to issue a recall before it's too late for millions of users."

Ashton looked at me. "It's not what we do."

"When I signed on, it was my understanding that stopping terrorism and other threats to public safety is *precisely* what we do. Sterilizing an entire generation of young women is terrorism at its worst."

My handler shook his head. "Go pack."

"By the way, did you know that the Sec Def's kid uses DermaZing? She had a design on her ankle during the wedding on Bald Head. You think he'd be happy to learn that his only daughter is being rendered sterile while you're trying to push the file into someone else's hands?" Cracker sauntered back in, stretched, and waited for somebody to pet him. "I'd imagine that he's hoping for a lot of grandkids."

Ashton rubbed bloodshot eyes. "Are you attempting to threaten me, Agent Barnes?"

I refilled his coffee cup and sat beside him. "No, but if you want a threat, here's one for you. I'm thinking of doing a television interview about my ordeal in the root cellar. Of course it would probably come out that the assailant was your *handpicked protégé* for the trial SWEET recruitment program, which you created. You know—the program that recruited agents from populations other than those already in military service? And that you not only found him, but kept him in the system despite reservations, because you wanted your new recruitment program to survive." I scratched Cracker's snout and watched his tail rev up. "Probably, the interviewer would find out that this former agent—your *handpicked recruit*—blew up my car, tried to murder the country's secretary of Defense and sank a container ship along with two Coast Guard boats killing more than ten crew members."

Ashton's head fell forward. "How did you find out?"

"Your people trained me, Ash, remember? I'm good and I surround myself with people who are even better. When you refused to share his recruitment details and you kept shoving Mason's innocence down my throat, I knew there was more to the story. Somebody hacked into SWEET's system and found the details of the now-defunct program. But they said that your e-security is top-notch."

"Soup," Ashton said to himself. He didn't bother to reprimand me and he knew they'd never be able to prove that Soup had been inside the electronic guts of the agency. Soup's reputation and abilities were well known at SWEET. "What is it that you want me to do?"

I planned to find the chemist, I said. And when I did, I wanted a local safe house ready—for her. We needed to keep her secure and keep her from bolting while we questioned her.

The phone behind the bar rang. I answered it.

"Jersey, where the heck have you been?" JJ said. "I thought you were coming by the agency last night, and I've been trying to reach you ever since."

"I got sidetracked by a bad man," I told her. "But at least now, he can't send me any more text messages because he smashed my phones."

"Listen, Peggy Lee Cooke called and wants to meet with you. We got a location on her. A pay phone outside Whiteville. She's in a motel but she wouldn't say which one. She won't talk to anyone except you."

I got the rest of the details from JJ, hung up the phone, and stretched my back, which was still stiff from sitting in the dirt hole. Another hour of sleep would have felt great. I peeled a banana and offered Ashton half. He declined. Cracker was happy to accept the snack, though.

I dropped a pinch of banana in his waiting mouth. "About that safe house?"

"I'll make it happen," Ashton said.

"Great. Because as luck would have it, the chemist wants to talk. I don't have to waste time tracking her down."

FIFTY-ONE

"*Please, let me* go!" Peggy Lee said from the passenger's side of the corpse caddy, struggling with the zip-tie restraint that secured her wrists together. "I was going to leave a letter for you at the café, I swear. I was going to tell you everything in the letter."

Instead of climbing back in bed after my chat with Ashton at the Block, I'd dressed and headed to Whiteville, a white Chevy Suburban on my tail. Using a prepaid mobile phone I bought along the way, I called the pay phone number that Peggy Lee left with the Barnes Agency. The chemist answered on the second ring. She told me to meet her at the Milky Way Café in Whiteville at eleven o'clock. Instead, I went straight to the street address of the pay phone and cruised nearby hotels until I found her Honda. Whiteville is a small town. At nine thirty, Peggy Lee emerged, looking ridiculous in an oversized hat and huge black sunglasses. The overcast sky and early hour didn't necessitate either accessory. She carried nothing but a purse and a shopping bag. Once in her car, she pulled off the sunglasses to study a road atlas. Figuring the woman wouldn't need a road map to find her way to a nearby café, I pulled in behind the Honda, sideways, blocking her.

She tried to run when she saw me get out of the hearse and I had to physically restrain her. I searched the Honda, collected her belongings, and asked the motel manager if the Honda could remain parked in his lot for a week or so. "Sure," he said and pocketed my hundred-dollar bill without missing a beat.

"You were going to write a tell-all letter?" I said to the chemist, pulling out of the parking lot. "How amusing."

She frantically tried to get the plastic cuffs off with her teeth.

"That's a very tough resin material you're trying to bite through, Peggy Lee. Pretty much impossible to do. A handheld pair of hedge trimmers works best to cut them off."

She went for the door handle. I slowed down, just in case she tried to throw herself out of the hearse. She did and hit the grassy shoulder of the road with a thud, not knowing how to break her fall with a roll. I pulled over as she struggled to her feet. The white Suburban stopped behind me and the two agents inside watched with amusement.

Running awkwardly, Peggy Lee tripped and fell. I planted a foot on her back before she could get up. Struggling, she ignorantly rolled onto her back and tried to kick at me. I pressed the sole of my shoe against her throat, just hard enough to get her attention. She stopped squirming.

"Here's the deal, Peggy Lee," I said, standing over her. "You are coming with me, one way or the other. If you keep acting stupid, you are going to hurt yourself. And if I have to, I will secure you with more than a couple of plastic strips and toss your ass in the back of the hearse for the hour drive to Wilmington. Is that what you want?"

She shook her head.

"I'm going to let you up now and you're going to walk back to the car and get in."

She nodded.

"He's going to kill me and my baby," she said when we were rolling again.

"We're not going to let that happen, Peggy Lee."

I sat the chemist at my kitchen table and, still not quite trusting her, cut off the zip strips and secured her hands behind her back with a new pair. I put a glass of ice water in front of her and stuck a straw in it.

When I went into the living room, I came face-to-chest with a giant. Close to seven feet tall, he had the build of a wrestler and looked like he'd just come from Maui in Bermuda shorts, a multicolored shirt with giant hibiscus blooms all over it, and some sort of a shell pendant on a leather cord around his neck. His thighs and biceps were as thick as tree trunks. Once I got beyond his body, I saw a pleasantly handsome face with light blue eyes.

"Who are you?" I said.

"Paul."

"*What* are you?"

"Your personal bodyguard."

"You're a SWEET agent?"

The corners of his mouth twitched briefly upward. "Something like that."

"Was that a smile?" I asked.

"Yes," he said.

"Huh," I said, noticing a variety of weapons strapped to his body, mostly concealed by the baggy shorts and bright shirt. His main piece, protruding from a quick-draw hip holster, was the size of a small cannon. I dialed Ashton, who verified that Paul was there for my protection.

I hung up and checked out the giant once again. "The boss says you're legit, so make yourself at home. The dog's name is Cracker. My father lives in the connecting apartment. His name is Spud. We usually eat at my pub downstairs. Oh, and the guest toilet runs if you don't jiggle the handle."

He followed me to the kitchen and leaned against a wall. Still sitting at the table like a good girl, Peggy Lee gasped when she saw him.

"Are you going to do that all the time?" I said to Paul. "Follow me from room to room?"

"Yes."

"What about bedtime?"

"Yes."

"Huh," I said.

The corners of his lips twitched again.

FIFTY-TWO

Ashton could be creative when the situation warranted and I had to give him credit for securing a safe house on short notice, even if it was a boat. Visible from the Cape Fear Memorial Bridge, the SS *Cape Pelican* was docked at the Navy's wharf as a part of the Maritime Administration's Ready Reserve Force. At port cities nationwide, RRF vessels sit empty while they await call-up, and it's not uncommon to see the same ship docked for several months at a time in Wilmington.

Almost seven hundred feet long and one hundred feet wide, the SS *Cape Pelican* was designed with a giant ramp to allow cargo to be driven on and off, according to one of the three crew members who was assigned to boat duty as long as Peggy Lee was aboard. Other than roving security and the two-person detail assigned to keep an eye on the chemist, the giant ship was eerily quiet. Peggy Lee's new temporary home was the captain's quarters, which included a living area and private head.

Paul towering behind us, Ox and I carried bags of takeout from the Block: shaved beef sandwiches with horseradish sauce, roasted red pepper and goat cheese quesadillas, a few six packs of cold beer, bottled water, and cartons of milk and juice for the mother-to-be. After distributing the food, we found a shady spot on the deck to eat what was left. While Paul and Ox did the male bonding thing, Peggy Lee and I had a chat.

She'd met Chuck Holloman at a conference, she said, and that's when she fell in love. The first night over dinner, they discussed her years of research that never yielded a fertility cure, her education and background, her hellish upbringing, and her appreciation for chemistry. Chuck was the first man to applaud her talents, the first man to show an interest in her, the first and only man she'd ever slept with.

A month into their long-distance relationship, Chuck quizzed Peggy Lee about her views on environmental preservation and when he flew to Wilmington later that week, he told her about Project Antisis.

"His vision seemed so admirable and so important to the health of the planet," Peggy Lee said. "We were in his hotel room, eating room-service food, when the idea came to him. A product using one of his company's adhesives and a synthetic version of the wild leafy shiff bush extract. Something that girls would put on their skin to ultimately reduce population growth and save natural resources."

I swallowed my last bite of quesadilla and started on a Coors Light. "That's when the two of you came up with Derma-Zing."

"Right. Derma-Zing was phase one of Project Antisis. Chuck had been planning the project for years. He already had the name, a play on the goddess of fertility. He just hadn't yet figured out how to implement his vision. Anyway, we discussed it and realized the skin adhesive idea would work. So he hired marketing people to handle the advertising and stuff. Once Derma-Zing ran its cycle, Chuck planned to move forward with another product. Phase two."

From my perch on the mammoth ship, a pleasure boat cruising

past looked like a toy. "And you went along with this plan, no questions asked?"

"He convinced me it was all for the better good," she said. "At that point, I'd have done anything for Chuck. Plus he said that the girls could get pregnant later on, after they'd stopped using the product. I guess I convinced myself that was true, so really, we wouldn't be doing any harm."

"But deep inside, you knew that the majority of the girls would never be able to have a child, didn't you?" Studying her, I couldn't grasp that the woman in front of me was capable of participating in such a horrendous act.

"I don't know. Maybe," she said. "I just loved him. I loved him so much and I believed everything he said. It's almost like I was under his control. I guess it took me getting pregnant to see things clearly."

She talked for another half-hour and finally, the story and the guilt purged from her system, Peggy Lee gained an appetite and dug in to her food. When she finished, she ate my leftovers.

I asked the chemist about the items they'd found in her apartment, including the book on depression. I'd seen the detailed list.

"There's nothing in my apartment on Project Antisis. Nothing. Not even my past research notes. Everything was at the lab. Chuck insisted on it. And the self-help book on depression? It's not mine. The only books I have are chemistry books."

I caught a glimpse of Ox and Paul out of the corner of my eye. Paul had barely said three words to me since he appeared in my home, but now he and Ox were laughing like old fishing buddies. Or in Paul's case with the hang-ten duds, old surfing buddies.

"What about your diary?"

Lines appeared on Peggy Lee's forehead. "I have a diary, yes. I used to call it my depression diary. It was sort of like going to therapy, I guess. Only I'd write my thoughts down instead of talking to somebody. When I met Chuck, I was happy and quit writing in it."

Ashton called to tell me he was on the way over with someone to take an official statement from the chemist. If there was enough evidence to do so, they'd arrest Holloman in Roanoke, Virginia. If not, they'd simply pick him up for questioning.

"He's going to pin everything on you, Peggy Lee. You're the chemist, and the lone employee at the Wilmington lab. You did the research on the shiff bush. There's incriminating verbiage in your handwritten diary. The notes on Project Antisis were found in your apartment. It doesn't look good."

"But it was his plan, not mine! And Chuck was sleeping with me, to make me fall in love so I'd go along with what he wanted. He said we'd get married."

I finished the beer and considered a second one. "So? He was sleeping with his live-in girlfriend, too. Not to mention the receptionist at ECH Chemical Engineering & Consulting. He'll say you were just another lay."

She let out a wail that turned into sobbing. I can't stand crying, especially when it's coming from an adult. I grabbed another beer and joined Ox and Paul at the deck's railing. A short time later, Ashton came aboard with an assistant.

He nodded in the direction of Peggy Lee. "Can you make her stop crying? We need to get a statement."

"Not my job," I answered. "But if you've brought some food, she may stop wailing long enough to eat again. She's eating for two, you know."

We looked up to see one of the security guards leading a group tour: Spud, Fran, Bobby, and Lindsey.

"For Chrissakes," Ashton said. "This is supposed to be a safe house, not a damn party pad."

"I overheard Jersey and Ox talking about this floating hideout." Spud's cane shrugged. "Doodlebug wanted to see the ship. And Fran made a pie for the chemist lady."

"It's lemon," Fran interrupted. "I must have gone through a lemon pie a week when I was pregnant."

"And Bobby's here because we drove his van," Spud finished. "We couldn't just leave him out there."

"There you go," I said to Ashton. "Problem solved. Feed the chemist some pie and you can get your statement."

The guard took my father, his girlfriend, Lindsey, and Bobby on a tour of the ship while Ashton's assistant carried the pie to the captain's quarters.

An hour later, we'd lost Spud and his entourage and we'd run out of beer, but at least Ashton had the statement he came for. As I figured, he said they'd question Holloman, but there wasn't enough evidence to arrest him. The crazy man with a God-complex would probably go free.

"What will you do with the chemist?" I asked.

"Keep her here for a few days. Most likely, she'll be imprisoned."

"What about the product?" Ox asked. "It's still on the shelves, being used by millions."

"The plan is for ECH Chemical Engineering to agree to a worldwide recall, pay for the advertising, and offer full product refunds."

I looked at my handler. "That's it? Give people their money back? What about all the affected teens?"

"It's a delicate situation, Jersey. First, we don't want to create panic. Second, we're still not exactly sure what we're dealing with. The chemist says Holloman told her to increase the amount of the suspect ingredient in the adhesive. Anyone who has used the latest Derma-Zing, according to her, could be sterile after one or two applications. Girls using the earlier product wouldn't be affected until three or four months of use."

We immediately thought of Lindsey, who was happily eating

lemon pie with the chemist in the captain's quarters. Of course she'd used the latest product because she was getting it for free, shipped straight from the production line. Once again, Ox faced the water with closed eyes, breathing deep, as if drawing strength from some unseen source.

"Peggy Lee says there's nothing to be done. For those users whose systems have already been affected, the damage is irreversible." Ashton wiped his forehead with a handkerchief. "We will implement a course of action that is in the best interest of the public."

I could read between the lines of Ashton's diplomatic double-talk. His superiors didn't want to create a nationwide scare. After all, if a simple cosmetic product could cause sterility, what other horrors might be present in unregulated personal hygiene items, makeup, or even clothing fibers? Not only would the United States' economy feel the impact, but there would be a public outcry for regulation of absorbable consumer products. The Food and Drug Administration is already understaffed, underfunded, and under fire from citizen watch groups. It wouldn't be good.

"Hey, you guys!" Lindsey called, skipping our way with the chemist in tow. "Listen up. She can fix things. She can make an antidote!"

"Is that true?" Ashton asked the woman, sitting her in a chair.

Peggy Lee nodded.

"She was like, all weepy and stuff," Lindsey said, "like it's the end of the world or something. Saying that a bunch of girls can never have baby and it's all her fault. Blah, blah, blah. So I ask her, how can she be pregnant, when she's been working with this bad chemical, right? And she goes, it's the by-product!"

"Explain," Ashton demanded.

"Basically, when you squeeze extract from the plant, there's a pile of stuff left over," Peggy Lee said. "Think of it as pulp, if you will. It's soft and waxy, and I've been rubbing it on my hands and arms because it's a wonderful moisturizer. Then I got pregnant. My doctor says it's a miracle, but Lindsey just made me realize that the by-product is the answer."

"Go on."

"I think I was on the right track all along, during those years of frustrating research. Purified extract from the plant produced the opposite result of what I wanted—it causes *infertility*—but something in the by-product holds the answer for fertility. It stimulates and heals the ova. It might be the seed casings or the woody stem bark. I'm not sure. But something created a reversal of my condition, my faulty eggs. If I can isolate it, I can create an antidote. I can undo all the damage that Derma-Zing has done."

Ox grabbed me and his daughter into a tight circle for a group hug. Lindsey never considered that she might be one of the infertile ones. I'd been agonizing over how to tell her that her ovaries were damaged. But Ox's faith in his vision remained strong—the one where he saw grandkids in his future—and he decided that Lindsey didn't need to know what the doctor's test results revealed. At least not until she was older. And now, not ever. Relief and amazement flowed between me and Ox. The embrace would have held much longer if Lindsey didn't wiggle her way loose.

"So all the kids who've used Derma-Zing can have babies if they want to," the girl announced. "I mean, you know. Someday. Like maybe when they're forty or something."

Spud, Fran, and Bobby slowly shuffled our way in one geriatric clump. "This ship is huge," Spud declared. "We need Fran's scooter to get around on this thing, for crying out loud. I'm exhausted."

"Have a piece of lemon pie," Fran said. "That will perk you up."

Lindsey shook her head. "Peggy Lee ate it all."

The chemist smiled. "And it worked wonders."

FIFTY-THREE

Edward Charles Holloman acted shocked when two federal investigators showed up at his office, escorted by a local city cop. A man and a woman, both wearing suits and stern expressions, flashed badges and asked for twenty minutes of his time.

He kept them waiting an appropriate ten minutes before buzzing his secretary to usher them to his office. When they explained they were there to discuss Peggy Lee Cooke and Derma-Zing, Chuck made a worried face.

"She tore up our new satellite lab and I haven't heard from her since. At first, I thought it was a burglary, but then I realized my own employee had done it. I didn't bother to file a report with the Wilmington police because it was more vandalism than actual monetary damages."

"Why would your employee do such a thing, Mr. Holloman?"

Chuck stood, shut the office door, and returned to his executive leather chair. "We were having an affair and I broke it off with her," he confided. "I know, I know. It's bad policy to date an employee and I shouldn't have allowed it to happen. But things were fine until recently, when she started making demands. She even bought herself an engagement ring and said she wanted to get married. I think she's delusional." He leaned on the desk and released a heavy sigh. "The next thing I know, she's demolished my lab, and trashed the computer."

"I'm curious," the woman interviewer said. "Why did you set up a lab in North Carolina to begin with?"

Chuck opened a desk drawer, pulled out a folder, and slid it across the desk. "I've had plans to open some satellite labs in the southeast for some time now. Those are the maps and demographic statistics of locations we've considered. The journals say that satellite labs are good for independent thinking and innovative research to generate new products. You know, get away from the status quo and all that. Strategically, Wilmington is a good location. It's the first satellite we opened." He waved a hand at the file of maps and demographic data. "But now, after this incident with Peggy, I'm no longer sure that satellite laboratories are a good idea." He chuckled. "I think I'll just stick with my real estate investments as far as out-of-state holdings."

One of them consulted a list. "Your company owns beach condos in South Carolina and Florida, land holdings in West Virginia, and a chalet in the Montana mountains. You personally own a soybean farm in Iowa, and a ranch in Texas."

Holloman tried to appear modest. "I don't like to play the stock market, but I've done very well with real estate. The condos and the ski chalet are wonderful write-offs because we use them to entertain clients." He stopped to ask if anyone would care for a bottled water or cup of coffee. Everyone declined. "After all, ECH adhesives can be found in products everywhere, from automobiles to airplanes to high-rise construction sites. It's good business to wine and dine the decision makers who buy raw materials."

The woman jotted something down. "Mr. Holloman, have you ever heard of Project Antisis?"

Chuck wrinkled his forehead in thought. "Project Ant-what?"

"Project Antisis." The woman spelled the letters out for him.

"We often assign nicknames to various research projects, or a new custom-manufactured adhesive," Chuck said, rubbing his chin. "But no, that name doesn't ring a bell. I've never heard of it. Why?"

Ignoring his questions, the two suits quizzed Chuck for another half-hour while the policeman looked on, seemingly bored. Finally, Chuck allowed some annoyance to show, and turned the questioning on them.

"Look, you said twenty minutes and I've tried to accommodate you. But I have a full schedule and I really don't understand why you've come all this way," the company president said. "I know I should have probably filed a police complaint about the damaged lab, but nobody was injured and it's not like the research was confidential or high-tech information. My company produces adhesives. Has the Cooke woman done something I don't know about?"

Looking at each other, the agents decided they'd already gotten all they were going to get out of Charles Holloman. He'd performed brilliantly and had a reasonable explanation for everything they'd thrown at him. The woman told Holloman that something in Derma-Zing might be toxic and harmful. Some users of the product had exhibited physical symptoms related to their reproductive systems.

"What?" Chuck stood up. "Derma-Zing is formulated with a nontoxic adhesive! It's been independently tested and proven safe. We took extra precautions with the formula, since it was our first product marketed to individual consumers. Are you sure these girls' problems are tied to Derma-Zing?"

"We're fairly certain," the man said, and explained that testing was in progress.

Chuck fell back into his chair. "It's inconceivable. But if there's even a chance that Derma-Zing contains a harmful ingredient, then we must do an immediate recall. It's going to cost the company a ton of money, but I don't know what else to do."

Once again, the two agents eyed each other. Holloman agreed to a recall, even before they'd suggested it.

"It must be the Cooke woman," Chuck mumbled to himself. "She must have altered the formulation somehow. But why would anyone do such a thing?"

Before the interrogators left his office, Chuck agreed to implement a full product recall, citing potential side effects. He agreed to refund consumers' money and postage costs if they mailed in their unused Derma-Zing, or even if they sent an empty package. And he agreed to halt further production, pending a complete investigation.

When the visitors had gone, Chuck sat back in his chair and smiled. The recall simply meant a delay in selling off the Derma-Zing division. Both retail buyers and consumers had short memories, he thought. As soon as he launched another advertising campaign, Derma-Zing sales would be stronger than before, at which point he could market the division for sale. Peggy had run off like a scared rabbit and he didn't get the opportunity to kill her as planned, which was a bothersome detail. But if agents ever did catch up with the woman, she'd go to jail for a long time. All the evidence pointed to her—he'd made sure of that. He'd even been so helpful as to provide the agents with a recent photograph of Peggy from her company ID card, as well as all the information from her personnel file, and the make and color of her car.

Outside, as they climbed into their rental car, the agents had a gut feeling that Holloman knew a lot more than he was telling. But they couldn't do a thing about it.

FIFTY-FOUR

The best thing about having a handsome, brightly clad giant shadow me is that Paul gave me something to think about other than sterile teenagers and a rogue former SWEET agent. And even though I found it disconcerting that Paul slept on a cot inside my bedroom by the door, the nearness of a mysterious hunk helped to keep my mind off of Ox and his night with Louise.

"Shouldn't you have one of those curly wires or something sticking out of your ear, like they do on TV?" I said to him, when I'd emerged from the bathroom and he followed me to the kitchen.

"I'm in direct contact with every operative assigned to coverage duty."

Maybe he was bionic. Maybe there was a communications device wired inside his head. Maybe he didn't really exist and I'd conjured Paul from my imagination.

Spud sat at the table with a nearly empty plate in front of him. Since my father isn't supposed to use any heat-generating appliances, I could only assume that Paul made breakfast. And since illusions can't cook, I decided that Paul wasn't a figment of my imagination, after all.

"Spud, you have got to get your trash off my property," I said, poring through yesterday's mail, which contained a written warning about the debris in front of the Block. Dirk had already stalled as long as he could, and said I would receive a citation and hefty fine if the abandoned vehicle wasn't removed.

Spud shook a bottle of chocolate Yoo-hoo, his breakfast drink of choice. "Even though nobody bid on it doesn't mean it's not art, for crying out loud."

"I don't care what you call it." I handed him the written warning. "Just get it off my property. I want it gone *today*!"

"Okay, okay. You sure are testy this morning, for crying out loud."

Paul handed me plate of food: omelet, fried potatoes, sliced tomatoes, and toast. He must've cooked breakfast while I was in the shower. I thanked him. Not wanting to go overboard with the conversation, he nodded. Checking him out, I dug in. This morning, the baggy shorts were a flowery part of his attire, complemented by a simple white shirt with bright yellow trim. I caught glimpses of leather straps and holsters and metal. He was a walking arsenal.

Spud used a piece of my toast to wipe up the remains from his plate. He finished chewing and made food appreciation noises. "Tall Paul is a great cook. Can we keep him?"

Paul's mouth did the twitch thing.

After breakfast, my shadow and I met Ox and Lindsey downstairs. Erring on the side of caution, Ox had pulled her out of school for the week. Unconcerned about the reason, Lindsey thought all the attention was pretty "rad," even if she did still have to complete her homework assignments.

In Ox's four-door truck, we spent the next hour running errands and ended up at Soup's place to retrieve the memory stick. Ox and Lindsey waited outside.

"Yo, Paul, whassup?" Soup said, when the flowered giant followed me into Soup's apartment. They did a handshake thing that ended with a fist bump.

Eyeing my bodyguard, Soup whistled. "You must be deep in some major shit, Jersey."

"Why's that?" I said.

He pointed at Paul. "To warrant this guy. He's legendary. Wow."

"He is?"

Soup whistled again. Paul did his version of a smile. Soup gave me the memory stick and a stack of printouts.

"You got most everything on the hard drive," Soup said, "but it's all gibberish to me. Data was password protected with the word *antisis*. All scientific notes, spreadsheets, a mathematic formulation program with a time line of entries."

"Bottom line?" I said.

"Nothing personal on there. Nothing connected to ECH or Holloman. No financial files, correspondence, calendars, viruses, keystroke-tracking programs. Nothing except working files that a chemist would use."

"Thanks, guy."

"You're welcome," Soup said. "Now would you please get out of here? No offense, but it's making me a little nervous, knowing they put this guy on you."

We climbed into Ox's truck and headed to the safe house.

Peggy Lee let out a shrill scream when I told her I had the entire hard drive from the lab. Weapons were instantly out and ready, aimed our way, in the hands of no less than four men. Paul gripped the minicannon in one hand and a second, shorter-barreled weapon in the other.

"It's okay, it's okay," I called out. "She's just, ah, excited."

The weapons disappeared.

"Do you realize how much time this will save? After the hard drive got destroyed, I thought it was all gone! This is great, Jersey." She rushed to her makeshift onboard laboratory, erected inside a cargo bay. Two tractor-trailer rigs that looked ordinary from the outside were buzzing with equipment, workstations, computers, and air-conditioning on the inside. Three motor homes, parked side by side, had been driven aboard for living quarters.

In the mobile lab, scientist-types huddled around Peggy Lee as she loaded the data into a computer. I wondered which agencies the chemists had come from and what other jobs they'd been pulled off of. But it didn't matter. They'd soon have an antidote. And meanwhile, every last bit of Derma-Zing was being removed from shelves and destroyed.

"Agent Barnes," Ashton called, poking his head in the lab. "You are aware that the SS *Cape Pelican* has been designated as a secure shelter, security clearance required."

I moved out of the lab. Paul, Lindsey, and Ox followed. "Yes, sir," I said.

"The girl, I can understand. Knowing Ox, I'll even make an allowance for him. But what in the hell is that?" Ashton pointed to another cargo bay, directly across from the one where we stood. Spud's demolished Chrysler and deformed alligator had been dumped there. Fresh tire marks—probably from a flatbed tow truck—could be seen on the deck.

"They're my father's sculptures, sir."

Ox's stomach moved with silent laughter. Paul's mouth twitched. Lindsey went to get a closer look.

"And they got on this ship *how*?"

"I don't know, sir." I made a mental note to kill my father. Or at least yell at him. As if I'd conjured him up, Spud rolled from behind the alligator and using his cane, hauled himself upright.

Wearing a tool belt, Bobby did the same. They'd been doing something to the animatronic animal.

"What's all the ruckus about?" Spud demanded.

"You, Spud. The ruckus is about you," I said. "What were you thinking, having this crap hauled to the ship? And what are the two of you doing with tools?"

"First off, it ain't crap. It's my artwork. Secondly, you said I had to move my sculptures away from the Block, remember? So I did." He wobbled for a second, caught his balance, and spun the cane around him in an arc. "This ship is huge, for crying out loud. Look at all this empty space. Bobby and I just figured we'd stash my sculptures here until they sell." He stopped to count on his fingers. "And third of all, we brought tools to fix the alligator. If we can get the tail to move again, somebody will buy it."

Ashton one-push dialed somebody on a digital phone. "Nobody else gets on this ship without the required clearance, you got me? Nobody," he said into the tiny phone and paused for the reply. "I don't care if he is Barnes's father! I said nobody! No old ladies with fruit pies, no kids, and no deliveries of totaled vehicles! If I so much as see a seagull on this ship without the required clearance, I will have your ass!"

Ashton flipped the phone shut harder than necessary and stalked off, dropping a file folder as he went. Its elastic band enclosure popped off and a single paper came loose to dance in the breeze. Lindsey snatched the sheet before it had a chance to blow overboard.

"Hey, is this something top secret?" she said, walking to Ashton but reading the paper instead of handing it back.

Ashton threw his hands up. Security had already been compromised so what difference did it make if a sixteen-year-old quizzed him? "That is a list of real estate owned by Charles Holloman."

"Man," she said. "He owns a lot of stuff. He must be pretty rich."

Ashton waited a beat, letting the girl read. "Take your time," he said. "No need to follow protocol. In fact, when you've finished with that, perhaps you can look at all the other documents in this folder while you run and play on the decks of a safe house. Maybe you can even fold some of them into paper planes and fly them off the deck."

"Who knew?" I muttered to Ox. "He has a sense of humor."

Lindsey sat down in place, legs crossed Indian style, to read. "Hey, wait a minute! The ranch in Texas? It's called Sisitna Ranch and Stables?"

Ashton squatted beside her. "What about it?"

"Peggy Lee said that Doc named the whole thing Project Antisis."

"So?"

Lindsey flashed her star-quality smile. "*Sisitna* is *Antisis* spelled backward."

FIFTY-FIVE

Chuck had prepared to leave for the day when his secretary called him on the intercom to announce that the visitors, the federal agents, were back.

"What can they possibly want now?" he mumbled to himself, irritated that they'd be taking up more of his time. The total cost of the recall would be into the millions, not including the public-service announcement spots he'd agreed to run on the music video networks. He'd given them everything he had on the Cooke woman. He even assigned the Derma-Zing public relations lady to the recall campaign. He'd done more than enough, Chuck decided, and pushed the intercom button to tell the secretary he wasn't available. Before he got a chance, the agents barged through his office door.

"Edward Charles Holloman, you are under arrest for endangering the safety of the public . . ." The voice kept going, but Chuck didn't hear the words. In disbelief, he racked his brain, trying to determine what they could possibly have on him. He'd been so careful. It had to be a mistake. "You have the right to . . ." the voice continued. *It must be a mistake,* Chuck thought.

The founder and president of ECH Chemical Engineering & Consulting remained speechless as the agents led him out in handcuffs, right past the management offices and the receptionist, whom he had planned to have dinner with that night.

"This must be a mistake," Chuck said from the backseat of an unmarked police car. "Why am I being arrested? This is ridiculous!"

A woman in the front passenger's seat turned to give him a smile. "You should have been more careful when choosing the name for your Texas ranch, Mr. Holloman."

Still smiling, she faced forward and adjusted her seat belt. A search of the ranch had proven quite fruitful, including a fully documented account of Project Antisis: conception date, mission statement, funding sources, and ideas for future consumer products. Figuring himself to be a genius, the authoritarian had created a running documentary of his work, complete with self-taped video segments, souvenirs including the prototype Derma-Zing packaging, and pages and pages of notes. He couldn't openly brag or submit his work to the worldwide scientific community, but Charles Holloman's arrogance dictated that he take credit for Project Antisis. Now he would have all the credit he could handle, the agent thought.

As he watched a blur of buildings and cars and people speed by, Chuck understood that life as he knew it would never be the same. Due to one ridiculous oversight, they'd searched his ranch. They'd found mission control. He wondered who might head up ECH while he lived in prison and decided that it probably didn't matter. He knew he'd have to sell the company anyway. At least they couldn't take away his money and when he got free, Project Antisis would live again.

FIFTY-SIX

With the data from her original lab computer, Peggy Lee and the other chemists were able to produce enough of the South American plant by-product, and quickly isolate the individual chemical that cured her infertility. A hormone-like substance found solely in the stem bark of the South American wild leafy shiff bush, it was in the process of being synthetically reproduced by a team of scientists. Since Holloman was no longer a threat and Peggy Lee was cooperating, their effort was moved from the SS *Cape Pelican* to a brick-and-mortar laboratory facility in Pennsylvania to allow for more production capability.

No longer needed, the floating safe house was being dismantled—a good thing since Ashton informed me that the ship had been called into service and needed to be ready to sail in ten days. It would only take one day, though, to remove all evidence that anyone had been on the ship. The assigned captain would probably never notice that a woman had occupied his quarters for two weeks.

Ox and I—with Paul in tow—went to the ship to figure out

what to do with Spud's sculptures. Spud and Fran had come to collect her pie plate. Since the sky kept spitting mist, she couldn't tote my father on the back of her Vespa scooter, so they recruited Bobby's van. And Bobby had tagged along as their official chauffeur.

Ashton, however, didn't need to be on the ship and I wondered why he remained aboard. Watching the man give orders, I wondered if he'd come to say good-bye. I sensed that it was time for him to head back to his regular office and move on to the next terrorist threat, leaving Sunny Point and his hand-selected recruit-gone-bad and the entire Derma-Zing horror behind. The coverage on me would continue until John Mason was stopped, or at least until a reasonable amount of time had passed. But Ashton could easily monitor that effort from anywhere in the world. At any given time, in fact, there were numerous people under constant threat during his watch.

We stood staring at *Road Rage* and *Nature's Wrath* when Ashton pulled me, Ox, and Paul aside.

"We believe that John Mason has been using an unauthorized password and an old digital security key to access our database. If that's the case, there is a possibility he knows about the ship, just by following the trail of supplies that were delivered to this location. Agent Barnes, I want you to take your father and his entourage and get off this vessel immediately. Paul, you will continue your coverage as assigned. A limited detail remains on the ship right now and they have been alerted to the potential threat. Reinforcements are on the way and will remain until the *Cape Pelican* sails. Crew members will begin arriving tomorrow to prep the ship for duty, but I don't want to see any of you back here, understand?"

"Yes, sir," I said.

"Got it," Paul said.

Ox nodded out of courtesy. He didn't report to Ashton and never would. But he understood the system.

"Forget about the scrap your father dumped," Ashton continued. "I'll have it towed to a recycling salvage yard."

"Thank you, sir," I said.

Ashton proffered his hand. It was an action of apology and acceptance and recognition of an unspoken friendship. I gripped his palm and we shook.

"Been a pleasure working with you again, Barnes. Happy trails," he said, referring to the old song by Roy Rogers. Ashton's way of telling me to stay safe until we met again, it is his trademark sign-off.

"Happy trails," I replied.

Ashton waited to see us vacate the ship as workers moved past hauling computers and other miscellaneous equipment. Two men carrying a folding metal table suddenly froze at the same instant Ox and Paul stepped in front of me and aimed their weapons. I turned to see John Mason, decked out in full body armor, including a helmet with a face shield. A rocket-propelled grenade launcher, resting on his shoulder, was pointed straight at us. A light antitank weapon that looks like a large tube, it could take out the entire cargo hold and everyone standing around me. I reflexively drew my own weapon but, glimpsing the target through Paul and Ox's crouched bodies, quickly realized why they'd held their fire. Mason's Kevlar gear would offer enough protection to give the maniac an opportunity to fire at us, even as he went down. Either one of the three men next to me could take Mason out with a head shot, which might give us a chance, but in all probability, he would manage to fire before he died. There was no other movement on deck. Mason had killed two or three men as he'd infiltrated the ship.

Across the wide deck—out of the corner of my eye—I watched Spud, Bobby, and Fran move behind the Chrysler. Their heads disappeared as they shimmied down a ladder.

Empty palms up and outward, Ashton took a step forward. "Just tell me what you want, John. I can help you. It doesn't need to come to this."

Mason shouted a string of observations that included something about greedy politicians and backward United States policy. Standing perfectly still, feet planted wide, he appeared as though neither the weight of the weapon nor the heat from the full body gear had affected him. He sounded like a mental patient in the midst of a full-fledged breakdown. But at least he was talking instead of activating his weapon.

"Stand down," Ashton said quietly and the three of us pointed our weapons at the deck instead of toward Mason. Ashton inched closer to the madman. "Violence is not the way out of this, John. Put down your weapon and we'll talk. We can fix this."

"No more talking," John Mason screamed. "And no more Jersey Barnes!"

By the slight shift in his stance and contracting of muscles, we all knew he'd decided to fire. In the instant everyone reacted by bringing up their weapons for a Hail Mary shot, Spud's alligator let out a screeching groan, its tail scraping across the concrete deck. Mason spun toward the sound behind him. The grenade blasted from his shoulder-mounted launcher in the same instant that Ashton drew a gun and shot the former SWEET agent in the exposed space at the back of his neck, just below the helmet. The four of us hit the ground as a ball of heat, fire, and exhaust shot out the back end of the launch tube.

The rocket impacted the Chrysler with an ear-splitting boom and both sculptures exploded into hundreds of flying parts. A variety of weapons were sighted on the man holding the launcher. But there was no need to fire. John Mason's knees buckled and his lifeless Kevlar-gray form folded to the ground, brilliantly backlit by a ball of darting flames.

Ashton stayed behind, staring at the man he'd just killed, while the rest of us went to locate my father. Once on the lower deck, we found Spud sputtering in the water, trying to float his way to the shore. Fran stood on the ship's giant ramp, calling to him. Getting a shuffling start, Bobby threw himself off the ramp into the river, to rescue Spud. Shaking his head, Ox grabbed a couple of life preservers and jumped into the water. He managed to get the flotation devices beneath each man's flailing arms before hauling them to the muddy shore. Fran ran to hug Spud, losing her balance in the silt, and the pair of them fell back into the water. Ox helped them to their feet.

Watching the show, Paul cocked his head and almost cut loose with a real smile.

"Welcome to my world," I said.

He made a phone call and hung up with a terse "Roger that."

"It's been fun, Jersey Barnes," Paul said. "But since the threat has been eliminated, I'm gone." It was the most words he'd used in one sentence since I'd met him.

"Don't you want to stay for dinner? You have to get your things out of the Block anyway."

"Already taken care of." The corners of his mouth twitched. "Tell the Spudster good-bye for me."

"That was another smile, right?"

"Yes," he said and vanished.

Ox and I got my dripping, muddy father and his friends loaded into Bobby's van. I drove them to the Block and Ox followed in his truck. A chorus of sirens grew loud as fire engines, police, harbor patrol boats, and seemingly anyone else with a set of strobe lights bolted to their vehicle passed us in the opposite direction, headed toward the SS *Cape Pelican.*

FIFTY-SEVEN

Nearly a month had passed since John Mason died while trying to kill me and I hadn't heard anything further from my former SWEET handler. I took it as a sign that my callback to duty was over and declared an official retirement celebration at the Block.

Lindsey and her new best friend, Cindy, played pool on the brand-new coin-operated table that they'd convinced Ox to install, and with fully functioning and healthy reproductive systems, the girls played eight ball. They were two of the first to be injected with the Antisis antidote. Dr. Pam Warner had called earlier in the morning to report Lindsey's current test results as perfectly normal. It was as though she'd never had any problems to begin with, Pam said, and if she hadn't overseen the testing herself, she wouldn't have believed it.

Ox's arm around my shoulders, we watched a national news report on a wall-mounted television while we waited for everyone to arrive. An evening news reporter smiled at us. "In other news,

Edward Charles Holloman, inventor of the wildly successful product Derma-Zing, was indicted today on federal tax-evasion and money-laundering charges. He faces up to thirty years in prison."

"That's right, Susan," the co-anchor said. "Viewers may remember that just last month, there was a worldwide recall of Derma-Zing, due to side effects including possible skin irritation."

One half of a two-shot, the woman on television nodded to her viewing audience. "Ironically, David, Derma-Zing has since been independently tested and proven to be perfectly safe. It's back on the market and Gail Sanders, marketing director for Derma-Zing, reports that sales of the tattoo-like, nonpermanent body art kits are stronger than ever. Sanders said that starter kits with three tubes of color are being offered absolutely free for the next thirty days, in an unprecedented promotion. Anyone wanting a free kit should visit the product's Web site or go to a store where the product is sold. The free gift is a way to compensate fans of Derma-Zing who were affected by the recall, according to Sanders."

The male anchor stared straight into the camera. "The company's founder may not get to enjoy Derma-Zing's success, however, if he gets the maximum prison term on the unrelated charges. Our independent panel of prosecutors believes that he will, indeed, be incarcerated for a long time. Tune in at eleven tonight for that exclusive."

The anchor tossed to a weatherman and I looked at Ox in disbelief. "They've put the antidote in the new Derma-Zing."

Ox nodded. "Avoid a public scare that way."

"And they've manufactured fake charges against Holloman."

Ox nodded again. "A good way to put him behind bars without letting parents know that Holloman tried to sterilize their daughters."

"Our government is nuts," I said.

Ox caressed the back of my neck. "Sometimes, yes."

I wondered where Peggy Lee Cooke would end up, but something told me that her life would turn out just fine. She was confined to a psychiatric facility, where she would undergo counseling during the term of her pregnancy. But thanks to a plea bargain, she and her new baby would be released once she was deemed a nonthreat to society.

JJ and Rita arrived with some friends I didn't know. Cracker pranced at our feet, and when Dirk and Soup showed up, Ruby made sure everyone had a drink in hand so they could toast to my bona fide retirement—the same retirement that had been slyly evading me for months.

Spud, his three poker buddies, and his new girlfriend ambled in from the Block's outdoor patio, carrying an assortment of walking aids and frozen drinks. Somebody made a second toast to include them and afterward, my father handed me an envelope.

"This was just delivered by a courier," he said.

I opened the envelope to find two checks. One, made out to me, read eleven thousand dollars—a lump-sum payment from the government for my contract job. The second check, signed with the same automated script from a laser writer, was made out to my father for thirty thousand dollars.

He snatched the check out of my hands. "It's about time, for crying out loud."

I almost dropped my beer. "What the—"

Spud patted my cheek. "I filed a claim with that boss of yours for my destroyed sculptures. Fifteen thousand dollars apiece is what I could have sold 'em for. And since the SS *Cape Pelican* was under government control when that madman blew up my personal property, I figured Uncle Sam owed me damages, for crying out loud."

"You got thirty grand for a wrecked car and a burnt, shot-up alligator." I yanked the check out of my father's hands and held it next to mine, studying the watermarked paper and the signatures. Both were real. Only his was nineteen thousand dollars more real than mine. Dropping both checks on the bar, I downed my beer and asked the bartender for a Patrón tequila straight up.

Fran fluffed her hair and kissed my father, straight on the lips. Bobby gave him a high five. Hal asked to borrow twenty dollars. And Trip demanded that Spud pay up the fifty dollars he borrowed during their last poker game.

Laughing, Ox pulled me outside and planted his mouth on mine in a long, tasty kiss. The late afternoon was just sliding into cocktail hour, a refreshing chill permeated the breeze coming off the river, and the scent of Ox's aftershave made me giddy. I closed my eyes to fully relish the moment when a dump truck pulled up to the curb in front of the Block.

Its driver proceeded to jam up traffic by backing up to the dirt area, where Spud's demolished sedan had sat for so long that it killed a patch of grass. High-pitched beeping noises sounded as the truck's bed tilted up in the air and dumped a load of unidentifiable garbage on my property.

"Hey!" I called and ran out to where the driver stood by the hydraulic controls. "What do you think you're doing? Stop that!"

He finished dumping the load, climbed in the cab, handed me an envelope through the window, and drove off leaving a blast of diesel fumes and a pyramid of debris in his wake.

Stunned, I read the note aloud as Ruby came outside to investigate.

"Thought your father would want the remains of his sculptures. Maybe he can recycle the parts into something new. Cheers, Ash"

"Spud!" Ruby hollered, reading over my shoulder. "Delivery for you! It's your Chrysler!"

"Oh, for crying out loud," Spud said and shuffled outside, walking cane leading the way. He stopped at the pile of trash and stooped to pick up a piece. It was the Chrysler medallion from the front grille. "It's the car from hell. From hell, I tell you!"

Ignoring the tirade, my best friend pulled me against his chest. Laughing, I wrapped my arms around him. My family and my friends were all alive and the Block was still standing. Life was good. Contented and cheerful, I looked into Ox's face and read the same sentiment in his expression. Just as he tilted his head to drop another kiss on my mouth, my phone rang. I separated myself from his body to answer and listened to the person on the other end.

"Look, I appreciate you thinking of me for the job," I said, "but I'm retired. There's a party going on right now to prove it. Got a cake and everything."

Ox's eyes seemed to twinkle as they reflected a faint glow of colors from the neon beer lights.

"You can't call in a favor after that person has retired," I said, knowing how irrational it sounded. "Okay, okay, maybe you can. I'll have to check the official retirement rule book. Is there such a rule book?"

We agreed to talk tomorrow and I disconnected, pledging to forget about the phone call, at least temporarily. For one night anyway, I was going to savor my retirement.